ALSO BY SARAH LOVETT

Dantes' Inferno

Acquired Motives

Dangerous Attachments

A Desperate Silence

DARK ALCHEMY

A DR. SYLVIA STRANGE NOVEL

SARAH LOVETT

SIMON & SCHUSTER

New York   London   Toronto   Sydney   Singapore

SIMON & SCHUSTER
Rockefeller Center
1230 Avenue of the Americas
New York, NY 10020

SIMON & SCHUSTER and colophon are registered
trademarks of Simon & Schuster, Inc.

For information about special discounts for bulk purchases,
please contact Simon & Schuster Special Sales:
1-800-456-6798 or business@simonandschuster.com

Manufactured in the United States of America

1   3   5   7   9   10   8   6   4   2

Library of Congress Cataloging-in-Publication Data
Lovett, Sarah (Sarah Poland).
Dark alchemy : a Dr. Sylvia Strange novel / Sarah Lovett.
p. cm.
1. Strange, Sylvia (Fictitious character)—Fiction. 2. Forensic psychiatrists—Fiction.
3. Los Angeles (Calif.)—Fiction. 4. Women psychiatrists—Fiction.
5. Serial murders—fiction. 6. Poisoners—Fiction. I. Title.

PS3562.O873 D39 2003
813'.54—dc21   2002036513
ISBN 0-684-85599-2

ACKNOWLEDGMENTS

VERY SPECIAL THANKS TO

David Rosenthal, Marysue Rucci, and Tara Parsons
Theresa Park, Julie Barer, and Peter McGuigan
Aileen Boyle and Loretta Denner
Miriam Sagan and Maggie Griffin
Michael Mariano
Saul Cohen
Mike Gelles
Reid Meloy
Pat Berssenbrugge
Susie and Brianna Johnson
Bruce Mann, M.D.
Barb Curry, M.D.
John Koch
Joe Prezioso
David Doughten, Esq.
Dr. James Eisenberg
Jay Milano, Esq.
Alice Dixon and Stan Cohen
Hank Blackwell
Annie Lindgren and Jill Ryan
John Wolcott and Jan Arrington-Wolcott
David and Peggy van Hulsteyn
Jude McNally
Dian and Saul Lieberthal
Tamara Kessler and March Kessler
Fritz Feltman
Oru Bose
Eve Velie
Rodney Barker
Danny and Laurie Lehman
Layne Vickers-Smith and Rick Smith
Richard H. Miller, Captain U.S. Navy Retired
Marilyn Abraham and Sandy MacGregor
Tim Thompson
Peter Miller and Jennifer Robinson

For my brothers and sisters
and for my husband, Michael

PART I

The Secret Art

Doug Thomas fed the cat, walked the dog, and left for work in his two-year-old Subaru Outback. It was business as usual for the thirty-six-year-old molecular toxicologist, except for the headache. A doozy. Gene Krupa playing sticks on his gray matter.

Doug popped two Extra Strength Tylenol and donned his sunglasses. Must be his sinuses acting up again; he'd been having trouble lately. His fingers had been tingling and now his field of vision was blurry around the edges. Bad headaches could do that. When his ex-wife called about the child support check, she always had the same three complaints: men, money, migraines.

Headache or no, Doug couldn't afford to stay home. No rest for the wicked, he thought to himself with a tight smile. Stay on schedule, business as usual, no break with routine. Nothing to tip them to the fact he'd pulled off another extracurricular assignment. Ten minutes' work—only moderately risky—and this time he'd bought himself the chance to erase his debts once and for all.

Keep up appearances—that's all I have to do. Can't afford to miss a minute at the lab.

This was a crucial window for Project Mithradates. The Mith Squad had made a major breakthrough—"Building a better biotoxin," he whispered. They'd developed an entirely new manufacturing process (not to mention quantum improvements in the delivery system) using their quarry.

And a fascinating quarry it was—a relative (third cousin twice removed) of *Gymnodinium breve,* the dinoflagellate responsible for red tides, and *Pfiesteria pisicida.* Lethal little bastard. Still, you couldn't help but admire its chameleon nature: opportunistic, unpredictable, changeable.

Got to hand it to their project head, the Ice Queen. For all her bitchiness, she is truly amazing—come to think of it, not unlike their killer tox: opportunistic, unpredictable, lethal.

What was a headache compared to everything he'd been through over the past months? he wondered bitterly. He'd vowed he wouldn't let the petty personality differences affect his concentration. Territorial disputes were part of every research project, federal, state, private—just like they were part of every family. In a field as narrowly focused as his, fellow researchers interacted like some extended clan, complete with feuds and alliances. He'd been down this road before. He told himself it would go no further than disputes over territory; in the end it would all work out. The bastards were always on his case anyway—he'd yet to see eye to eye with his supervisors on any project.

But hell, a little bickering never killed anyone.

In fact, all in all, Dr. Doug Thomas was looking forward to his day. His thirty-five-minute commute—he lived in a sweet little river valley, and the lab was on a mountaintop—allowed him to organize and prepare mentally for the work ahead.

He usually finished his PB&J sandwich before he reached the main highway, and he almost always swallowed the last of the Earl Grey tea in his thermos at the alpine treeline, where the view was awesome.

But this morning he'd forgotten to make his sandwich; the jar of Jif was sitting on the counter at home, as was the milk for his tea. And when Doug tried to open the thermos, his fingers felt stiff.

He spilled half of the contents into his lap; the other half tasted like bitter water, and it was *cold*, not hot. A sudden, fleeting bout of nausea hit—he managed to keep from vomiting. He did not remember that he'd been sick the night before.

In fact, by the time he approached the main highway, Doug Thomas wasn't registering much of anything. He was functioning on autopilot. A faint internal voice warned him that he should take his foot off the gas pedal. The voice was meaningless because Doug could no longer respond to voluntary commands from his brain. He was traveling in a deep fog.

The thermos toppled, spilling the last of the tea onto his thigh, but he didn't feel the liquid contact. Sunglasses couldn't ease the bright, blinding light because it came from behind his eyes, an explosion of illumination. Fear came and went. Terror turned his skin cold—and then that emotion receded, too.

A weary sigh escaped his lips. A heavy calm slowed his body. He moved through molasses. His right foot grew heavy as it pressed down on the accelerator. The dark blue cross-trainer with the white laces seemed to belong to someone else.

As Doug Thomas drove his Subaru across four lanes of oncoming traffic on the highway, he did experience a moment of bewilderment: *You'd almost think I was poisoned.*

The two-ton truck hit the Subaru broadside and Doug Thomas was killed almost instantly.

redrider: well done! bravo!

alchemist: have we met?

redrider: call me an admirer

alchemist: ?

redrider: I was impressed with the way you handled your associate

alchemist: sorry?

redrider: Dr. T—brilliantly done

alchemist: don't know what you're talking about

redrider: I'm still not sure how you managed the exposure

redrider: hello . . .

redrider: I know you're there

redrider: take all the time you need I'll be waiting

"One of the most problematic aspects of the case is the longitudinal factor; the deaths have occurred over a span of at least a decade," Edmond Sweetheart said. He was standing by the window of his room at the Eldorado Hotel. Behind him the New Mexico sky was the color of raw turquoise and quartzite, metallic cirrus clouds highlighting a blue-green scrim.

"Why did it take so long to put it together?" Dr. Sylvia Strange had chosen to sit at one end of a cream-colored suede sofa in front of a polished burl table, the room's centerpiece. For the moment, she would keep her distance—from Sweetheart, from this new case. Her slender fingers slid over the black frame of the sunglasses that still shaded her eyes. Her shoulder-length hair was slightly damp from the shower she'd taken after a harder than usual workout at the gym. She studied the simple arrangement of flowers on the table: pale lavender orchids blooming from a slender vase the color of moss. Late-afternoon sun highlighted the moist, fleshlike texture of the blossoms. The air was laced with a heavy, sweet scent. "Why didn't anybody link the deaths?"

"They were written off as accidents." Sweetheart frowned.

"Everyone missed the connection—the CID, FBI, Dutch investigators—until a biochem grad assistant was poisoned in London six months ago. Her name was Samantha Grayson. Her fiancé happened to be an analyst with MI-6—the Brits' intelligence service responsible for foreign intelligence. He didn't buy the idea that his girlfriend had accidentally contaminated herself with high doses of an experimental neurotoxin. Samantha Grayson died a bad death, but her fiancé had some consolation—he zeroed in on a suspect."

"But MI-6 chases spies, not serial poisoners." Sylvia stretched both arms along the crest of the couch, settling in. "And this is a criminal matter." She was aware that Sweetheart was impatient. He reminded her of a parent irritated with a sassing child. "So who gets to play Sherlock Holmes, the FBI?"

"As of last week, the case belongs to the FBI, yes."

She nodded. Although the FBI handled most of its investigations on home turf, in complex international criminal cases, the feds were often called upon to head up investigations, to integrate information from all involved local law enforcement agencies—and to ward off the inevitable territorial battles that could destroy any chance of successful closure.

"And the FBI is using you—"

"To gather a profile on the suspect."

Sylvia shrugged. "Correct me if I'm wrong, but the last time I looked, you were a counterterrorist expert. Is there something you're leaving out of your narration?"

"There are unusual facets to this case."

"For instance."

"The suspect deals with particularly lethal neurotoxins classified as biological weapons. As far as we know, at this moment, there's no active terrorist agenda; nevertheless, more than one agency is seeking swift resolution."

Sweetheart settled his full weight on the window ledge, which looked too delicate to support his 280 pounds. "The suspect is female, Caucasian, forty-four, never married, although she's had a series of lovers. She's American, a research toxicologist and molecular biochemist with an IQ that's off the charts."

"You've got my attention."

"She received her B.S. from Harvard, then went on to complete her graduate work at Berkeley, top of her class, then medical school and a one-year fellowship at MIT—by then she was all of twenty-six. She rose swiftly in her career. She cut her teeth on the big shows—Rajneesh, Aum Shinrykyo, the Ventro extortion. She had access to the anthrax samples after nine-eleven—worked for all the big players, including Lawrence Livermore, the CDC, WHO, USAMRID, DOD. As a consultant she's worked in the private sector as well." Sweetheart knew the facts, reciting them succinctly, steadily, until he paused for emphasis. "Two, maybe three people in the world know as much about exotic neurotoxins and their antidotes as this woman. No one knows more."

Sylvia set her sunglasses on the table next to the moss-colored vase. She rubbed the two tiny contact triangles that marked the bridge of her nose. "How many people has she killed? Who were they?"

"It appears the victims were colleagues, fellow researchers, grad assistants. How many? Three? Five? A half dozen?" Sweetheart shrugged. "The investigation has been a challenge. Five days ago the target was put under surveillance. We both know it's a trick to gather forensic evidence in a serial case without tipping off the bad guy. Add to that the fact that she doesn't use mundane, easily detectable compounds like arsenic or cyanide. Bodies still need to be exhumed; after years, compounds degrade, pathologists come up with inconclusive data. Think Donald Harvey: he was convicted of thirty-nine poisonings; *his* count was eighty-six. We may never know how many people she's poisoned."

"Who is she?"

"Her name is Christine Palmer."

"Fielding Palmer's daughter?" Sylvia was visibly surprised.

Sweetheart nodded. "What do you know about her?"

"What everybody knows. There was a short profile in *Time* or *Newsweek* a year ago—tied to that outbreak of environmental fish toxin and the rumors it was some government plot to cover up research in biological weapons. The slant of the profile was 'daughter follows in famous father's footsteps.'" Sylvia shifted position, settling deeper into the couch, crossing her ankles. She toyed restlessly with the diamond and ruby ring on the third finger of her left hand. "That can't have been easy. Fielding Palmer was amazing. Immunologist, biologist, pioneering AIDS researcher, writer."

"Did you read his book?"

Sylvia nodded. Fielding Palmer had died of brain cancer in the early 1990s, at the height of his fame and just after the publication of his classic, *A Life of Small Reflections.* The book was a series of essays exploring the ethical complexities, the moral dilemmas, of scientific research at the close of the twentieth century. He'd been a prescient writer, anticipating the ever deepening moral and ethical quicksand of a world that embraced the science of gene therapy, cloning, and the bioengineering of new organisms.

Sylvia frowned. It jarred and disturbed—this idea that his only daughter might be a serial poisoner. The thought had an obscene quality.

She saw that Sweetheart had his eyes on her again—he was *reading* her, gleaning information like some biochemically sensitive scanner. Well, let him wait; she signaled *time-out* as she left the couch, heading for the dark oak cabinet that accommodated the room's

minibar. She squatted down in front of the cabinet, selecting a miniature of Stolichnaya and a can of tonic from the refrigerator and a bag
of Cheetos from the drawer.

"Join me?" she asked as she poured vodka into a tumbler.

"Maybe later."

Sylvia swirled the liquid in the glass, and the tiny bubbles of tonic
seemed to bounce off the oily vodka. She turned, holding the glass in
front of her face, staring at Sweetheart, her left eye magnified
through a watery lens. She said, "That's the beauty of poison—invisibility."

"Toxicology protocol is much more sophisticated than it used to
be," Sweetheart said. "But there will always be undetectable poisons.
Even water is toxic in the right dose. You have to know what you're
looking for—there are new organisms, new compounds discovered all
the time. You have to know what to culture, what to analyze, which
screens to run."

When Sylvia was settled once more on the couch, she balanced her
heels on the table and tore the snack bag open with her teeth. She ate
a half dozen of the orange puffs before tossing the bag onto the polished wood. "Okay." She held up her index finger: "Why you?" Her
middle finger: "Why me?" Her ring finger, complete with precious
stones: "Why now?"

"The FBI has a problem—their strongest tool is a psychological
profile, because there are no eyewitnesses; no secret poison cache
turned up in Palmer's basement. All the evidence is circumstantial.
The purpose of the profile is twofold: to track her patterns, her M.O.,
to look for a signature—and to prime investigators for the interrogation process. I'm their profiling consultant, I've got carte blanche."

"And you want me because—"

"Adam Riker."

The answer in a name.

Sylvia nodded, not surprised, but discomfited all the same. Months after the investigation, she still had nightmares about the Riker case. Adam Riker had been a nurse, a hospice specialist, who'd worked at nursing homes and V.A. hospitals in Texas and California, and most recently at an Indian hospital in New Mexico. He'd had another speciality in addition to nursing—serial murder. He'd poisoned at least thirty-five victims, ranging in age from an unborn child to a ninety-nine-year-old war veteran. And Sylvia had been part of the profiling team. In they end they'd brought him down—but not before more victims died.

"The Riker case is fresh in your mind," Sweetheart said, interrupting her thoughts. "You know better than I do that poisoners have their own special *tics*."

Sylvia didn't respond; she was looking straight at Sweetheart—seeing not his face but the faces of Riker's victims.

"You'll work with me on the psychological profile—that means some intensive travel, interviews, assessment of the data we've already got, and retrieval of new data. It will be down and dirty, no time for anything *but* down and dirty. We'll stay in close touch with Quantico—running our data past their guys—and our local contacts will be the field agents on surveillance and their S.A.C. It's a short list—intentionally short—to avoid attracting attention. We'll have to give the investigators the tools they need for interrogation. We'll give them her stress points, her soft spots, her jugular. Once they have enough to bring her in, they're going to have to break Christine Palmer."

"A confession?"

"As I said, so far all the evidence is circumstantial."

"They'll need hard evidence."

"What they need is a homicide on U.S. soil."

"Are you certain she's your poisoner?"

He barely hesitated. "Yes."

"So Palmer had the expertise and the access, the method and the means. What about motive?" Sylvia thought Sweetheart's energy belonged to a caged cat—behind steel bars he was pacing a path in concrete.

He turned his head, avoiding her scrutiny, and said, "Before Samantha Grayson's death, she confided in her fiancé—the analyst; his name is Paul Lang. Samantha said she'd been spooked by Palmer. There was an incident where Palmer criticized Grayson's protocol—she flew into a rage and threatened Grayson. At the time Lang encouraged his girlfriend to go to someone with more authority to mediate the dispute. Grayson said nobody had more authority than Palmer."

"That's unpleasant, but it's not motive."

"After Samantha Grayson died, Lang started investigating on his own and found a string of incidents: abrupt arguments, paranoia, accusations of misconduct and negligence leveled by Palmer against her coworkers. He also found a disturbing number of 'untimely' deaths—accidental and 'natural.' Together, the incidents and the deaths began to carry weight."

"Were the accusations of negligence and misconduct groundless, or did Palmer have a point?"

"Either way, a punishment of death is a bit harsh," Sweetheart said, his expression flat, his voice deadpan.

Sylvia took a drink of her vodka tonic. Ice beaded on the glass, dripping onto her fingers and then onto the deep mahogany wood. "In her line of work, psych screens are a given. Is she a full-blown psychopath? Paranoid? Schizotypal?"

"Her test scores fall within normal range."

"So she's smart enough to fake good."

"As far as the world's concerned, she's hyperfunctional. She's *abnormal* only because she's brilliant, ambitious, highly moral, and charismatic."

"Since when do you care what the world believes? What's the real story?"

"The surveillance team has seen some eccentric behavior." Sweetheart crossed his arms over his broad chest. "And there have been fleeting rumors of a breakdown, time spent at private retreats—we'll have to look more closely at the rumors. It's our job to figure out why she kills, her pattern, her particular system of reference." He paused, his expression shrewd, then opted for understatement. "It's an interesting case."

Sylvia didn't speak immediately. In her glass, the last of the ice was melting in front of her eyes. *What's there, what's not there?* It took her a moment to focus on Sweetheart's face. She said, "Why do I have the feeling you've left something out?"

He didn't blink, didn't react. From a distance Sweetheart could almost pass for a tourist. *Almost.* He was dressed in slightly rumpled gray linen slacks, his broad, muscled shoulders softened by a casual yellow shirt. But even in shadow, his symmetrical features teased the viewer with alternating glimpses of European and Polynesian ancestry; the power of his body was undeniable, and the dark eyes gleamed with extraordinary intelligence.

The dead cases, the inactive files—there were no such things in Sweetheart's language. She'd heard whispers of his alliances with the CIA and MI-6, as well as the FBI. (She didn't know how much was truth.) But his specialty could be summed up in the phrase "the ones that got away."

She stared at him. She didn't know exactly what drove him—hadn't figured it all out yet. But she would. She was filling in the pieces slowly. Constructing her own profile of the profiler. The ice clinked softly in her glass as she set it down.

The first fugitive she'd known about was Ben Black, a terrorist with ties to the IRA and Osama bin Laden. Sweetheart had pursued Black for years—he'd seen Black "killed" more than once. In the end, Black had died in an explosion of his own design.

And there were others on his most-wanted list. A bomber responsible for a plane crash in British Columbia that claimed 221 lives.

A sixties radical who had participated in a bank robbery that ended with three civilians dead, including a pregnant woman. (This one arrested a month ago, tracked down with the help of Sweetheart's profiling system, MOSAIK.)

And now this—a serial poisoner . . .

Sweetheart shook his head, a gesture meant to dismiss her appraisal.

But Sylvia felt his hesitation. She considered the fact that he hadn't told her the whole truth; she didn't press him. She'd learned not to push Edmond Hommalia Sweetheart.

As partners she and Sweetheart made interesting chemistry. *He*— analytical, obsessed with empirical data, prone to intrapsychic denial. *She*—an equal mix of intellect and intuition, capable of faith under pressure.

Officially, Sweetheart was an expert in psycholinguistics, an antiterrorism specialist, and the creator of the multitiered computer profiling system known as MOSAIK. In his spare time he practiced sumo, collected rare timepieces, and consulted with federal and international agencies.

Officially, Sylvia was a forensic psychologist who had extensive experience with criminal and institutionalized populations; she was the author of several books, including one that had brought a popular readership. She had a mother in San Diego and a father who'd been missing for more than two decades. She had a highly perceptive eleven-year-old foster daughter named Serena, two dogs, and a lover named Matt England, whom she adored and was about to marry and who shared her tendency to prefer an adrenalized life in the trenches over mundane, day-to-day problems. In her spare time she ran miles, played Mom, and consulted with law enforcement agencies and private parties.

Placing the empty glass on the table, Sylvia stood and stretched her arms above her head. "You haven't asked about my life." She crossed the room to join him at the window. When she reached his side, she waved her ring finger in front of his nose. Light made the ruby shimmer. "You haven't said a word about my wedding."

"How was it?"

"Do you work hard to be this—*obtuse*—or does it just come naturally?"

"I want you on this case."

"Why?"

"Because you'll understand Palmer in a way I can't." He waited a beat, waited for the question she refused to ask, before he finished his answer. "Because you worked Riker."

Sylvia turned away from him to stare out at the city—a shadowy, muted Santa Fe at sunset, purple and peach waves across a turquoise sea. Sounds drifted up from the streets: a car horn, laughter, radio songs. At that instant she felt poised between two worlds, between dark and light, between bad and good. "Hey, Sweetheart." Her voice was soft and flat. "What do you think of my city? How do you like this view?"

He shook his head, his gaze impolite in its intensity. His carotid artery was responding visibly to his heart. She felt as if she'd been penetrated and recognized.

"You want me on this case because of what I saw in Riker," she said. "It's what I saw in *me* that gives me nightmares. Riker made me touch a place within myself—a place without compassion, without mercy." She turned away and her eyes were drawn toward the glass, but what she saw was her own reflection, her face distorted, a softening that read as compromise, a blurring of line. Her voice came out as a whisper. "That's a horrible realization when compassion is what separates you from the monsters. And you know mercy and compassion must be the lifelines that offer the only glimmer of salvation—if not humanity, what's left? But all I touched was emptiness. Do you understand why I can't keep going back?"

"I know you can't turn away." He reached toward her; she shook her head and he said, "You're burned out from the Riker case, I understand that. You've lost your balance, but just for a moment—"

"It's more than that."

"I need you, Sylvia."

She heard the urgency in his voice, and when she looked into his eyes, she saw an almost desperate entreaty that left her shaken. She took a breath, trying to retreat but feeling the internal pull. Strong. Sharp.

She sighed, abruptly exhausted—taking the first step in his direction. "What's the time line on Palmer?"

"Four months ago she joined a team of researchers who've been working on a highly sensitive contract for the DOD—potent marine toxins, analyzed and manipulated in a way that's cutting-edge. There's no evidence to arrest, and she's too valuable to freeze off the project."

"I can spend the next few days reviewing the files. I'll let you know . . ."

"Not acceptable. I need you now."

"I can't do that." She pushed away from the window—physically distancing herself once again, as if freeing herself from some invisible force field. "Not until after the wedding."

"As of last Friday morning, we have a new victim. A molecular toxicologist. Part of the original research team in England."

"What did she use?"

"A neurotoxin—" He faltered.

Sylvia shook his head, and Sweetheart countered harshly: "You said it yourself, the beauty of poison is invisibility. The toxicology screens will take time. They're not looking for the standard compounds."

"What happened to him?"

"The victim drove his car at seventy miles per hour directly into the path of oncoming traffic. Yes, it might have been a vehicular malfunction, it might have been an accident, it might have been suicide. But I'll stake my career it was murder."

"Can't they shut down the project on some excuse?"

"They'd lose invaluable research, and they'd tip her off." He shook his head. "She's under twenty-four-hour surveillance. The feds need to catch her in the act. Or they need a confession. That's where you and I come in. Sylvia, I'm asking you—give me five days, then go have your life."

"She's in England? What—London?"

Sweetheart shook his head. "Dr. Thomas died on U.S. soil—and his murderer's in your neighborhood. Why do you think I'm here? Dr. Palmer's heading up this project at LANL."

redrider: are you ready to talk?

alchemist: what do you want?

redrider: a civil response

alchemist: who are you?

redrider: friend / no I confess a fan!

alchemist: colleague?

redrider: we travel in concentric circles

alchemist: then we've met

redrider: not so fast

alchemist: introduce yourself

redrider: not yet

alchemist: why not?

redrider: you'd have to kill me

alchemist: repeat what do you want?

redrider: to earn your trust / the feds are watching

Since the Cerro Grande fire of 2000, the vast tracks of acreage surrounding Los Alamos National Laboratory, fifty miles north of Santa Fe, had resembled the dark side of the moon. The isolated lab located near Technical Area 58—once enclosed by dense forest—stood out against charred tree stumps and singed earth. Moonlight only intensified the atmosphere of ruin.

B-30/T, part of the facility's bioscience division, looked more like a war-era bunker than a secure biocontainment lab equipped to handle lethal microorganisms. Lit by a dozen halogen lamps mounted on the necks of thirty-foot steel poles, the single-story structure had originally been designated as an interim lab, to be in use only until construction of the three-thousand-square-foot $4 million biosciences secure-containment complex was complete. But demand—due to the escalating threat of biological terrorist attacks and the beefing up of the nation's biothreat programs—had outstripped supply, and the "temp" BSL-3 lab had remained in operation long past its original date of obsolescence.

The building had no true windows; instead, narrow plastic casements and electricity provided light, while a ventilation system of pumps, filters, exhaust shafts, and fans ensured breathable air.

Ongoing maintenance of the artificially balanced environment of B-30/T—the monitoring of closed-air systems and hazardous materials containment and disposal—was provided by workers in the facility maintenance unit. Periodic full-systems inspections were carried out in B-30/T after the last member of the research team had logged out for the day or night.

For more than forty-eight hours the lab had been functioning at basic survival level as dictated by security protocol: researchers and technicians would not be allowed on-site without authorization. When anything unusual happened to a member of a team working on highly sensitive, potentially lethal microcritters, people got nervous. Doug Thomas's death—a headlong Subaru dive into high-speed traffic—was definitely unusual. In search of *cause*, basic HazMat and HHAS inspection protocol could rule out chronic environmental exposure to toxins: toxins that might create any number of exotic and unpleasant symptoms—toxins that could *effect* death.

This particular security protocol—and the resulting vacated lab—provided a rare window of opportunity for Edmond Sweetheart and Sylvia Strange. They could tour the lab with minimal possibility of contact with their surveillance target, Dr. Christine Palmer.

But they were on-site only after a round of complex jurisdictional wrangling between FBI and DOE bureaucrats.

They were on-site under the watchful and wary eye of LANL's internal security division.

"We've completed checks on air-filtration systems, power sources, containment areas," Drew Dexter said. "All systems are clean, which tells us environmental exposure ain't the culprit." Dexter—buff, late forties, with a close crop of wheat-colored hair, a permanent sunburn, and a soft Louisiana drawl—had recently retired after two decades with the U.S. Army's criminal investigation division to take over as LANL's deputy division director of internal safety and security.

The lab was Drew Dexter's turf.

He announced that fact loud and clear before his actual appearance—he made them wait: five minutes, ten minutes, fifteen dragging into twenty. No apology, no explanation, when he finally deigned to meet them in a gleaming white all-terrain security vehicle.

It took Sylvia less than a minute to sum up Drew Dexter: possessive, proprietary, agressively polite, smart, and vigilant in the way guys who've spent a lifetime weathering intelligence bureaucracies are. Dexter had survived the fall of the Wall, Cold War meltdown, and the fallout after September 11. He didn't give two hoots about civilian consultants to the FBI.

She watched Sweetheart, curious about his initial reaction to the deputy division director. But whatever feelings Sweetheart had, he kept them to himself, controlling any stray urge to engage in a futile pissing contest.

They followed Dexter and two uniformed men from the maintenance unit along the cement walkway leading from the parking area to B-30/T's main entrance. The night air hummed with the sound of electrical systems. Overhead, insects and predatory bats swarmed the powerful lights. The high mountain air had a crisp, wintry edge.

For all the years Sylvia had lived in Santa Fe, the lab was foreign territory. In spite of having close friends who'd worked there, she thought of it as one massively dysfunctional family, complete with patriarchy in denial, brilliantly eccentric firstborns, their less brilliant and sometimes jealous siblings, a slew of distant relations (usually grumpy and less privileged), a black sheep or two, and finally the "help"—those people who arrived each day to clock in for an eight-hour shift sorting radioactive scrap metal or logging urine samples from the plutonium facility.

LANL made news when computer disks disappeared or when

physicists were suspected of becoming spies. On a more positive note, scientists moved from Los Alamos to Santa Fe's "Silicon Mesa," where they opened up nonprofits (the Santa Fe Institute) and technology transfer businesses (GenTech and NightSky).

Sylvia knew LANL was still under the administration of the University of California; she wasn't surprised to learn that a small city of fifteen thousand scientists, technicians, administrators, and support staff worked at LANL's one thousand facilities, which included labs, a hospital, industrial sites, administration buildings, and utility units. Researchers from around the world came here to study the business of cryogenics, supercollider magnets, linear proton acceleration.

And, more recently, biohazards.

B-30/T was secured by an alarm system as well as physical barriers. The FMU workers led the way; Dexter, Sweetheart, and Sylvia followed. Inside, the air was cool, not cold, and the light was uncomfortably bright.

Beyond the protocol security barrier, manned by a blue-blazered guard, there was a small reception area where workers and visitors could discard the superficial trappings of the outside world—coats, boots, backpacks, hats. The next six hundred square feet were taken up by common areas, storage units, bathrooms, a small kitchen, and offices. Computer monitors glowed like huge eyes, desks were surprisingly free of clutter, perhaps in preparation for the security clampdown.

Dexter opened a glass door and flipped a switch. Fluorescent lights buzzed to life, illuminating a narrow hallway with fractured brightness. As he led them all the way to the end of the hall, Sylvia noticed the thick gold wedding band on his manicured finger, the heavy-duty watch cuffing his broad wrist. "Palmer's administrative office," he drawled as he unlocked the second-to-last door.

Sylvia followed Sweetheart inside the office while Dexter waited in the hall. The space was about ten feet square; the ceiling was particle tile vented in two places, the floor was light blue industrial linoleum.

A large desk faced the door; a computer and monitor snoozed on the desktop; a long table lined one wall; filing cabinets covered the lower half of the opposite wall. A cardigan sweater had been left behind, draped over the shoulders of the desk chair, as if the wearer had just stepped out. Presumably the sweater belonged to Palmer; it was quality cashmere, quite new, the color of pale jade. When Sylvia ran her fingers along the edging, the delicate mother-of-pearl buttons felt cool to the touch.

Sweetheart seemed to catalogue each item carefully, but now his attention had been caught by a painting, the only decoration on the walls. Sylvia moved to his side to examine the small oil of a New York street scene: brick buildings, the glow of streetlamps, a solitary woman standing expectantly on a snow-covered street corner. A Wiggins. The mood of the painting was wintry and mysterious.

"She looks lonely," Sweetheart said softly.

"You think so?" Sylvia glanced at him in surprise. "I think she's meeting someone. It's evocative."

And Sylvia realized—was startled to realize—that although she'd never met Christine Palmer, she already admired the woman's taste.

At first glance, painting and sweater were the only two non-work-related items in the office, which was neat to the point of obsession. Books were arranged by size, files by color, while the surfaces—desk and cabinets—were clear of all clutter, all papers, all folders. The cabinets, marked with alphabetical tags, were unlocked. When Sylvia pulled out a drawer, she scanned the tags and saw what she presumed were test sequences—pages filled with comparisons, biochemical analyses, protocol notes. To truly evaluate what was here, she'd need a translator fluent in hard science.

Cutting through her thoughts, Dexter said, "This area is cold space."

For a moment Sylvia thought he was referring to the obsessively ordered office, then she realized he was discussing containment.

"Before we head downstairs," Dexter added, "I want you to understand what we're equipped for here: zootoxins, phytotoxins, viruses, microbes—we have the capabilities to handle them safely."

"Handle *some* of them safely," Sweetheart clarified. Biological hazards were rated from one to five—the higher the number, the greater the risk—all part of a rating code established by the CDC and the NIH. "I assume you're referring to those organisms permitted in labs rated at biological safety level three."

"That's a given." Dexter didn't try to mask his impatience. "For the most part, our scientists are working with DNA amplification. You'd be surprised—journalists, other civilians, are almost disappointed because it's *not* Ebola."

"But you do store live toxins on-site," Sylvia said, thinking of Dr. Thomas and the possibility of his exposure to a neurotoxin.

"We store toxins in this lab, yes, but it's important to have a realistic perspective. As I said, we are *not* talking Ebola virus, level four."

"But level three toxins can be lethal . . ."

"Table salt will kill you if you swallow enough."

Dexter ushered them back into the hallway, where they didn't have to venture far to reach the first barrier; Palmer's office was adjacent to a locked metal door, which had been plastered with warnings: a black skull and crossbones; STOP! BL3; CAUTION—CHEMICAL STORAGE; BIOLOGICAL HAZARDS ON SITE; NO EATING OR DRINKING; DANGER—HIGH VOLTAGE! Dexter tapped on the emblems. "Even in level three, the standard is to separate hot areas from cold. Hot being where we're headed right now, y'all."

While Dexter punched a security code into a digital pad, he kept talking. "Now, *if* a research team has to cope with viable pathogens, there's a remote possibility of aerosolization. That's where the ventilation system comes into play. Clean air pumps from the cold rooms to the hot rooms, in five-minute cycles. If the system were to back up—it's happened at other labs—then you'd get workers breathing pathogens. To guarantee that doesn't happen, this air cycles only once from intake to outtake"—he swirled one index finger overhead—"and then it's processed through a series of filters that trap hot substances before release."

"*Release* where?" Sylvia asked.

"Into the environment. The system is state-of-the-art."

"Is your background in science, Mr. Dexter?" Sylvia asked.

Dexter's gaze was impersonal, detached. She was startled to recognize that he didn't categorize her with the good guys: she was an unknown. Her fiancé did the same thing when he met someone for the first time. A suspicious mind—a trait of career cops, state or fed.

"I went to college, Dr. Strange. I completed a master's in science before I decided on a career in investigation and enforcement. I can't adequately protect what I don't understand."

Sylvia nodded, impressed, but also aware of the lab's imperfect track record. "What about malfunctions? What about human error or deliberate sabotage? You're staking fifty, a hundred thousand lives on your state-of-the-art-system. Don't you ever lose sleep wondering if this research is as safe as the party line claims it is?"

Except for his eyes, which narrowed and seemed to darken, Dexter's expression remained neutral—but passion bled through his words. "My daughter sings with the church choir, my son's a fullback for the Hilltoppers, my wife teaches second grade. I make it my business to *know* that the air they breathe is safe."

The silence lasted only a few seconds, but it felt like ten minutes to Sylvia. She was grateful when Sweetheart drew Dexter's focus.

"What can you tell us about Palmer's research?" he asked.

Dexter blinked, seemingly relieved to move on. "From what I've been told, it follows two tracks. The first—amplification—is basically innocuous. You can't make the organism from scratch, and the DNA's in a stable form—you could spike your martini and pretty much all you'd have is a bad taste in your mouth."

"The first track's DNA analysis," Sweetheart prompted. "What about the second?"

"Where time is a crucial element—the anthrax cases after September eleventh—the DNA analysis happens simultaneously with work in other areas, such as toxin isolation, serum formulation, and then it's necessary to have whole animals on site."

"What kinds of animals are we talking about?" Sylvia asked.

"Two years ago, spores of *Bacillus anthracis.* Today, other microorganisms." He turned his attention to the sterile, packaged protective gear in the dispenser mounted on the wall. "We'll skip the respirators tonight because we've been given the all-clear. Pick yourself booties and gloves—one size fits all."

In the hot sector of B-30/T—the inner sanctum—the air was thick with misty blue-white twilight, and the world was made of unforgiving chrome, steel, tempered glass, plastic, and tangles of rainbow-colored wires.

At the core of the hot sector, labs reserved for physical research and analysis were filled with equipment: the traditional stuff of beakers, thermometers, centrifuges.

Smaller rooms surrounded the labs: offices, isolation cells, and animal containment areas, where the metallic hiss of running wheels, the chatter of rodents, and the plaintive cries of other living creatures created eerie white noise. Limited animal research had been approved only within the previous six months—another sign of the escalating war against terrorism.

The hallways were mazelike, and the air smelled stale and slightly chemical. Their footsteps sounded with a hollow echo. Instinctively, Sylvia felt restless, on edge, impatient to return to the outside world. Instead, they were heading deeper into alien terrain—a world where research supported diverse fields such as biowarfare and ecology. They were heading for Christine Palmer's lab.

As Dexter led them down another hallway, Sylvia heard Sweetheart asking about the facility, general security protocols, and the late Dr. Doug Thomas. She was trying to absorb the conversation and, at the same time, glean a preliminary sense of Christine Palmer, the person she now considered their quarry.

She almost bumped into Sweetheart; the men had come to a stop in front of a large, glassed-in laboratory.

"This is where Palmer does the bulk of her work," Dexter said.

"You said she was involved in two tracks of research," Sylvia said. "What's going on in here, specifically?"

"I can tell you what I know: Dr. Palmer and her team are in the process of isolating a potent neurotoxin."

With that, Dexter punched a code on the keypad and, opening the door, allowed both profilers to pass with the admonition "Do not touch."

Sylvia took a deep breath, then began to look around. The lab (approximately twenty square feet) reminded her of a morgue, with its stainless steel counters, massive sinks, and storage units. Glass isolation boxes, complete with gloves, occupied two corners. A large overhead flue provided extra ventilation for especially toxic samples. White plastic trays were filled with culture plates, and red buckets contained swabs, syringes, and filters. Storage tanks were marked LIQUID NITROGEN and CRYO. Behind a thick glass barrier, a dozen numbered boxes housed albino mice; most of the animals seemed healthy, but when she looked more closely, she saw that several boxes contained dead and dying mice.

Sylvia turned away to find Sweetheart and Dexter gazing into one of three glass-walled, isolated, adjacent subrooms where level three toxins were stored, maintained, and manipulated in refrigerators, freezer units, and storage cells.

"This is what you've been waiting for, Dr. Strange." Dexter's drawl sounded like warm taffy. "If Doug Thomas was contaminated by something in this lab, you'll find it there."

"Give me an idea what we're talking about," she said.

Dexter pointed to a small freezer behind safety glass. "A substance classified as an antidote for a specific biochemical contamination, which means it's also a toxin." He indicated another container, marked BIOHAZARD in orange letters. "That one has a toxicity level of six—it's classified as supertoxic: less than five milligrams per kilogram will produce lethal results."

"And Dr. Thomas had access?" Sylvia asked.

"Only with approval of his supervisor—Dr. Palmer," Dexter said.

"But he had access."

"Yes. He was an integral team member of Project Mith—that's what they've tagged Palmer's project. Short for 'Mithridates.'"

"King of Pontus, one hundred B.C., king of the universal antidote," Sylvia murmured. She saw Sweetheart eyeing her—deciding she'd come across this fact in his case files—and she smiled slightly, knowing she'd trespassed on his territory. *He* was the font of archaic facts and figures.

"Dr. Thomas's lab is a few doors down," Dexter said sharply. "Whenever you're ready." Meaning now.

"Good," Sweetheart said, following the cue.

Sylvia shook her head. "I need another minute."

Sweetheart nodded. "Join us when you're ready."

Dexter hesitated, eyeing her. "Do not touch," he finally repeated on the way out.

When the two men were gone and Sylvia was left alone, she perched on the edge of a work stool and waited for her thoughts to tear loose, for her mind to begin spinning. She tried to imagine what it was like to dedicate one's life to the study of poisons and toxins.

Scientists were compulsive people; it took a certain level of obsession to focus your entire life on something that fit inside the lens of a microscope or a test tube, or simply into a theoretical formula—the task of counting angels on the head of a pin.

Christine Palmer was good at her job. She was one of the best toxicologists in the world. Was she a murderer? If so—had something turned her toward darkness, or had she always lived with the shadow of pathology?

It was too early to answer any of those questions, but already, Sylvia felt a deep curiosity—a *yearning*—to understand Christine Palmer.

She shook her head at her own arrogance: she could be accused of counting angels from time to time, and certainly she was obsessive when it came to her work as a psychologist.

Sylvia closed her eyes to let her senses register the background noises of the lab: the rustling of mice, the soft sounds of distress from dying animals, the hum of electrical systems—and the regular *shush* of air being circulated and filtered. She shivered. Dexter had explained that the room was pumped with pressurized fresh air, which ensured that old air moved *out* of the lab. A backdraft would allow pathogens to enter the lungs before the victim was even aware of exposure . . .

"I think it sounds like the room is breathing."

Sylvia started forward, opening her eyes abruptly, pivoting around. She found herself standing less than three feet away from Christine Palmer. Recognition was instinctual: this woman *had* to be

Palmer—the force of her personality, the obvious charisma, the powerful presence.

Sylvia could feel her heart pounding against her rib cage. "You startled me. I didn't expect to see anyone here." She held out her hand, half afraid it would tremble. "I'm Dr. Strange. You must be—"

"Dr. Christine Palmer." The toxicologist kept her arms at her sides. "What are you doing in my lab?"

"I'm sorry—I assumed you'd been informed." Sylvia found herself talking fast. "Due to the circumstances of Dr. Thomas's death—"

"Multiple agencies will conduct inquiries," Palmer finished tersely. "I'm familiar with the protocol. You're not physical security; not internal security—and that leaves DOE's administrative security, but I don't think so." Her eyes—intelligent and perceptive—were a deep smoky blue. At the moment they were communicating a direct challenge. Her features were symmetrical, slightly delicate, almost perfect. "So which agency are you with?" Palmer asked, scanning the lab.

"I didn't touch anything," Sylvia said, palms up, trying out a smile. "Actually, I'm a psychologist—part of a joint effort—"

"DOD? DOE?"

"—to study industrial accidents associated with toxic materials, toxic contamination."

"Do you have some ID, Dr. Strange?"

"I'm on contract with the health department." That much was true. Sylvia dug into her pocket and pulled out a business card. "My associates are working under the DOE," she said—at least that was somewhat true of Dexter. "As I said, we understood the lab was off-limits until morning. The FMU crew let us inside. Listen, I understand your attitude. I'd feel the same way in your shoes. I'm sure you need to call security. Clear this up." Sylvia moved briskly toward the telephone mounted on the wall near the door.

Christine Palmer held up one hand, the business card trapped between her fingers. "That's not necessary."

But behind those blue-gray eyes, Sylvia knew that Palmer was running scenarios, trying to identify an intruder in her territory. The black dots of the woman's pupils expanded and contracted infinitesimally.

"You said you're a psychologist?"

"In this case it's my job to look at the psychological state of victims," Sylvia said, warding off another challenge. "Did you know Dr. Thomas well?"

"We were colleagues—we did not socialize. He was a meticulous researcher." Palmer removed the cover from the first of the plastic trays.

"His death must have come as a terrible shock."

"Actually, no. I assume you're looking for indicators of emotional instability, substance abuse, life stressors?"

"Among other things."

"So you're conducting a psychological autopsy?"

"Yes." Sylvia pulled back a few inches; she was giving Palmer plenty of room. "Do you have any insights to share?"

"As team leader, I have insights into all my coworkers," Palmer said softly. She was more than confident—she was arrogant. "Doug Thomas had troubles with his personal life. He was recently divorced, he drank too much, and he liked to play the casinos."

"Did he confide in you?" Sylvia asked, silently deciding, *unlikely*.

"No. But I make it a point to pay attention to details. It doesn't take a genius to notice deteriorating personal hygiene, phone messages from ex-wives, casino matchbooks." Dr. Palmer washed her hands carefully at the decontamination sink. "What else would you like to know, Dr. Strange?"

"I was wondering where toxic exposure on the job was most likely to occur."

"Wouldn't it be more helpful to use Dr. Thomas's lab for his—*autopsy?*"

"I needed a sense of the overall structure of B-30 before I zeroed in on his work area."

"I see," Palmer said, nodding. "For the sake of this project, I want questions around Dr. Thomas's death answered as soon as possible. If you're interested in possible symptomology from exposure to neurotoxins—"

"I'm interested."

"I've been involved in after-the-fact analyses of a number of accidental exposures. The most recent was a lab in England."

"What types of symptoms?" Sylvia asked, watching Palmer move around the space.

Palmer pulled gloves from a dispenser as she said, "The symptoms may be fleeting, and they are varied: tremors, blurred vision, headaches, vomiting, weight loss, lesions, short-term-memory loss, general cognitive deficit. At their most acute, seizures, heart failure, total paralysis."

"Would those symptoms relate to this project?"

"Are they relevant to Dr. Thomas? Possibly. But the lab is clean."

Sylvia didn't acknowledge the statement. She forced herself to wait out an uncomfortable silence while Palmer examined several trays of cultures.

After almost a minute, Palmer turned to face Sylvia. "In the case of Dr. Thomas, you can't rule out suicide."

"Why not?"

Palmer looked surprised by the question. "He was unstable." She shrugged—*case closed.* "Now that I've answered your questions, perhaps you'll return the favor. Can you give me any information about the accident?" Her voice was soft, almost insinuating. "Was Dr. Thomas conscious at the time of impact?"

"I don't know."

"Is there any evidence of convulsions? Seizures?"

"I'm sorry . . ." Sylvia shook her head, uncomfortable with the level of Palmer's curiosity. "I have no information to share at this time."

Palmer was staring at Sylvia. She frowned, and the skin at the corner of her eyes tightened. "Have we met before?"

"No. I'd remember."

Palmer took a step forward. An arm's length separated the two women. Sylvia could hear Palmer breathing under the sound of the lab mice and the hum of equipment. She could see a dark speck in the iris of Palmer's left eye; the woman didn't blink.

The hair on the back of Sylvia's neck stood up.

Footsteps sounded in the hallway, and Sylvia jerked forward—feeling released—moving quickly toward the exit. She didn't want Palmer to encounter Dexter and Sweetheart.

"You've been helpful," Sylvia said, pushing the door open. "I appreciate the fact you didn't tear my head off. I know what it's like to work with sensitive material. I'd love to talk with you some more about exposure scenarios."

Palmer just stared at her as the door closed with a soft hiss of air.

Sylvia hurried down the hall to intercept the men. She had the distinct impression that Palmer was following her—but there was no one there when she turned to look back.

Special Agent Darrel Hoopai spoke quietly into his transmitter. "The Target caught Pest Control in the Web."

"Web" meaning laboratory, "Pest Control" referring to LANL security and the two profilers, "the Target" being Dr. Christine Palmer—the whole incident adding up to one big snafu.

As he listened to his superior read him the riot act, Hoopai walked, tracing a circle, trying to get his circulation moving again, to pump the blood out of aching feet.

At this moment his partner was in position behind the Nest, his vantage point allowing him to cover all three rear exits.

Hoopai listened for another fifteen seconds then said, "Target departed the Web at twenty-three hundred and came home to Nest."

Silently, he agreed with his S.A.C.: there was no excuse.

But whose fault was it ultimately? They'd tried repeatedly to contact LANL's deputy director of security—by the time their message was received, the Target was already inside.

How had Palmer sweet-talked her way past protocol security? And why hadn't protocol security notified internal security?

If LANL was sloppy . . .

But it was S.A. Hoopai who was taking the brunt of the heat. As the special agent paced, he shook his head and the transmitter moved like some alien appendage. "Three hundred yards from the Nest," he said, "we have clear skies."

The cul-de-sac—deserted except for a convention of feral cats, and surrounded by twenty-five-foot pines—gave them an uninterrupted view of the two-story home where the Target resided. Lights were on in several rooms, and the Target's vehicle was parked in the driveway. Agents Hoopai and Weaver had followed her home, put her to bed from a distance.

The house was situated in a Los Alamos neighborhood that was a few miles north of the lab's hospital and administration buildings. A number of homes in this area had been destroyed by the Cerro Grande fire (the wildfire had prowled like a ravenous beast, taking bites from forest and town); most homes had been rebuilt, but a few lots remained empty.

"The diner, that's a roger," S.A. Hoopai said slowly, responding to a question. The Target had ordered takeout. "We attempted to establish audio contact regarding ETA with Pest Control—transmission unsuccessful."

S.A. Hoopai liked the whisper of wind through the trees, liked the scent of pine and wood smoke—unlike his friends and fellow agents who'd been born in cities. They'd never gotten used to space that wasn't covered in concrete.

"The Target is stable in the Nest," Hoopai said in response to a query. He nodded. "Oh-eight-hundred in your office, roger that." Terminating the transmission, he made a long, doleful face.

He walked over to the van and retrieved the single can of Diet Coke he'd been saving. He swirled it, held it to his ear, and slowly put pressure on the punch lid. The can opened, and air escaped with a satisfying belch.

After he finished off a third of the Diet Coke, Special Agent Hoopai directed his surveillance glasses at the two-story house, the Nest.

The Target—clearly visible through her office window—was seated at her desk, posture rigid, eyes on the open book in front of her. She was writing, her hand tracing a continuous scrawl across the page. This could go on for hours. It often did. Until she stopped abruptly at 0100 hours—her bedtime.

Hoopai settled in for a long night.

But tonight she wrote for thirty minutes—and then she flung the book across the room, bolted from the table, and disappeared inside her bathroom. When she reappeared a few minutes later, she was naked.

Hoopai whistled. He kept his voice low and spoke to his coagent via the transmitter: "Big Daddy to Little Daddy—she's doing that thing."

S.A. Weaver's voice was faint and scratchy. "Again?"

"Take a look." Hoopai adjusted his own glasses, catching the bare breasts of Dr. Christine Palmer—the Target—squarely in both eyes. As he stared across the distance, she began *pacing* the length of the room—arms at her sides, back straight, eyes forward—only to turn and retrace her steps again and again and again.

At one point she stopped on a dime, pivoting to face the plate glass windows.

Hoopai shrunk back unconsciously, even though he would not be visible from this distance, in this darkness.

The Target pivoted again, as neatly as a dancer. She stooped down to retrieve something from the floor.

"Whoa," Weaver breathed, his voice traveling the distance.

But it was Hoopai who got the benefit of the perfect moon shot—full, milky white ass.

Another thought crossed S.A. Hoopai's mind—just for an instant: *We've been made.* But then the thought evaporated, gone.

She was back to her pacing.

It could go on until dawn.

"Come on, Sweetheart," Sylvia snapped. "Do we have to rehash this all night? What the hell did you want me to do? Palmer found me trespassing in her level three lab."

"And you gave her your business card? One or two phone calls, five minutes of her time, and she knows you're lying."

"Are you afraid she'll connect me with you and blow your cover?"

He shot her a dark look, and Sylvia wondered if her words had hit the mark.

She said, "If Dexter's own guys didn't stop her, if the feds can't keep track of her—"

"Either way, you end up as bait."

They'd begun the argument on the drive down the hill; they'd reworked it on the bypass ten miles later; they'd worn themselves out on the outskirts of Santa Fe, settling into a sulky silence.

But now the argument resurfaced as they stood in shadow—out of range of the twenty-foot lamps and the slivered moon—in the parking lot across from the Eldorado Hotel.

"Blame the feds, not me," she said.

"I blame myself. I'm having second thoughts."

"About?"

"Your participation."

Sylvia's eyes went wide, and thoughts raced through her brain. This was the perfect opportunity to walk away. For the last seven hours she'd been vacillating, simultaneously drawn to and repelled by the case. This *split mind* wasn't limited to the Palmer case. Since her very first class in abnormal psychology, more than fifteen years ago, she'd been aware of the appeal and the cost of a career in forensic psychology. The years of delving into shattered psyches had taken their toll—and her ambivalence had grown. In fact, it was the Riker case that had pushed her to a new level of misgiving. Nightmares, the brutal nature of the murders, and Riker himself had all overloaded her system to the point where she'd thought of giving up the work completely. *Burnout.* But she'd never gone that far. Always—without fail—she'd found the strength to pace herself, to go beyond the point of no return, to go all the way to the end.

"You practically begged me to work on this case, you said you needed my help. I believed you." She shook her head, confused, reproving. "Now, a few hours later, you're over the top, semihysterical because Christine Palmer intimidated the hell out of me in that lab, but I'm a big girl, so—"

She bit down on her lower lip, going silent as she noticed a woman in flamenco dress emerging from a dark Cadillac. The sharp, impromptu clack of castanets punctuated her next words, which were delivered sotto voce. "Do not ask me to walk away."

They were standing so close she could feel his breath on her face. In the artificial light cast from overhead, she thought she saw fear in his eyes, but she couldn't tell if he was afraid for her or if the fear belonged to something else. For several seconds, he was silent, then he whispered, "All right."

And she jumped right in—as if the moment had never happened—saying, "I have no problem envisioning Palmer as an aggressive opponent, a professional I wouldn't want to cross, but I'm standing here in the dark trying to believe she's a serial murderer. Where's the pattern? With her lineage, her brilliance, her career—what does she gain by killing?"

"You're letting your mind be clouded by those very things: career, brilliance, scientific lineage, which are all irrelevant—"

They both stood mute while the dancer—heels clicking out sharp notes on asphalt—passed them by. When she walked beneath a lamp, the glow was a spotlight illuminating a scarlet ruffled dress, red lips and black eyes, a coiled snake of black hair.

"—because what she gains is power. And *pleasure.*"

"You really believe it's that basic?"

"Absolutely." Sweetheart's eyes followed the dancer as she disappeared through an alcove. He refocused on Sylvia. "How could you believe it's *not* that basic?"

"But you've barely begun to cover even the most obvious aspects of victimology and . . ." Sylvia trailed off, feeling oddly perplexed, as if she'd missed the moment when they'd changed tracks. She frowned. "This is a last-minute scramble to gather data and fill in the blanks, you said so yourself."

"Data won't change the primitive schematic. Palmer's a psychopath. Brilliance, privilege, and beauty are part of the package—but at her core you'll find psychopathy. Don't get sidetracked."

"You know this for a fact already? Let me in on your secret. *Please.*"

"Don't be stupid." He set his mouth, tightening his body, shutting her out. "I expect you to use your intelligence."

"Maybe you're right," Sylvia said slowly. "You've got it all figured out, maybe you don't need my participation."

But when she saw his relief, she knew she didn't want to let him push her away, didn't want to be barred from the investigation, wanted to stay *in*—most of all because her deepest instinct told her Sweetheart needed her more than he realized.

So she shoved him verbally into a defensive posture. "You sound like an embittered lover."

"And you sound like a disappointed fan." He snapped up her bait almost greedily. "A schoolgirl with a crush."

Their eyes met. She knew Sweetheart was driven by a level of obsession that was off the charts. Well, if anybody could match him, she could. But once again, it wasn't ambition or hunger that made her refuse to back off; it was the nagging sense that her friend and colleague was on the edge.

But on the edge of what? she found herself wondering—and that thought alone seemed melodramatic.

The stubborn silence was punctuated by the distant sound of a flamenco guitar, and then a Gypsy singer began his melancholy canto. Sylvia shivered, not from cold but from a sense of disturbed equilibrium. She turned away from Sweetheart toward the music, toward the hotel. Lights were on in some of the rooms, a woman strolled past a sliding glass door, a lone figure stood watch from a fifth-story window.

"It's possible that Palmer got it right," she said in a low voice. "It's possible Doug Thomas committed suicide. Or maybe he was accidentally exposed—we don't even have confirmation it *was* a toxin. And Dexter gave us nothing." She shook her head, and her volume built. "How are we supposed to sort through classified information and *dis*information?"

"Keep your voice down," Sweetheart hissed. "Dr. Thomas had toxin in his blood." He held up his Palm Pilot, displaying the glowing green alphanumeric remnants of a message. "A reaction on the final blood analysis detection assay. There was enough luminescence to indicate exposure to a neurotoxin."

"Do we know which one?"

"No." He paused. "But I pushed for information through my own channels, and I found out what Drew Dexter wouldn't—or couldn't—tell you in the lab. The focus of Palmer's projects over the past eight years has been the study of toxic dinoflagellates."

"Dinoflagellates—algae?"

"Single-celled microorganisms, very primitive, with qualities that can be used to identify them as either plant or animal. With few exceptions, dinoflagellates are basic and beneficial to both fresh- and saltwater food chains. Palmer's interested in the exceptions: the rogue dinoflagellates, capable of producing highly lethal neurotoxins." His eyebrows dipped together. "These same toxins have been used to produce nerve gas for military research—vomiting, paralysis, psychosis, death—typical symptoms that could explain why a man would drive head-on into a truck."

Restlessly, Sylvia shifted her weight. This time the horror had hit home. "Jesus, that's what they're playing with on the hill?" She pushed her dark hair from her cheek. A Spanish song, something in a nine-eight rhythm, lingered faintly in the air.

Along the side streets the traffic signals had begun to blink, a sign it was nearing midnight. She'd have to move soon, go in search of Matt. She'd tried to reach him on his cell phone several times during the past forty minutes—no answer—and she'd left a string of messages flavored by Sweetheart being by her side the whole time: *"Hey, it's me, call me back when you get a chance. Tell me where you are. I hope your dinner in Albuquerque went well. Love you."*

Then: *"Maybe you're already home in bed, but call me if you check messages."*

And finally: *"It's a good thing I'm not stranded by the side of the road or something. Where are you?"*

Thinking about him, about his voice, his laugh, she felt a yearning so sharp it hurt. When they'd first met, several years earlier, the circumstances were anything but romantic—her life had been fractured by a psychotic inmate, a prison riot, and grief over the death of a man who had been her lover, colleague, mentor. Her attraction to Matt had been prompted by his strength, his integrity, his basic goodness. Her great-grandmother would have called him "salt of the earth"— and she would've been right.

Those thoughts raced through her mind in the time it took to breathe, and she felt herself mobilize—her priority was to let Matt know about the change in their prenuptial game plan. He wasn't going to be thrilled by the news.

For an instant, she saw herself telling Sweetheart he was right after all—she should forget the case—but even as she felt the instinct, she knew it was too late. She'd already taken her stand. She was on board for the ride.

"Sylvia, I want to get back to the question of your continued participation."

"So do I." She was already moving toward her truck, keys in hand. "I *refuse* to participate in a witch-hunt. As it is, there aren't enough women in Palmer's scientific league. She's brilliant. She could discover the antidote to any number of biological threats, could save thousands of lives. Even a tinge of suspicion—if this *ever* gets out, and if we're *wrong*—it will ruin her."

In contrast to Sylvia's restless motion, Sweetheart stood without moving, without appearing to breathe. "I understand your concerns," he said, "but the evidence points to our target."

"The evidence is circumstantial. Don't forget what happened when the FBI was trying to track down the perpetrator of the 'anthrax letters.'" Sylvia unlocked the door of her truck, opened it, and hoisted herself up into the seat. She pointed a finger at Sweetheart. "They burned poisoners during the Inquisition. If you want me along for the ride, *no* witch-hunts." With a quick toss of her head, she slammed the door shut.

Sweetheart closed his eyes, and oddly, his entire face seemed to disappear in shadow. "No witch-hunts," he murmured softly.

From a distance, the old adobe in La Cieneguilla resembled a Moorish castle as much as the ruins of a nineteenth-century coach stop. The thick mud bricks had been patched and replastered countless times over the decades; more than thirty years ago, Sylvia's own father had added a long, sloping *portal* and an extra bedroom (now used by Serena); within the past six months, Sylvia had supervised the addition of a second-story master bedroom and bath, a walled garden, and a separate studio for writing, research, and seclusion.

All this change was her version of *nesting*.

Shifting into second gear, then third, she guided the truck along the quarter mile of gravel that led to the driveway. She was impatient to see Matt, looking forward to the haven of home.

The house sat in the middle of a twenty-acre parcel that included pastures, a stream, two small calderas, and a geologic ridge resembling the backbone of a giant Pleistocene creature.

Sylvia loved the house for its history and its high-desert setting. She and Matt had agreed they would continue to call it home after their marriage. Although he still maintained a trailer in Santa Fe, he spent most of his time in La Cieneguilla.

The truck bounced over a rut created by the roots of the oldest cottonwood on the property, her "grandfather tree." She passed the red-and-white mailbox, turned in to the driveway, and parked next to Matt's Ford. As she climbed out, she could hear the faintly frantic welcoming cries of her two dogs. She could picture exactly where they were at this moment: dog snouts pressed to the living room picture window, front paws propped on the big jade's ceramic pot.

She approached the front door; no lights went on inside the house. She knew Matt had driven to Albuquerque for dinner and a meeting with the state's lieutenant governor and Lucia Hernandez, the governor's smart and gorgeous aide-de-camp, the woman who definitely had his ear. A cozy tête-à-tête. Strictly business, of course— on the political and budgetary implications of a new command center for the state's special operations officers. Matt's bailiwick these days.

Not that she was jealous.

She unlocked the door and greeted her dogs in the usual order: Rocko, the scrappy terrier with bad hair, then Nikki, the three-legged Belgian Malinois. Except for the dogs' muffled greetings, the house was silent.

But clearly not empty.

She followed the trail of Matt's clothes—jacket tossed over the leather couch, shirt in the kitchen, boots askew in the hallway, socks on the recently built staircase that led up to the new master bedroom.

With both dogs quietly in tow, she tiptoed up the stairs and into the room.

He was fast asleep, snoring faintly, his naked body akimbo, filling most of the king-size bed. His eyes were shut, his mouth open. His palms were up, his fingers curled, as if he were holding on to something. A faint illumination from the overhead casement highlighted his torso—the broad, muscular chest, the lightly defined ribs, the dark hair that curled from the hollow of his throat to his groin. His penis was half erect.

Sylvia thought, not for the first time, that this was any man's most vulnerable moment.

She stood for a minute or so. Just watching, taking him in. She felt the energy of her own desire—a nice chemical and emotional scramble of love and lust. The dogs had settled on the floor next to the bed. Once or twice, Sylvia thought that she saw Matt open his eyes; but it was her own eyes playing tricks.

When she had undressed, she stepped forward, shifting her weight carefully onto the bed so her breasts rubbed his belly and her lips touched his skin.

He moaned, shifting, reaching out instinctively.

He felt hot to the touch. In an instant he was hard.

She took her time, lingering for several minutes before she finally began to work her way up his abdomen. She nipped his earlobe and whispered, "I thought you might want a last fling before you get hitched."

Apparently he did.

Alchemist

I can read your mind although I don't dare share the depth of my knowledge with you. Not yet.

There is always the hunger to understand:

—while poison courses through veins, is absorbed into organs, reaches the cells and synapses of the brain.

You ask:

Where does it hurt the most? Are you shivering from heat, or cold? Is that flickering of your eyelids the first sign of convulsions to follow? Is your mouth dry? Is your brain exploding with pain? Is your stomach tied in knots? Are your thoughts fractured? Are you going blind and deaf?

Do you know death is with you . . . do you know death is with you . . . do you know death is with you?

Are you afraid?

M oon shadows through the skylight. The room glowing with light. Sylvia pushed herself reluctantly off the bed and away from the warmth of Matt's body. She'd almost fallen asleep in the wake of making love.

But now to business—the need to tell Matt about the impending trip, the collaborative work with Sweetheart couldn't be postponed.

"We've got to talk," she said softly. "Babe?"

"Mmmm."

She opened her mouth, then shut it again. The words stuck in her throat. *Don't be ridiculous,* she told herself, *jump in.* "I left messages on your cell. I need to talk to you about tomorrow."

"Shhhh. I'm dreaming. Good one." He rolled over, eyelids squeezed tight. "Give me a minute . . . find out how it turns out."

She sighed. Another minute couldn't hurt—then she heard a truncated snore. Make that another five or ten minutes.

She slipped into a well-worn terry robe and slippers, retrieved her purse from the top of the dresser, and padded across the room to the bathroom. The door squeaked slightly as it shut behind her. She washed her face, brushed her teeth, and surveyed her image in the mirror—did she look like a liar?

She opened her purse to retrieve the small pharmacy bag; she'd refilled two prescriptions earlier in the day. From the bag she pulled out the container of antihistamines and set it on the middle shelf of the medicine cabinet. There was one more item in the bag—the pink plastic case of contraceptives.

Quickly she slid the pink case into a zippered compartment in her handbag, as if out of sight were truly out of mind. Not this time. The guilt had kicked in: she was lying to the man she was about to marry.

As far as Matt knew, she'd finished her last prescription of birth control pills. With marriage on the agenda, they'd agreed to try to get pregnant. At least she *thought* she'd agreed. But when it came down to the final few pills, she'd found herself calling in a refill. And she'd done it furtively—horrified by herself, by such a deep untruth.

She sighed, studying herself in the mirror. She wanted children—most of the time. She pictured Rosie Sanchez, her best friend, sitting on the edge of her desk, wagging tiny feet in very spiky heels, ankle bracelet sparkling: "You'll make a fabulous mother, *jita*. Trust yourself."

But each time she believed she'd resolved all remaining child-rearing conflicts, some internal beast raised its doubting head. She knew—no matter how much Matt assured her he'd carry fifty percent of the load—that the weight of parenting would fall most heavily on her shoulders. She'd seen it over and over again; her close friends joked that after the first eighteen years it got easier. Despite all the planning and good intentions and political awareness, nature had an ancient and basic agenda.

But her doubts ran deeper, to more complex issues than child care—issues of suitability and desire.

The woman gazing back at Sylvia from the mirror looked miserable. She certainly didn't want to put off motherhood until it was too late. And Matt felt time running out even more acutely than she did. He'd survived the death of his first wife and son years ago. And he wasn't one of those men who wanted to be Grandpa to his own child. He didn't want to be too old to keep up with his son or daughter.

She pulled away from the mirror, crossed her arms under her breasts, and frowned at herself. She knew what she would tell some other woman in the same circumstances, knew what advice she'd give a client who showed up for counseling.

Be honest. Be truthful. Tell your husband, your lover, your boyfriend about your worries and your conflicts. Don't withhold, don't lie.

Good advice. The woman in the mirror stood up straight and nodded.

But the internal voice that whispered in Sylvia's ear—the voice that rationalized, and made deals, and struck bargains—said, *Just one more month. By then you'll be ready to commit to motherhood, and you'll spare Matt the needless worry caused by your neurotic doubts.*

She swallowed the first pill in the pink container, dropped it back into her purse, and zipped the compartment shut, ready for travel.

When she left the bathroom, Rocko followed at her heels. Nikki watched their progress from her favorite spot, a threadbare oversize pillow next to the bed.

As Sylvia walked downstairs, she ran over a mental list of last-minute wedding details, the numerous favors she would ask of Rosie Sanchez: problems with the florist; the dress (currently with the seamstress for minor alterations) that needed to be picked up; the issue of whether to have the mariachi play before the salsa band or during the meal; and the burning question of whether or not her all-time favorite caterers, Josie's Casa de Comida, should make the enchilada plates with red, green, or Christmas.

On ground level Rocko took the lead from the hallway to the kitchen. His ears cocked forward and his little tail twitched as he moved with a stiff, tightly sprung gait. Sylvia switched on the light, opened the refrigerator, and gazed blankly at a leftover turkey and green chile sandwich, a quart of milk, strawberry yogurt, black pepper goat cheese, and martini olives.

She pulled out the milk and let the door thump shut as she took a box of Grape-Nuts from the pantry shelf. She shook the box, gauging from the rustle that there was enough cereal for one bowl.

At her side, Rocko gave a low growl through his whiskers. He sat up on his haunches, begging shamelessly.

"You know that's not allowed," she chided gently, nevertheless reaching into the cereal bowl to flip him several hard nuggets. He caught them neatly before they hit the floor.

At the table she settled down to eat. It was an ordinary moment that had been repeated so many times in her life, she sometimes failed to realize how much it meant—this kitchen, this view of the cottonwood and the salt cedar (a pretty but dangerous interloper in the desert ecosystem), this piece of land that had been in her family for over fifty years.

Her gaze continued around the room—cheerful and utilitarian at the same time—before settling on a glittery blue-and-green jacket that belonged to her foster daughter. Serena was staying with her father for the next four days. Although Cash Wheeler had legal custody of his daughter, he showed no signs of veering from the shared custody that Serena enjoyed. The back-and-forth arrangement had worked fairly smoothly for the past year. Perhaps trading houses and sharing families suited Serena because her first ten years had been spent in such intense isolation. She'd grown up just across the U.S.–Mexico border, in a barrio in Juarez; human contact had been limited to a handful of people. She'd survived by using her imagination, her incredible talent as an artist, instead of words.

In exchange, sharing families had allowed Sylvia the pleasure of contact and love without the full responsibility a child of her own would require. She smiled now as she pictured Serena today, at twelve years old: confident, intuitive, filled with light and grace. The transformation had taught Sylvia to believe in miracles.

She had no doubt that Serena would understand her decision to work with Sweetheart on the profile, but Rosie Sanchez was another matter. She would do all she could to make Sylvia feel guilty, as if she were running away.

Sylvia sighed, then stood to carry her dishes to the sink. She could see the eyelash moon hovering in a blue-black sky. It was very late, but for some reason she wasn't tired. Perhaps her energy was actually leftover adrenaline from the events of the afternoon and evening? For an instant, she was transported back to the dark lab with its dying animals, its deadly toxins; she *felt* her encounter with Christine Palmer— and a shiver ran from her butt to the top of her head. The dish slipped from her fingers, clattering to the sink.

"Hey, babe." She heard Matt's voice echoing down the hall, then his arms slid around her waist. He buried his face in her neck and said, "You okay?"

"Maybe a little bit spooked—fine now." She turned to smile at him. "Love you."

"And I love the way you wake me up. But it's the middle of the night."

She offered him a kiss, took her time, and then tilted her head to see into his eyes. "You really awake?"

"You sound like my grandma Effie: 'Hey, Frank, you awake?'"

"I am *now*." Sylvia finished the familiar line with a smile. She kissed Matt again, and then her expression turned serious. "What do you know about that LANL scientist who died up on 285?"

He took a moment, knowing she wasn't asking an idle question.

He said, "He was dead at the scene. The oncoming truck pushed his vehicle three hundred feet past the intersection into a ditch." He shrugged, a wary look in his eye. "Why are you interested?"

"Promise me you'll listen to what I have to say."

He stepped back, his hands sliding from her waist to his sides. "Listen before *what?*"

"Before you say anything."

He nodded, watching her, one brow arched in a question mark. His expression had shifted from wary to openly suspicious. "Talk to me."

"I need to do a little bit of traveling—two, maybe three days tops."

"Why?"

"A serial poisoning case at LANL. I've been asked to help put together a profile for investigators. I've got to visit a previous job site, another lab, do some document review, some interviews."

"Which lab? Sandia?"

"Porton Down." Sylvia tried to sound casual. "Outside London."

Matt's jaw tightened, and he spoke slowly. "London."

"There was another death about six months ago, and it's connected to the case."

"So it's multijurisdictional—"

"And the FBI has the case, yes."

"And who enlisted your help?"

"Edmond Sweetheart."

"Sweetheart's consulting for the feds?" Envy darkened Matt's voice—he resented Sweetheart's high-profile connections at the same time he coveted the free agent's ability to pick and choose investigations. It was a sharp contrast to a career with the state police, even at the rank of major, even with his lateral promotion to special operations. These days Matt was much more entrenched in the political arena than ever before. The hostage negotiation team, the dive team, special rescues all came under the umbrella of special ops—which meant time spent lobbying, making sure the governor's office was in the loop, co-ordinating with narcotics, as well as recruiting and training.

"This is all connected to the death of the LANL scientist last Fri-day?" he asked sharply.

She nodded. "The feds stepped in to begin surveillance after the collision—they believe he was poisoned and that's why he lost control of the car."

"You said *serial* poisoning."

"Apparently the deaths stretch back years—in Europe and the U.S."

"Then the FBI's facing a jurisdictional nightmare," Matt said. "Unless they've got hard evidence of a murder on U.S. soil, they won't make charges stick."

"You're right. They need this profile." She crossed the kitchen to check the lock on the sliding glass door. "I'll be back Wednesday night, Thursday at the latest."

Silently, Matt tracked her restless circuit.

"Seventy-two hours at most," she said, talking too fast because she felt awkward and because she hated having to rationalize her actions. "Listen, I know the timing isn't perfect."

"Isn't *what?*"

"Okay, okay, the timing sucks," she said quickly. "But it won't interfere with the wedding. I won't let that happen."

"What time is your flight?"

She glanced automatically at the big white clock. "I need to leave here by seven-thirty at the latest. The flight isn't until midday, but I've got to finish writing up an evaluation for the courts and drop it off." Rocko followed her gaze; a faint worried whine escaped his jaws.

"I don't believe this," Matt said.

The grizzled terrier looked at the man and then back at Sylvia as she said, "Matt, please understand."

He shook his head, turning away from her, heading back down the hall.

"Hey, can we *not* argue about this? We're both adults. If a case comes up—if you have to go to Las Cruces or Denver—I don't give you a hard time."

"That's big of you." He kept walking.

"All right. Wait." She followed him, Rocko at her heels, still acting like her shadow. "I know it's short notice."

"Short? What if I'd stayed in Albuquerque tonight? Were you planning to call me from London?" Matt's voice always grew deeper when he was angry. Right now he was a bass. "You casually mention it's a serial poisoning case—which makes me think there may be some risk involved—Jesus, you just finished going through the Riker ordeal—but who cares what I know, right?"

"I care. I don't blame you for being upset."

"I can't believe you're taking on a case right now." He saw that she was about to respond, but he cut her off: "Don't tell me it's a matter of days. I know you, Sylvia. Once you commit to something, you hang in to the bitter end."

Now she didn't try to interrupt; she knew it was best to let him have his say.

"If you're too scared to do this wedding, tell me now," he said. "I don't need excuses. Let's hope there's no Leo to keep you distracted—"

"Leo Carreras isn't connected to this case," Sylvia protested. "You know I wouldn't do anything to jeopardize us, the wedding, our marriage."

Matt shrugged. "You've done a pretty good job of avoiding the altar up to now."

"I'm sorry," Sylvia said softly. She knew he'd felt the sting of their on-again, off-again engagement. She watched as he reached the foot of the stairs and stopped. "Don't you understand?" she asked. "I need to put my energy into one last case—it may be a big one—before I retire."

"You're not retiring."

"A sabbatical, then. We're getting married. We've decided to try for a baby. Virtual retirement. At least for a while."

He nodded. Neither of them spoke for several seconds. Rocko whined softly. Finally Matt sighed. "You'll be back by Thursday?"

"Probably Wednesday."

"I can work out arrangements with Cash about Serena."

She took a deep breath, realizing only as she exhaled that she'd been holding air in her lungs. "That would be great."

"If I have to take off to Albuquerque—"

"Cash will bring Serena by to pick up the dogs—she loves to have them at her dad's."

He nodded. Outside, somewhere in the distance, a dog was barking, a hoarse and frustrated repetition of sound.

Matt started up the stairs, stopping again when he heard her voice.

"Matt? I'm sorry for the times I hurt you."

"You ran out on me once," he said as she closed the short distance between them.

"I love you." She reached out, touching him gently on the temple with one hand. "I'm marrying you one week from Saturday."

Rocko stood on his hind legs, balancing his front paws on Matt's knees. The terrier let out a quick, demanding bark.

She watched Matt grapple with conflicting emotions, his internal struggle evidenced in his eyes. She had no doubt he loved her—he'd been far more patient than she would've been if the situation had been reversed.

He looked into her eyes, searching for fear. "I wish I could say it was fine; I wish I could let you off the hook, but I can't. I don't have the energy to go through another Riker case—or another round of *Runaway Bride.*"

She began to speak, her voice—faintly pleading—barely rising above a whisper. "If you tell me to stay home, forget this case, I will."

"Don't lay that responsibility on me." He shook his head. "You need to go. You said so yourself. So go."

The glow of the digital clock cast a reddish burn on Sweetheart's half-closed eyelids. He was sitting lotus style in the center of the massive hotel bed. Internally, he had made the transition from full meditation to the next best state, a notch down, still focused on breath but the frontal lobe actively engaged. The way he did his sharpest thinking.

The day, the night, had triggered old memories. Sonobe, Japan. The rain never stopped the whole time he was there. The Hayashi investigation—a housewife imprisoned for poisoning her fellow villagers during their spring festival. The investigation had been a circus, every international agency wanting in, most getting their wish.

The *fujin-kai,* the ladies' league, and Masuma Hayashi, killing everyone with her *kaari raisu.* All part of the puzzle. The rigid social hierarchy, the drive for prominence, feelings of entitlement. And always—he could hear Sylvia voicing his thoughts—*always* narcissism. It didn't matter who died or how many, because they were of no consequence. Most normal people found it almost impossible to relate to the worldview of the narcissist. Sweetheart found it too easy.

The detail that stood out clearest in his mind was the fact that Masuma Hayashi mixed up her cyanide stew and served the village elders and the children first—

The phone bleated softly, but he didn't react immediately. One, two, three bleats, sounding plaintive by now. Moving only one arm, he connected to the material world.

"I just got your message," Drew Dexter said.

"Late night."

"I had to follow through on tonight's problem." The deputy division director of internal safety and security at LANL paused. In the background the faint chatter of voices was audible. "That little run-in, Dr. Palmer and your gal. Shouldn't have happened."

Sweetheart said nothing, waiting to hear what Dexter would say next. He was more than curious. Dexter kept himself very well informed; Sweetheart made it a point to look closely at well-informed people.

He'd run a background check in MOSAIK—updated his files—and knew that Dexter was near the top of the food chain at the lab. He was southern blue-collar stock (hence the accent); both his parents were Louisiana natives. He'd done a tour of duty at the end of Vietnam, when the troops were coming home; upon his return to the States, he'd completed college on the G.I. Bill. Then he had spent most of twenty years with the army's criminal investigation division.

"The feds screwed up," Dexter was saying. The pronouncement was delivered in a derisive near-whisper. "But so did my guy on protocol." Equally derisive. "He should've kept Palmer at the door and contacted me. It won't happen again. As of thirty minutes ago, he's out of a job."

Sweetheart grunted. *Not good enough.* He knew firsthand what Palmer was capable of—don't touch, don't get burned. Several times tonight he'd considered taking Dexter down verbally—Sylvia and Palmer had made contact because Dexter's security had performed badly—but a takedown wouldn't win points, not in the end. He said calmly, "I'd consider it a personal favor if you keep this number at hand. If Palmer makes a move, any move—"

"You hear it ASAP," Dexter said, the drawl thicker than usual.

"Quantico will finish the formal pathology report on Doug Thomas in the next day or so," Sweetheart said, casting out a line—information on the death of Dr. Thomas—as a return of favor.

After he'd disconnected, he reached across the night table for his

Palm Pilot and sent a message. Forty minutes later he received a response.

The message waited for Rikishi, "Strong Man." It came from Toshiyori, the "Elder," a man whose elite position in Washington made him an invaluable source for extremely sensitive intelligence.

Encoded data led Sweetheart to two newpaper articles: an announcement of the employment of the American scientist Dr. Douglas Thomas by a Hong Kong biologicals company in 1990; the other, a brief article about a business consortium in Hong Kong—a company that dealt with biologicals—and possible connections to the Triads.

Sweetheart closed his eyes again, exploring the jagged pieces of the puzzle. It never looked simple, but in the end it always was.

His mind strayed back to Japan, back to the incessant rain and the fact that Masuma Hayashi had served the village elders and the children first. The complex answer: the desire to annihilate the innocent and the old.

The simple answer: serving children and elders first was considered *polite*.

If she was anything, Masuma Hayashi was polite.

Sylvia barely slept the few hours until her alarm went off, but when she rose, she found Matt already gone. There was no note. A miserable start to a new day, the new case.

As she showered, she thought about a conversation she'd had with Rosie Sanchez just last week, after she and Matt had argued over—what? She couldn't remember anymore. Something trivial and unimportant, no doubt.

He: "Don't leave a sink filled with last night's dishes and cold, greasy water."

She: "Throw your dirty clothes in the hamper, not on every available piece of furniture."

They rarely argued over anything major. They were compatible. So why, when it came to marriage and children, did she still have those shadowy doubts?

She reassured herself they'd work through this; they'd have a serious talk—and make love and make up—as soon as she returned from London.

She packed her bag: an extra pair of black slacks, sweater, tuxedo shirt, shorts and running shoes for the treadmill (although experience told her the Brits weren't fixated on their gym experience the way Americans were), umbrella and slicker. She almost forgot her underwear and her passport.

She had two hours of work to complete in town, and then she would be on her way to the airport. Sweetheart had mentioned their flight was booked through Houston.

It was barely six-fifteen when she stowed the garment bag behind the front seat of her truck and drove off the property. The sun seemed to struggle to rise over the Sangre de Cristos.

She pressed autodial on the cell phone—waiting while it rang—until a sleepy voice said, "Hello."

"Serena?"

"Sylvia?"

"I woke you up, honey. Sorry."

"That's okay." The yawn was audible. "What time is it?"

"Early. I'm on my way to London for two days. I wanted to give you the skinny myself."

"Is Matt going with you?"

"No, this is work."

"What kind of work? Are you going alone? What about the wedding? Your dress, *Sylvia*." Serena drew out the last syllable on a plaintive note.

Sylvia was amazed at the abrupt transformation from sleepy child to attentive adult. She said, "I'm going with Edmond Sweetheart—you know, the Professor."

"Professor Sumo!" She yelped excitedly and so loudly that Sylvia jerked the phone from her ear. Serena had actually attended a sumo match in L.A.; she'd seen Sweetheart in a *yokozuna tsuna*, the ceremonial belt—quite a sight. When she'd regained her calm, Serena asked, "When will you be back *exactly*?"

"Thursday night *exactly*."

"As long as you're back by Friday." Serena waited, letting the point settle. "You remember what's happening Friday, don't you?"

"Absolutely." Sylvia searched her brain for enlightenment; she heard her foster daughter inhale just as it came to her—the presentation for Students Against Drugs. "I'm speaking to students at your school."

"SAD's even putting an ad in the paper," Serena said proudly.

"I wouldn't miss it for the world."

"Sylvia?"

"Yes, honey, what is it?"

"Matt's not happy about this going-away stuff, is he?"

"No, he's not." Sylvia's eyes widened; sometimes the child was too perceptive. "But he's okay."

And then Serena turned into a grandmother, wagging a verbal finger, saying in a wise voice, "Is this one of those adult things, when you pretend it's work but it's really being afraid?"

Sylvia opened her mouth to say no.

Instead, she took another breath and shook her head.

"Everything's A-okay. I'll be back by Friday to talk to the kids at Cristo Rey. And the weekend after that, I'll be at the church to get married to Matt, with you and Rosie as my maid and matron of honor. Deal?"

"Deal."

PART II

Chemeia, Chumeia

redrider:	working late again?
alchemist:	you too
redrider:	you can do better than that
alchemist:	enlighten me
redrider:	you're *fishing* / need my time zone just ask
alchemist:	??
redrider:	not yet
alchemist:	name?
redrider:	let's establish rapport
alchemist:	is this blackmail?
redrider:	never / oh god / you misunderstand
alchemist:	what then?
redrider:	homage / worship
alchemist:	boring
redrider:	. . . then you'll welcome no contact for a day or so
alchemist:	?
redrider:	preparing for visitors
alchemist:	explain
redrider:	let the facts speak for themselves

A t 8:55 A.M. on Tuesday, in front of baggage claim in Gatwick Airport, a rather sheepish-looking little man stood holding a cardboard sign inscribed with one word: SWEETHEART.

"Isn't that nice," Sylvia teased, stifling a yawn. "Wherever we go, people love you."

The little man introduced himself as Eddie and explained (in an almost incomprehensible Cockney accent) that he would collect their luggage and stow it in the boot. He steered them vaguely toward a hired car parked at the curb outside the terminal before disappearing in the crowd.

As they dodged pedestrians, Sylvia found herself longing for an icy Coke or a very black, very tall cup of espresso, but there were no food purveyors in sight, not even vending machines. In lieu of caffeine, she discovered a battered stick of Juicy Fruit in her coat pocket. She stopped in front of the exit doors, stripped off the wrapper, and popped the gum into her mouth. She caught Sweetheart watching her, and she made a face as they stepped out into the damp English air.

While Sweetheart appeared inhumanly alert, she felt muzzy and sleep-deprived. (The slight drizzling rain didn't help.) The flight had been turbulent, warm, airless, and it had offered few opportunities for discourse with her traveling companion. Sweetheart had been tight-lipped, in another world, during all but takeoff and landing.

At least she could think of one plus: the undisturbed and inescapable confinement had allowed her to focus all her restless energy on Palmer's thick case file, as well as a chilling text on the investigation of criminal poisoning—a text edited by none other than Palmer herself.

She'd come away with wary respect, even more than she'd already gained from the Riker investigation, for the poisoners' craft. It was adaptable—death could be virtually painless or so excruciating that it made a gun or a knife seem merciful. It was versatile—the toxin of choice could be mundane, as in cyanide-based rat poison, or exotic, as in radioactive P-32. It was flexible: death could take months or minutes.

As they approached a line of vehicles at the curb, Sweetheart pulled up short, and Sylvia saw that he was reacting to a tall, gaunt cipher of a man who had seemingly appeared from nowhere and was now intent on intersecting their path.

"Follow me," the man hissed in a low whisper.

To Sylvia's surprise, Sweetheart did, urging her toward a battered Bentley that was double-parked beyond the hired cars. "Paul Lang," he informed her, just as the tall man ducked behind the steering wheel of the car.

"What—?"

"I'll explain later."

Sweetheart took the backseat. As Sylvia slid breathlessly into the worn leather passenger seat, she found herself staring directly at Lang's armband, a black stripe encircling his soiled gray sleeve, a symbol of mourning worn six months after Samantha Grayson's death.

"Who's she?" Lang demanded, eyes in the rearview mirror on Sweetheart.

"Dr. Strange is my colleague—a profiler from America."

"FBI?"

"Free-agent."

"What the hell took you so long?" Lang barked, shifting gears and accelerating into airport traffic. His hands were trembling on the wheel, his pallid complexion had the dull sheen of old sweat, and though he wore a tailored gray suit and a hand-painted silk tie, he smelled—the odor a combination of cigarette smoke, perspiration, and something faintly chemical. As he cut across lanes, Lang amazed Sylvia by inquiring politely and incongruously about their flight, jet lag, and any plans to see the sights of London.

"We slept on the plane," Sweetheart said.

"Speak for yourself," Sylvia said, glancing over her shoulder, already knowing she would find that curiously intent gleam in her colleague's eyes—sure enough, like diamonds in onyx. She tried to catch his attention, wanting to know what the hell was going on, but he kept his focus on Lang.

Sylvia mentally reviewed the files she'd accessed on Samantha Grayson's fiancé: thirty-four (although he looked older), never married, a ten-year employee of MI-6, the British agency responsible for monitoring foreign intelligence. Lang had no glam job; he was no James Bond; his specialty was intelligence analysis (usually from behind a desk), and according to all accounts, he did his job well and was respected by his colleagues.

Up until a few months ago, when he'd gone off the deep end. His reaction to Samantha Grayson's violent death had been so intense—depression, paranoia, insomnia—that MI-6 had placed him on medical/compassionate leave.

Oncoming traffic streamed past, and Sylvia experienced a sense of displacement. Why did the Brits stubbornly insist on veering to the left instead of driving in the *right* lane like most of the civilized world? She was startled when Lang's voice filled the car's interior.

"I need your schedule."

"Our first stop is BioPort," Sweetheart said, naming a private for-profit company so closely tied to England's most famous chemical and biological defense establishment, Porton Down, that its head-quarters was on government grounds.

BioPort also happened to be the institution where Dr. Christine Palmer had completed her last research project, and presumably where Samantha Grayson had been exposed to the toxic organism that caused her death. Those thoughts raced through Sylvia's mind as Lang interrogated Sweetheart. "Porton Down? How'd you get access? Not through the FBI's legal attaché—"

"I worked with one of their people in Hong Kong, a sticky case involving black market biologicals. Turned out for the best."

"And they owe you a favor." Lang had a feverish glow. "What are they offering?"

"Interviews with personnel."

"The place was tight as a drum—you won't get near the secure lab, but check out the working proximity between Palmer and Sam." Without glancing at the side mirror, Lang changed lanes abruptly. His maneuver was greeted by horns, but he seemed oblivious to the noise outside the Bentley. "PD's in Wiltshire County, that's roughly a hundred fifty kilometers west of London. Lots of traffic. What time are you due?"

"Eleven hundred hours."

Lang cut in front of a massive truck. "I won't keep you much longer."

"What have you got?" Sweetheart asked.

Lang reached beneath his seat, produced a manila envelope, held it over the seat in front of Sweetheart.

"What's this?"

"Not yet," Lang said, pulling the envelope out of reach just as Sweetheart tried to take it, then sliding it back under the seat. "First things first. What do you know about Porton Down?"

It took Sylvia a few seconds to realize the question was directed at her, and she stumbled a bit, then caught her breath. "It's military; biological and chemical research; controversial—at the moment because somebody discovered a series of tests performed on human subjects during the nineteen fifties; at least one soldier died from sarin gas exposure. And now there's a question if the experiments on humans spanned other decades."

"What else?" Lang asked harshly. Over the course of the last few miles, he'd grown increasingly tense, as if his inner timing mechanism had been notched up and his synapses were carrying more volts.

"It's also where Ms. Grayson was exposed to the neurotoxin—"

"Bloody *bullshit*."

Adenaline jolt. Sylvia realized she'd reacted physically to Lang's outburst. She took a breath, glancing at Sweetheart, but he offered no guidance, refused to run interference.

Now Lang seemed to be sulking, and he kept silent until Sylvia began to wonder if he was going to speak at all. Where was he taking them? The traffic had thinned, and the streets were lined with light industrial warehouses, shipping offices, machine shops. The few pedestrians had the numb expressions of people who work long hours repeating themselves.

"You know where Sam and I met?"

Quickly, Sylvia refocused her attention on Lang. Apparently he'd decided to let her be the sole contestant in his personal production of *Survivor* meets *Weakest Link*.

Bzzzzzz! Are you stupid? She'd gone blank, couldn't remember if she'd seen anything in the file, shook her head.

"Basson investigation. Bloody bastard, Basson."

She nodded, shifting in her seat, making an unsuccessful attempt to find a tolerable posture for her long body. Her underpants were trapped between her butt cheeks, her mouth had gone dry, and she recognized the first strokes of a headache. In the next lane, a goggle-eyed child peered down at her from a double-decker bus.

"The South African general," Sweetheart interjected. "In two thousand he was tried for his participation in Nazi-type experiments and assassination attempts against antiapartheid leaders. Basson and his people were experimenting with cholera, anthrax, and assorted biological agents—and they showed a preference for human test subjects."

"MI-6 was tracking Basson for years," Lang said. His attention was now focused on Sweetheart; he seemed to have forgotten that he was driving, and his voice faded as he said, "Bioterrorism is an incestuous world . . ."

"Weren't Basson's suppliers black marketeers, pharmaceuticals, governments?" Sweetheart was trying to jar Lang back to the present. It worked.

"That's right." Lang shook his head sharply, as if he had to physically adjust, get back on track. He'd come down a notch. "The investigation made everyone damn nervous. But Samantha was just beginning her postgraduate stint when we approached her, and she welcomed the chance to consult on some of the scientific and technical data. She was assigned to my division."

"If it was risky, why did she agree?" Sylvia asked, realizing too late that this might set him off again.

But Lang was oddly distant now. "Sam liked risks; she was easily bored." He turned toward Sylvia. "Do you know Christine?"

She shook her head, frowned, gave a half-nod. "I've met Dr. Palmer—once."

Lang returned his eyes to the road. He'd taken his foot off the accelerator and the Bentley coasted slowly along the almost deserted street. "Then you know her," he said finally. "The same way you know a cobra when you meet it."

The car rolled to a stop. He switched off the engine. Sylvia was acutely aware of the sound of the ticking engine. Sweetheart seemed primed for just about anything.

Anything but the matter-of-fact delivery: "I became familiar with Christine Palmer when she was still at Lawrence Livermore." Lang spoke as if, after the slightest pause, he'd picked up a thread in an ongoing conversation. While his voice revealed shadings of weariness and sadness, he sounded completely controlled, perfectly sane. (Or would have, Sylvia thought, if he hadn't been working up to a frenzy just minutes before.)

He ran long slender fingers through his every-which-way hair. "She provided data for an analysis—we were tracking bioweapons. I'm familiar with anyone working with rare biological agents, especially when their work, like Palmer's, is cutting edge." He sighed— "Incestuous world"—then paused, possibly reviewing the chronology in his head.

"Sam started at Porton Down just after we'd become an item," he said. "She'd admired Palmer's work, had applied for projects before, *worshiped* her, in fact. For the first few months everything went well."

"What changed?"

"Palmer changed. Bloody nightmare. Logical one day, a row over nothing the next. She blamed Sam for everything: mistakes in protocol, measuring and recording data. The other team members noticed, and it undermined morale." He shook his head. "Sam even thought about resigning."

"Was there any basis for Palmer's concerns?"

"No."

"What did Ms. Grayson think was going on?"

"Sam imagined she wasn't working at the caliber Palmer was used to, but then she began to think *jealousy* on Palmer's part."

"Jealous of . . . ?"

He paused just long enough for the beat to be noticeable. "Didn't want to share credit for the research with her colleagues. All too plausible. When it comes down to grants, funding, reputation, it happens."

Lang went silent, his expression shifting subtly, revealing internal rehearsal, a gearing up. He took a quick breath, began, "The day Samantha died, I was—"

"Hold that for later," Sweetheart interrupted. "After Ms. Grayson's death, you opened an *un*official investigation?"

Sylvia caught her breath at her associate's abruptness. *Cold* technique. She knew what he was doing—taking charge, controlling the interview. If it was hard on Lang, so be it.

Lang's fingers tightened on the steering wheel, then loosened as he surrendered. "This was no case of accidental exposure. I never believed it for a minute. Sam was meticulous about procedure. I don't mean careful—I mean *meticulous*."

"But others didn't see it your way," Sweetheart said.

"True." Lang adjusted the rearview mirror. "When my superiors didn't respond to my suspicions, I began to look at Palmer's history, each facility where she'd done research. I looked for deaths, accidents, unusual events. I didn't have to look far. In ninety-eight there were cases of contamination and a lab death in the Netherlands—an epileptic scientist who died from a grand mal seizure. The local chaps, dead man's mates, queued up, talked his mum and dad into exhumation."

As the grim story unfolded, Sylvia found herself longing for a cigarette, her first craving in ages.

"Pathologist found traces of antimony. If the FBI was going to get involved, we needed a minimum of two exhumations, two victims, two jurisdictions."

She heard Sweetheart asking about the second body, heard Lang's response: California, 1995, Lawrence Livermore, Palmer's coworker suffered a fatal heart attack.

"The man had a history of heart disease. When I couldn't convince the family to proceed, I kept digging, if you'll pardon the pun. In ninety-two her fiancé died of lung cancer. Avery Winter. The family is prominent; they also refused to consider exhumation, even though there was speculation at the time of his death that *someone* helped him along."

"Two strikes," Sweetheart said.

"But then I got lucky." Lang glanced at his watch, and the ornate ring on his finger caught the light. He turned the ignition key, the engine purred to life. As he accelerated, he said, "When Palmer was at MIT in eighty-seven, the only other finalist for a spectacular grant award died of a sudden heart attack. There, too, a history of heart disease, but the family couldn't fathom it, paid a visit to the local coroner." Lang looked harshly satisfied. "His bone showed evidence of sodium fluoroacetate."

"Isn't that used as a pest killer—rodents, coyotes?" Sylvia asked, primed from her research in international airspace.

"Crude but fitting," Sweetheart said. "From a poisoner's perspective, it's pest control."

Lang drove silently for several miles. Sylvia recognized enough of the landscape to know they were returning to Gatwick. Row houses strung together with lines of damp laundry passed in a gray-blue blur.

"Tell us about her death," Sweetheart said abruptly, with artful timing.

Because there was no rehearsal Lang struggled to keep his voice steady. "She . . . it was a Thursday. She left work early, she wasn't feeling well. I'd been in Paris for a few days on business. I flew back the next morning, Friday—changed my schedule, you see, delayed it by a day—and I found her that afternoon. If I'd kept to schedule—but I couldn't . . ."

The business of driving, changing lanes, turning, gave Lang a reprieve, and when he spoke again, his emotions were in hard check, his voice was flat. "Her death wasn't quick. She'd suffered. She'd probably fallen into a coma early Friday. She'd been dead several hours by the time I arrived."

He braked hard, knuckles white on the wheel, tires screeching, to avoid a truck that had stalled out in traffic. Nobody spoke for several moments.

The worst question yet came from Sweetheart. "Before her death, was your fiancée sick? Did she have bouts of flu? Headaches? Nausea?"

Lang slowed to make a turn. "She missed work several times, and we thought she couldn't shake a bit of flu going round. I was ill myself."

"Could you have been exposed to a mild dose of toxin?" Sweetheart asked, displaying no apparent emotion—unless, Sylvia thought, you watched closely enough to see the slight dilation of the nostrils, the tightening of the muscles around the eyes, the contraction of the masseter muscle, all idiosyncratic signs of extreme concentration.

"My blood was screened, nothing showed up. But that doesn't mean there was nothing there."

Sylvia felt her skin prickle. It was more than possible Samantha Grayson had been exposed to toxins before the final, acute attack. It was common for poisoners to administer multiple doses. She shifted again, uncomfortably. It wasn't easy to fathom the kind of mind it took to socialize with, and work next to, the person you were slowly killing.

"There was another death," Lang said finally. "In eighty-eight. Palmer's father."

Sweetheart frowned. "Fielding Palmer was diagnosed with a brain tumor . . ."

"That's true." Lang turned from the main thoroughfare into airport traffic. "He was undergoing chemotherapy, and his condition had stabilized. But he died very suddenly. One night when his daughter was visiting. Christine was alone with him in the house."

"Was there any proof?" Sweetheart asked softly.

Lang guided the Bentley around the corner, passing an idling black cab, braking for a pedestrian who carried a bouquet of red roses, before he said, "The body was cremated."

Sylvia shifted in her seat to study Lang's face. "You went to your superiors with your information?"

"That's right. And then I went to the American legal attaché in London—he works hand-in-glove with MI-6. To a man, they told me to shape up and bloody get over it. Next thing I know, the FBI's taking over."

Sylvia glanced at Sweetheart as she addressed one more question to Lang. "Have you ever doubted your instinct? Do you still believe Palmer's a murderer?"

"Oh, she's a murderer, all right. And she enjoys the killing. She poisoned her father, God knows how many colleagues, and the woman I loved. Which leaves only one question: Who's *next?*" He slowed the car, just as fat droplets of rain began to drum against the windshield.

As the noise of the rainstorm increased, Sylvia studied Lang—moody, vigilant, guarded, rigid, erratic, volatile were a few of the adjectives she might use in a psychological evaluation of the MI-6 analyst. But he was complex; she knew there was more. And she didn't like the fact that she wasn't getting a clear read on the man.

Lang retrieved the envelope from under his feet, but this time he shoved it over the seat. Sweetheart unfastened the metal clip. The envelope slid open. He examined the contents slowly, taking his time, even as his face registered shock.

After a moment, he handed Sylvia the photographs, but they slipped from her fingers and fell into her lap. She caught her breath. She was staring at color portraits of Samantha Grayson's corpse. The face was shockingly grotesque in death. Muscles contracted, features contorted. Skin mottled. A yellowish foam extruding from discolored lips.

She heard Paul Lang's flat, lifeless voice. "Do you see?"

She looked up sharply and found herself trapped by his eyes. This time there was no mistaking what she saw: a man intent on revenge.

"These weren't in the police file," she said slowly.

"They aren't police photographs. I took them." Lang shrugged. "I thought it would be best if I recorded the evidence. I was first on the scene of death, after all."

Lang dropped them off almost exactly where he'd picked them up, on the airport throughway just outside their terminal. The rain had slowed again, but there were plenty of puddles to dodge.

He said, "This is as far as I go."

Sweetheart asked, "How do we contact you?"

"I'll find you." With that, Lang shifted into gear and pulled out into the stream of traffic.

Eddie, their driver for hire, was waiting placidly beside a sturdy-looking sedan. He'd already loaded their bags into the boot, except for Sylvia's small roller bag, which he was using as a stool. When he saw them dash across the road toward him, he stood and dusted off his rump.

"Thought I'd lost you," was all he said in his thick Cockney accent as Sylvia and Sweetheart climbed into the back of the cab and settled in.

The main entrance to the Chemical and Biological Defense Establishment, Chemical and Biological Defense Sector, Porton Down—one of the world's largest facilities for the R&D of chemical and biological weaponry and warfare—was marked by protestors who carried signs, graphic duotones of animals suffering tortures in the name of science.

Eddie, their driver, braked to pass through the small crowd, and Sylvia forced herself not to turn away from the images. She thought she noticed Sweetheart's palms press together, as if he was offering a silent prayer.

"It's been all over the telly," Eddie said, frowning in concentration. "Viva-exceptionists."

"Antivivisectionists?" Sylvia ventured, aware that preclinical protocols were part of almost every research project.

"They're acting up about them poor dogs and cats," he explained solemnly, turning onto military grounds.

Sylvia stared out the window as they approached the sentinel post. A sentry greeted them with the cold steel of an M-16 rifle held to ready. Eddie identified himself as a licensed chauffeur; Sylvia and Sweetheart produced their passports and IDs, signed an entry sheet, destination BioPort; and then they all waited, engine idling softly, while a second sentry made the necessary phone calls.

A minute passed. Two minutes.

Outside the vehicle, the gray gloom turned to drizzle.

The sound of the protestors' voices penetrated: *Stop the murder of innocents before it's too late—stop the military-industrial killing machine before it kills us all!*

The guard with the M-16 gave Eddie a small plastic card and cautioned him not to stray from a direct course to BioPort's headquarters. The heavy security arm rose stiffly in wooden salute, allowing entry into the "military-industrial killing machine." Through the rain-misted rear window Sylvia watched the security arm fall again like a slow axe.

Eddie followed the main road for several miles. The oldest buildings, dating back to 1916, having suffered the degradations of industrial vogue and age, made no claim to architectural merit. Newer buildings, lacking such temporal excuses, seemed to exhibit existential and structural angst in lieu of design cohesion; then the buildings gave way to storage lots and scarred fields. Although the facility was vast, it had the air of a city recently deserted.

The car slowed to cut sharply into a narrow lane lined with war-era dormitories. Just beyond the dorms, at the dead end, a two-story fortification stood surrounded by twelve-foot barbed chain-link.

Eddie pulled the car up at an "electronic soldier" and plunged the plastic card into the mouth of the machine. Sylvia thought she heard him mumbling to himself. The wide gate rolled open, Eddie drove through, and the gate closed again.

A small black-and-silver sign above glass doors announced the headquarters of BioPort International. Although BioPort was a privately held company, it maintained a research facility on the grounds of the military center. A similar arrangement was in operation with companies at LANL and various national laboratories in the United States. Proximity of private to public encouraged technology transfer; it also provided sophisticated technical and scientific support for mixed-funding projects.

Sensible. Incestuous.

"Welcome to Project Nicander," Sweetheart said quietly as Eddie parked the car between a motorcycle and a military van.

"Nicander?"

"You didn't come across him in your Riker research?" Sweetheart asked—a tiny jab.

"Afraid not."

"Valet to Attalus the Third, king of Pergamum, second century B.C." Sweetheart was staring out at the foreboding façade. "Nicander developed an extremely popular and long-standing antidote made of venomous tissue, herbs, and fruits, used to counteract almost any poison." He paused, his fingers wrapped around the door handle. "Unfortunately, his recipe was useless."

"Who named the project?"

"Christine Palmer."

"Then she has an interesting sense of humor."

Sweetheart and Sylvia stepped out into a day turned damp and cold. Sylvia clutched the collar of her leather jacket and suppressed a shiver, but Sweetheart appeared unaffected by the drop in temperature. They kept to the curb, passing beneath a leafless elm to reach the main door of BioPort. Inside, they found a man in a gray suit waiting for them in an otherwise deserted tile-and-steel lobby. He said, "Professor Edmond Sweetheart? I'm Dr. Curtis Watley. I've been assigned to escort you around the facility." Dr. Watley, a soft, pasty man in his late fifties, spoke to them from behind a large handlebar mustache. His voice was tight and peevish.

Sweetheart said, "I was expecting Colonel Smythe."

"The colonel sends his regrets—speaks highly of you, by the way—but he's out of the country. Left at the crack of dawn; I'm sure you saw that unfortunate business in the news about Sierra Leone." He glanced pointedly at his watch. "I must say, I'd almost given up."

"We were forced to make a detour," Sweetheart answered—not exactly a lie but an oblique reference to their interlude with Paul Lang.

"Really? I had no idea they were diverting traffic anywhere en route from Gatwick. That must have been inconvenient." He looked as if he were personally affronted by any and all delays. "The colonel asked me to assure you that BioPort will do everything it can to be helpful, including cooperating with the FBI whenever possible. Samantha Grayson's death was a blow to Project Nicander—a horrible accident—but I must say, I thought we'd left that behind us . . ."

Sweetheart didn't respond to the prompt—and Sylvia could almost hear his mute warning: *Watley's an unknown.*

The doctor cleared his throat. "We've arranged for you to meet with former members of the project, those who worked with Ms. Grayson. Naturally, we're limited by the fact that many project members have moved on to other facilities. Dr. Christine Palmer, for instance. She's on your side of the ocean, I believe?"

"That's right," Sweetheart said. "Dr. Palmer is currently directing a project at Los Alamos National Laboratories in New Mexico."

"Ah, yes, *Mexico*." Dr. Watley turned to lead the way down the longest corridor. "We were sorry to hear about Dr. Thomas," he added, a frown creasing his broad forehead. "I watched one of your news shows and learned your highways are quite deadly."

"That's right," Sweetheart said. "Doug Thomas worked at Bio-Port."

"In close collaboration with Dr. Palmer, yes."

Cozy, Sylvia thought.

They followed Watley along the hard-tiled corridor to a stairwell, where their footsteps created an echoing cacophony as they descended one level. The basement was even colder than the rest of the building.

"Can you tell us about the project?" Sweetheart asked. "Did you work with Dr. Palmer and Ms. Grayson?"

"Unfortunately not. My work these days is in public information. But I can tell you BioPort researches and develops antidotes to chemical and biological agents that might be used in warfare situations." Watley spoke over considerable noise—an amorphous mix of cries, shrieks, and moans—emanating from somewhere at the end of the hallway.

Sylvia tipped her head toward the racket. "What's that?"

He made a rueful face. "Some of the preclinical subjects are still being housed down here until construction on a new facility is completed."

Preclinical subjects meant lab animals: rabbits, mice and other rodents, cats, dogs, primates. Sylvia thought of their driver, Eddie, of his reference to the antivivisectionists, and of the demonstrators outside Porton Down.

Dr. Watley picked up his pace. Apparently he didn't like the din of caged creatures any more than they did.

"I have the vaguest sense of Dr. Palmer's project, Samantha Grayson's work." Sylvia matched stride with their guide.

To her surprise, Watley didn't appear to hedge. He said, "Dr. Palmer's project was based on a cooperative grant from BDH, the British Department of Health. Its mission involved the analysis of zootoxins for medical applications—level three biological specimens. Specifically, for Dr. Palmer that meant some very rare species of dinoflagellates." The visceral shriek of an animal punctuated his words.

As they turned a corner, Watley paused to say, "Here we are, then." He pushed open steel doors, leading them along a short corridor that ended in front of a glass wall. Here, the corridor opened into a T—both wings marked the glass boundary through which they could see several employees dressed in lab coats but lacking protective clothing or goggles.

"This is BioPort's primary research area." Removing his horned-rim frames to chew on one earpiece, Watley gestured vaguely. "Of course, most of the work you see going on has only a tangential relationship to the research culled from Project Nicander."

"But these aren't hot areas," Sylvia said.

"Heavens no. The researchers you see are working in a BSL-one lab. We have several level-two labs. Our BSL-three areas are restricted." He sensed Sweetheart's protest and added firmly, "I'm afraid there's absolutely no way we can allow access to anyone but staff."

Sweetheart remained silent, so Sylvia asked, "They're in this building?"

"Oh, yes. I'll take you into this initial area—if we kept on walking, we'd reach the restricted labs." He moved toward the door.

"Was Project Nicander brought to successful completion?" Sweetheart asked.

Watley frowned. "The project reached its planned termination date; I've been told the research is promising, although I'm not privy to the details." He gestured for them to follow him along the glassed-in passageway, through the lab, into yet another hallway. Watley stopped at the door to an office, opening it wide, allowing them entry.

"We'd been led to believe the project was still active even though Dr. Palmer had completed her work," Sweetheart said slowly.

"You've been misinformed. Project Nicander is inactive; it has been since Dr. Palmer's departure. In fact, we're in the process of clearing out this office." Watley gestured around the room.

Sweetheart stepped up to a large metal filing cabinet. Sylvia crossed the room in the opposite direction, reaching a stack of boxes and lifting the lid of the uppermost box. It was packed with files, and she began to select random folders. She found computer printouts that appeared to be test protocols.

Sweetheart appeared at her shoulder and confirmed her guess: "Someone who worked on the project would have to decipher the data."

"That could easily be arranged," Dr. Watley said. He had moved to another box, where he lifted the cover to reveal several dozen videotapes labeled in ascending numerical order. He selected a tape— 16-32R—and held it up. "Recordings of the preclinical trials," he said. "Nothing revelatory, I'm afraid. But a glance will give you an idea of Ms. Grayson's work on the project."

"We'd appreciate it," Sweetheart agreed.

"You're welcome to view them all," Watley said, smiling tightly. "The monitor's in my office. If you're quite finished here, your interviews with project members are scheduled to begin in the next half hour."

Sweetheart didn't budge. "Before we leave, we need to get a sense of the jeopardy surface."

"Sorry?" Watley appeared genuinely puzzled.

"In an inquiry such as this, where large amounts of data are generated, geographical profiling is useful," Sweetheart explained. "The jeopardy surface refers to the area where an event occurred. In this case, an exposure incident."

Watley hesitated, then flattened his mouth and nodded. "Will a diagram suffice?"

"Where was Samantha Grayson doing most of her work?" Sweetheart asked once they were viewing a blueprint of the lab's floor plan mounted on the wall of the maintenance office. A small headline at the top of the map read: IN CASE OF AN EMERGENCY EVACUATION.

Watley frowned, and his thick fingers slid over the embossed chart. "Dr. Palmer's team members pursued several avenues of research." He pointed to one of two BSL-3 labs.

"What was Ms. Grayson's primary job?" Sweetheart asked.

"If I'm not mistaken, Ms. Grayson was assisting Drs. Thomas and Cray for most of the project."

Sweetheart nodded. "Where was Dr. Palmer working?"

Dr. Watley squinted at the blueprint as if his vision had been abruptly impaired. "I believe she was here." He pointed to the second BSL-3 lab.

"So Samantha Grayson's work space and Dr. Palmer's work space were separated by a hallway."

"Correct. In fact, they were in different labs."

"But wasn't there interaction between researchers in both labs?"

Watley shook his head. "It may not appear so, but in a lab such as this, schedules and physical security barriers keep interpersonal contact to a minimum." His eyes narrowed, creasing at the corners. "I believe she spent the bulk of her time monitoring and recording test batch data."

Sweetheart frowned. "You're certain?"

"Reasonably so." But Watley's voice definitely hitched. "Samantha Grayson worked with Dr. Cray for *almost* the entire project." He turned to stare at Sweetheart and Sylvia. "Two or three weeks before she died, she moved across the lab to work—*here*." On the diagram, he indicated the space that would have been directly adjacent to Dr. Palmer's lab.

"Why did she make the move?" Sweetheart asked.

"I can't tell you the exact reason. But Dr. Palmer would have final say. She might've requested the move so that she could more closely supervise some of Ms. Grayson's work on test protocols."

Or to keep an eye on Ms. Grayson. Sylvia stared silently at the diagram. *Which meant they were working side by side.*

Dr. Watley's office was located three floors above BioPort's basement laboratories. They found themselves with a few minutes to spare before the first interview. They raided the vending machines, purchasing stale sandwiches and bitter coffee. Sylvia stared dispiritedly at a soggy cheese sandwich.

"I'd heard the food in England was improving," she whispered to Sweetheart.

"Sssh, you'll hurt Watley's feelings."

When they returned to Dr. Watley's office, he was waiting with videotape 16-32R in hand. With a look that said they were wasting his time as well as their own, he slid the tape into the mouth of the machine.

An image filled the screen. A fixed camera had recorded a test protocol: a small monkey—a sign on the glassed cubicle identified the animal as "*(Saimiri sciureus)* 16-32R"—gazed at the camera with huge golden eyes.

The date—approximately eleven months earlier—and the time appeared in the lower right-hand corner of the picture.

The image jumped, and a woman dressed in a standard lab coat appeared on-screen. She offered a smile and a small wave to the video camera.

"Samantha Grayson," Dr. Watley said in a hushed tone.

In the dim light of the office, Sylvia watched as Watley stared intently at the monitor. Then she sat forward, her own eyes drawn to the video image.

Samantha Grayson looked very much alive: young, attractive, apparently affable, and unremarkable at first glance. But before a viewer might turn away dismissively, a certain intensity drew the eye back. Sylvia tried to catch what it was that made Samantha Grayson intriguing, at the same time tracking the woman's casual dialogue with someone off camera—"You watching the championships tonight? These things never fit . . . Got it . . . Hi, Mom"—that was audible while she donned protective booties and gloves.

There was something speculative and energized about her interactions—in the voice, in the eyes, in the body, the way she carried herself and managed to look casual, almost earnest. For all her ingenuousness, there was an underlying shading to her personality.

The camera followed her beyond a door marked DANGER—NO ENTRY—TEST AREA. Through a glass partition she reassured the tiny monkey, "We won't hurt you, Annie." Then she addressed the camera: "She's doing fine, she's relaxed. Time to go undercover."

The image jumped again: the isolated monkey was the star of the show.

Directly above the glass cage, a large round clock marked the passing of minutes. As the black hand approached the twelve, Sylvia braced for something to happen.

There was an audible click, the faintest hissing sound—and *nothing* else.

"The test substances were aerosolized," Dr. Watley explained quietly. "Administration was automatic. Through a small valve in the wall."

For the next several minutes, the monkey actually seemed to play to the camera, smiling and cooing. She appeared energetic, healthy, apparently unaffected by whatever substance had been administered.

As revealed by the digital numbers in the corner of the screen, the image jumped forward in time.

Now Samantha Grayson appeared again, speaking to the camera. "We've gone eight hours with no noticeable effects. We're reviewing blood assays."

One more jump—according to the timer another six hours had passed—and the little squirrel monkey hooted for an invisible audience. The tape ended.

"They're all like that," Watley said. "The videos were made each time the team administered a compound. But they were testing toxins reformulated for medicinal uses, not deadly bioagents."

Containing her disappointment at the same time she suppressed a twinge of guilt over what felt like ghoulishness, Sylvia glanced at her watch.

Watley said, "The interviews will take place in this room, if that's all right with you." Without waiting for confirmation, he said, "You'll be speaking with Dr. Harris Cray, one of our molecular toxicologists, among others. He's been in charge of closing down the project since Dr. Palmer's departure." He paused, then added (a bit disparagingly, Sylvia thought), "Although he's not as well known as Dr. Palmer, Dr. Cray is also a specialist on marine neurotoxins."

Then Watley looked uncomfortable. "The remaining project members have been told these interviews are part of an inquiry into involuntary contamination incidents—hence the questions about Ms. Grayson's death."

Sweetheart nodded reassuringly. But when only Sylvia was within earshot, he said, "Round up the usual suspects."

In total, Sylvia and Sweetheart spoke with a half-dozen people who had been connected in some way with Project Nicander and Samantha Grayson.

One of the first lessons of investigation: there is *always* some relationship between victim and killer, even when the crime appears to be an act of random violence.

Sylvia focused on questions about Ms. Grayson—*victim*. She

needed to gain a mental picture of the murdered woman. But Grayson was also her conduit to Christine Palmer—*killer*—the real subject of the inquiry.

Sweetheart sat by her side, and together they had their act down, asking an inventory of questions: How strictly were lab standards maintained? Did Ms. Grayson adhere to standard protocols? Did Ms. Grayson seem to have personal problems? How did she relate to others in the project? How would you evaluate her as a professional? What was she like to work with?

When the mood shifted and the interviewees relaxed: Did she seem happy? Did you ever notice that she seemed dissatisfied with her situation? Did you notice if others were taking extra sick days?

Important to know if project members were being poisoned.

The interviews began with Ole Jorgensen, biologist, molecular chemist—all smiles, loved everyone (including Sylvia, by the look of it) and the fact that the Americans were monitoring the international safety standards in high-level labs.

Dr. Jorgensen added that he had *liked* Ms. Grayson very much. His smile grew larger. "But Dr. Palmer let her get away with murder," he added, shaking his head.

"In what way?" Sylvia asked, a bit taken aback by the morbid cliché delivered with a strong Scandinavian accent.

"Samantha Grayson was the toxicologist's pet." Dr. Jorgensen laughed at his own joke, and his eyes twinkled.

"Was Ms. Grayson's work substandard?"

"Oh, no." Jorgensen nodded adamantly. "Her work was fine—but she was missing days, staying home, to play *hooky,* perhaps."

"Was she ill?" Sweetheart asked quietly; a vital question around the subject of repeated exposure to toxins.

Jorgensen tipped his head, smiling widely. "She looked healthy to me."

Next came several interviews with researchers whose work had been peripheral to the project and who had had little contact with team members.

There was a brief break between interviewees before they got to Julie Talbert. Ms. Talbert was a safety technician who had almost nothing positive to say about anything, including being forced to take time away from her current project. Impatiently, she summed up her views. "It was a case of airborne contamination, aerosolization—pouring liquid from beakers, you get aerosol accumulation of hot cultures—oh, never mind, it's a common enough occurrence in large laboratory settings, just check the data."

But as she left the office, Ms. Talbert sent a parting shot zinging toward the profilers: "We have an odd sort of tunnel vision, you know—those of us who work here—and we all get very protective about our research. But Samantha wasn't like that. She always seemed more interested in what everybody else was doing than in her own projects."

Dr. Harris Cray was the last interviewee. Sylvia marveled at his distinctive red hair and goatee. His responses were neutral and unenlightening—until they asked about Samantha Grayson's work standards.

"She was sloppy," he said bluntly.

"Can you give us specifics?"

"She mixed up slides, lost things, certainly didn't keep to safety protocols. No one else wanted to go near her work space." His eyes shifted from Sylvia to Sweetheart. "When I confronted her about her lapses, she denied them."

"Did those lapses in safety protocol endanger others in the lab?" Sweetheart asked.

Harris Cray frowned. "Everything you do in a lab affects everyone else."

"Did you report your observations to administrators?" Sylvia asked.

"Of course." He nodded curtly. He had a voice that made Sylvia think of dry ice. "I made a full report to the project head, Dr. Palmer."

"And what was Dr. Palmer's response?"

"She said she'd take care of it. Said she'd had her eye on Ms. Grayson for several weeks."

"What's your opinion of Christine Palmer?"

"She's a brilliant researcher."

"Did you ever question her integrity?"

"Never." He squinted through his glasses.

"Were you familiar with any stories of dissatisfaction among her peers?"

Suddenly Harris Cray's eyes widened. The internal "aha" was almost audible. "Ever since Christine's father died, there have been nothing but ugly rumors, innuendo—and the press makes money selling grubby little stories, accusing her of—" He broke off.

"Accusing her of what?" Sweetheart asked quietly.

Harris Cray was silent for a long beat, then seemed to collect himself and said, "There are politics in any research project. If you collect a dozen people and lock them away each day in a space this size, there are bound to be problems. Competition. Backbiting. Worse than the lab rats." He ran his fingers over his rusty goatee. "The project would never have existed without Dr. Palmer."

"You feel she was responsible for keeping Project Nicander on track?"

"Christine deserved a medal. Samantha Grayson was not the sweet little thing she pretended to be. She was ambitious, a party girl who stirred things up when she got—" He again stopped abruptly, as if he'd shocked himself. Finally, he said, "I'm only repeating what the investigators discovered after the trouble."

"By trouble, do you mean Ms. Grayson's death?"

He shook his head, looking from Sweetheart to Sylvia and back again. "I mean before her death, the internal investigation. The *thefts.*"

"Thefts," Sylvia echoed, nodding.

"It's no secret." Harris Cray shrugged. "It was covered by the press—at least as much of the story as they could get—along with that ancient sarin gas business. Some things went missing from the labs. Files, disks, tapes." He stood to leave.

Sylvia stood with him and asked, "Was the thief uncovered?"

"I wouldn't be the one to ask about that."

"Who would be the person to ask?"

"Her boyfriend, the one in the spy business. He all but accused Dr. Palmer of murdering Samantha. What's-his-name, Lang. Paul Lang."

"Why didn't Lang tell us that Samantha was suspected of stealing from the project?" Sylvia asked. They were outside the building, alone. Eddie was waiting beside his car roughly five hundred feet away, definitely out of earshot.

"There were rumors, but they were never confirmed," Sweetheart said.

"You knew about it? Why didn't you tell *me?*"

"It's not really pertinent to our mission, which is to gather data for the profile," Sweetheart countered sharply.

Sylvia stared at him in disbelief. "I can't believe you'd even say that—you're not serious. Everything is pertinent. If Christine Palmer felt threatened by someone on the project, that's pertinent. If she felt her research was jeopardized . . ."

Sweetheart shook his head impatiently. "At the time of the thefts, there were rumors that the Koreans, the Chinese, Iraq—someone—had a fixer in place. On top of that, a top-secret military-based research center is a hell of a place to conduct an investigation. The whole thing blew over anyway—put to bed as a case of carelessness and coincidence."

Sylvia began to walk away, but Sweetheart called her name and she turned. He waited until she took the few steps back to him, where he could speak in a low voice. "This isn't the first time there have been rumors of theft surrounding Palmer's research." He shook his head. "At the moment you're not here to worry about issues of security. We need to stay focused on the issue at hand—too much irrelevant information can cloud perceptions; too much information can throw us off scent. I'm asking you to trust me when I say the rumors of theft are not pertinent."

She stared at him, her mouth a straight line, and then she nodded once.

The drive back to London was interminable. This round, Sylvia had the backseat. As the miles passed, she fought off car sickness and fatigue; jet lag was setting in. She craved the only accessible remedy she could think of—a coffee or chocolate biochemical boost. She felt cranky and exhausted.

She closed her eyes, wishing she were home in New Mexico attending to wedding details. She felt a sharp twinge of guilt for running out on Matt; she couldn't wait to call him when she reached their hotel. She'd worked out the time difference and had a good idea where to find her family, at least by satellite transmission. She hungered for a simple conversation based on trust and the normal things of life—nothing to do with theft, murder, and military research projects.

Finally, the outskirts of London gave way to increasingly busy streets. The rain had settled in to stay. The city was slick with a dark sheen. Pedestrians dodged showers and huddled under umbrellas. On a corner, a raggedy busker was performing an odd song and dance, tapping and shuffling his way from puddle to puddle.

For some reason, while she watched the dancer fade into the rain, she remembered Dr. Watley, his instant of recognition when he told them about the lab.

She knew now what Sweetheart had been probing for—what he needed to see with his own eyes: the jeopardy surface, *Christine Palmer's physical territory.*

At Los Alamos, the late Dr. Douglas Thomas had worked in the lab directly adjacent to Palmer's.

And now the pattern had begun to form. Christine Palmer liked to keep her victims close when she moved in for the kill. The better to monitor any suspicion or distrust, Sylvia thought. But more than that, Palmer liked her victims close in order to watch them die.

redrider: the Americans have been to visit

alchemist: feds?

redrider: no

alchemist: who?

redrider: you know them

alchemist: what do they want?

redrider: evidence

alchemist: nothing to find

redrider: they want to dissect you insult you / just say the word

alchemist: I can take care of myself

redrider: enemies appear in many guises

"Cold to the bone," Sylvia muttered, shaking off rain as she and Sweetheart marched through the lobby of the stately Claridge's Hotel.

She was startled by the deep, resonating chime of a massive grandfather clock: 9:00 P.M. Tuesday, going on 1:00 P.M. *Tuesday.*

Try explaining time zones to your body.

Sweetheart shot her a glance, leading the way to registration.

She had to concentrate in order to keep from swaying on her feet. She was so numb, so tired she could taste clean sheets. She managed a spare smile for the bellman, who reminded her of a pug standing guard over their bags.

"Your key," Sweetheart offered, heading toward the stairs.

"Oh, no." She shook her head, making a beeline for the elevator. "I'm taking the *lift.*" The bellman held the door open for her, then followed with the luggage cart.

Inside the brocade closet, the lift attendant gazed down the length of his nose. "Damp evening?"

"More like a bloody bathtub," she said, trying out the colloquialism.

"What was that, madam?"

"You're right, it's a damp evening." She smiled politely, resting her weight against the banister, mustering her energy when the elevator stuttered to a stop on the third floor.

She followed the bellman down the hallway to her room. Sweetheart was waiting inside.

"Adjoining suites," he said, looking pleased with himself. Incredibly, he still appeared awake and focused. "What took you so long?"

"Oh, leave me alone," she sighed. The bellman raised his eyebrows, and she shrugged. "He's not human. You've heard of those cloning experiments?" She tipped the man—"Is this enough?"—hoping she got the money right, pound for dollar, pence for cents—and watched the door close behind his back.

She shrugged off her jacket, tossing it over a chair. "What the hell happened today? I feel as if I'm traveling in a country where I speak just enough of the language to know I'm clueless." Moving restlessly, she surveyed her surroundings. The room was divided into sleeping chamber and parlor. The long curtains were drawn, and when parted, they revealed a view that was nothing but yellow mist. The door to Sweetheart's room was open and she glanced inside, catching sight of his jacket, a book, and files already spread across his double bed. She continued exploring—closet, tiny bathroom, extra blankets—speaking on the move: "Porton Down is terrifying, Bio-Port is creepy, and Paul Lang is a casebook study in morbid, pathological grief."

Looking through cupboards, she discovered the minibar hidden beneath the television and VCR. She took inventory, selecting the half bottle of French chardonnay and the Violet chocolate bar.

"The clincher was when Lang showed us his photo album," she decided, slumping onto the bed, coming to rest for an instant before she leaned down to attack the laces of her black boots. First left, then right, the boots flew across the room to smack against the old-fashioned radiator. Socks followed. She flexed her bare feet, flashing plum-enameled nails. "He was so detached from any real feelings—that level of denial is frightening. Lang scared me." She looked up at Sweetheart. "What I saw at BioPort scared me." She shook her head, but it was almost a shiver. "If I didn't know about Christine Palmer, I'd look long and hard at Lang as Samantha Grayson's murderer."

Sweetheart's eyebrows rose. "I admit the photographs were unsettling, but Lang is not a murder suspect."

"Believe me, after we considered the 'jeopardy surface'—the way Palmer moved Samantha Grayson into close proximity before her death—I don't doubt for a minute that Palmer murdered her." Sylvia sat still, then said, "What's your read on Harris Cray? When Palmer left for LANL, he remained at BioPort, but he strikes me as the type who's always second gun and resentful." She whistled softly. "No love lost between Harris and Samantha Grayson. And when it comes to Christine Palmer, he's beyond loyal, he's gaga. Lovesick." Sylvia's facial expression shifted between distaste and surprise. "Do you suppose they had an affair?"

Sweetheart gave her an odd look. "You heard the results of the MOSAIK search. Nothing came up in Cray's history to indicate a relationship with Palmer—in fact, there's some question as to whether or not he's gay."

"He's not gay, I'm telling you. But forget sexual preference for the moment. Something's going on with Cray—maybe he's a closet gambler, maybe a drug addict. He's got something up his sleeve, even if it's his rigid ego."

She stretched, easing the tension in her shoulders and neck. She was studying Sweetheart intently. But now she picked up a hotel postcard from the table beside the bed and guided it gently through the air. "If Samantha Grayson had been a diabetic, I would've used the new super insulin—drain the contents of her regular script and refill it with double potency. The next time she injects, bam."

"Nice touch."

"Or, even nastier, steal a tampon from her purse, open it, dose the cotton with heavy metal, reseal the paper wrapper with some wax and an iron, sneak it back into the purse, and"—she snapped her fingers—"be in another country when she dies by a self-administered dose."

Sweetheart's eyes narrowed. "Then you'd miss out on the experience of watching her die. Don't forget, Christine Palmer has an insatiable curiosity."

Lifting the telephone receiver, Sylvia scanned the labels on the various buttons, punched one, and waited. "Yes, hello, that's me. I need a pot of very hot, very strong tea and a sandwich of some kind that's not too fattening so I'll be able to fit in my wedding dress back home. No—oh—*yes,* grilled ham, cheese, and tomato is perfect. A glass of milk and something sweet." She waited, then said, "Just a tiny serving of trifle, that would be lovely. You have my room number—twenty-five minutes? *Please* hurry, I'm famished, I may die of hunger."

"Trifle?"

"It's light. All that whipped cream." She replaced the receiver and eyed Sweetheart. "Order your own. I'm headed for a hot bath, after which I'm going to open my wine and slide under the covers." She fell back on the bed and, after a moment, spoke to the ceiling. "Lang is lying or at least censoring. Watley's lying. What's all this about Bio-Port and Dr. Thomas? And my feet hurt."

"They're lying, you're whining."

"I know. But my feet really do hurt."

"I can fix that." He had seated himself on a green silk love seat and smiled slightly when she raised her head to stare at him. "Nothing more exotic than shiatsu massage."

"Pressure points, right?" She rolled over, burying her face in the knobby spread.

"Right." He moved to the edge of the bed.

She felt his weight shift the mattress and her equilibrium. When his fingers slid knowingly along the arch of her left foot, she melted. "*Oh*. That's good." Her words were muffled by a mouthful of fabric. "Wheredidyoulearn—"

"Japan." He pressed the tip of her big toe, then whispered, "*Shindeshi*, eh."

"Yeow." She squeezed her eyelids tight. She could hear his breathing, feel his other hand begin to enclose the heel of the same foot.

"You're holding too much tension," he said, his voice soft.

She didn't answer; she was too busy dissolving into liquid. Her body was disappearing. Electricity traveled from her feet up her legs, butt, shoulders, neck; her brain tingled.

"You can adjust the entire body through the feet," Sweetheart said.

"Mmmm." As he worked, she drifted to the edge of consciousness. Here and there, something pulled her back. His hands moving to her other foot. His fingers sliding around her ankle, returning to her toes. She floated away again.

Almost missing his quiet words, "Why are you getting married?"

Still caught in the liminal space between sleep and waking, she let the question settle, thought about answers, took her time. *I'm getting married because it's time . . . because we want to try for a child . . . because I need family . . . because I want to be normal, lead a normal life . . . because I'm in love, because he makes me content.*

Because there was no single answer—and because Sweetheart was really asking another question altogether—she didn't respond.

. . .

The knock on the door brought her around.

She sat up slowly, rubbing her eyes. Alone. Had she slept?

Her stomach growled. *Room service.*

"I'm coming," she mumbled. Second knock. She stumbled toward the door, calling hoarsely to the next room, "Sweetheart?"

The waiter set the tray on the table in front of the green love seat. He removed stainless steel covers with a flourish, explained that the Lapsong souchon was steeping, adjusted the single pink rose in the narrow vase, and disappeared when she blinked.

She grabbed a half of sandwich, devoured it in a minute, and downed the milk, only then beginning to feel human again.

She heard faint sounds in the other room. Sweetheart moving around. He appeared at the door, entered the room. "I fell asleep," she said, dazed.

"You're *still* asleep." He looked at her in a way that left her self-conscious. The look wasn't inappropriate, it wasn't sexual, but it implied intimacy—and he was *reading* her again.

"It's too late to call home right now, isn't it?" she asked hurriedly, feeling exposed. "Too *early*, I mean." She caught it now—his expression was almost *needy*, definitely vulnerable behind the tough-guy warrior.

"You have a yellow dot on your chin."

"Cheese," she said, dabbing herself with the napkin.

"It's gone." Still he stared at her, his mouth softening. "You look like a *shindeshi*, a new recruit. Sumo." He almost smiled.

"Chow Yun Fat," she countered. "In *The Killer.* That's who you remind me of tonight. That's a compliment." If he responded she didn't hear him, because she'd retreated into secret thoughts. She knew almost nothing about Sweetheart's life, his past, his family. What was it that he pursued so desperately? He'd made a life tracking down the *bad* guys.

For his part, he knew what his research and his database told him about her, which was not enough. She'd made a career of trying to understand what drove people to do *bad* things.

Which meant they were most closely related through their obsessions, a dark connection: the drive to go after the pathologically narcissistic, those who are very dangerous to the world, the twisted and the greedy.

And greed brought Sylvia right back in a tight circle to Samantha Grayson.

She picked up the fork from the tray, examined the tines, and guided them gently through the air. "Maybe Samantha was an industrial spy."

"Maybe she was. Gretchen and Luke are running the background checks—queries into her financial affairs, et cetera—through MOSAIK," Sweetheart said, referring to the assistants in his California office.

"Good. To see if she was buying Ferraris, caviar, and diamonds on a technician's salary? I'd like a Ferrari. What do *you* think of Lang?"

"I don't *think*, I know," Sweetheart said. "Gray and red: he's a repressed British bureaucrat, a *gray* man, who had his world turned upside down by a sexually adventurous woman. The *red* is passion, and now a hunger for revenge. That's Paul Lang."

"In other words, a Brit on emotional steroids," Sylvia said. "I have a stomachache."

"You ate too fast."

She sighed, picking at the remaining sandwich. "What do we know about Lang's work, his area of expertise?"

"Among other things, his speciality is the analysis of international weapons trafficking: NBC—nuclear, biological, chemical."

Sylvia yawned. "What did Samantha Grayson see in him?" She followed up with a stretch. "I got the definite impression, she was attracted to the more obvious pleasures of life. Lang doesn't strike me as the type she'd go for."

"Then she was drawn to the allure of MI-6."

"So, Samantha liked her fiancé's connections."

"Social?"

"Professional." Sylvia considered the idea. "You said it: the allure of MI-6. It's possible, the fact he worked in international affairs—even if it was a desk job—"

There was a sharp bleat from the cell phone clipped to Sweetheart's belt, and he put it to his ear and grunted a greeting. Reading conversational fragments, Sylvia realized he was talking to Luke or Gretchen, his assistants in Los Angeles.

"She said she was from where?" Sweetheart asked.

Indecipherable noise from the phone; it actually sounded as though tiny chipmunks were trapped inside the earpiece.

"Save the rest for later, but put her through *now*," Sweetheart said, abruptly pushing a button on the phone. He turned toward Sylvia, opening his mouth to speak, but was interrupted by a voice emerging from the handset. A woman's voice, heavily accented, breathless. "Don't say my name."

"Fine. We'll do this in a way that makes you comfortable," Sweetheart agreed.

"I hear an echo—is this a conference call? Are you alone?"

"I'm here with my associate." Sweetheart nodded, as if the speaker could see him, then said, "I understand that you were a colleague of a certain party at a Danish lab." As he spoke, he scrawled on a piece of notepaper so Sylvia could read: *Gisla Schmidt—worked with Palmer.*

"Yes." Schmidt hesitated, then relayed a shorthand history of her association with Palmer. They'd worked together five years earlier. Zootoxins. A project with several employees logging in too much sick time.

Schmidt explained, "I'd been sick for three days—muscles rubbery, pains in my chest, it hurt to breathe, my legs half numb, scared to death—and I get this call from *her*. She's sympathetic, she asks how I am, I say I feel lucky, because I'm alive. She starts asking me questions. When did I first feel sick? Where did the pain start, in my stomach or in my head? How quickly did my illness proceed? Did I vomit? She even asks how much I vomited and how many times. How did my head feel? What was I feeling? I mean, she wants exact symptoms, *precise* symptoms.

"When I tell her it upsets me to talk about it, she apologizes. But she insists. She says it's for documentation, a requirement of the lab's internal safety, standard operating procedure. Well, that makes sense to me.

"And I don't think anything about it until two days later, when someone from administration calls me. He has a report to file. 'Standard,' he says. When I tell him I've already done the SOP questionnaire for *her*, he says he doesn't know what I'm talking about. He says she must be doing her own research, because he's never heard of a lab questionnaire."

"Did you report the incident to anyone else?" Sweetheart asked.

"Sure." Schmidt hesitated. "The division director was all worked up, said he'd go to the lab's deputy director." She went silent, then said, "I don't like talking about this."

"I understand, but the circumstances are exceptional."

"I shouldn't have called."

"We appreciate your candor and your concern."

Schmidt took an audible breath. "It stopped there."

"We didn't get that."

"Nothing happened. It was all written off, blamed on a defective fume hood. Aerosol accretion of toxic cultures. A month later, she announces she's going to England. She was gone two weeks after that."

"And there was never any other feedback from your supervisors?"

"Nothing," Schmidt said. "She did it to others. She made them sick, and then she asked for intimate details about their illness, their symptoms. She's like a cannibal—one who treats you like an honored guest, who offers you food and drink—but all the time it's a way to fatten you up for the kill."

"Let me get this straight. You're saying the director of the lab ignored the complaints against your colleague."

This time the silence stretched almost forty seconds. "After I hang up, don't try to reach me. I can't talk to you again." The sound of her breathing filled the space; finally she relented. "How do you say it? Friends in high places? Somebody up there likes the doctor."

After Gisla Schmidt had disconnected, both profilers sat for almost a minute. Finally, Sylvia said, "I'm beginning to get the feeling that once Christine Palmer touches your life, it's never the same again. *You're* never the same again."

Sylvia is alone. Her house. Her hands shake as she reaches out to open the closet door. Her clothes hang neatly, pants on the left, shirts in the middle, jackets on the right. Her shoes are lined up in rows, eleven pairs. Everything's just ducky.

She closes the door—comes face-to-face with her own reflection.

Not her face, not her hair.

Who are you?

Pale golden skin; blond hair; long, slender neck—a hand reaches out, fingers curl around a hypodermic needle.

What are you looking for?

Trespassing!

Someone is banging on the door. She wants to cry out for help— too late—they're going away. She's alone with this woman . . .

Sylvia sat up abruptly. She was breathing fast, almost hyperventilating, and she was damp with sweat. *Dreaming. It was only a dream. Catch your bearings.*

Hotel room. London. Sweetheart.

A noise drew her attention. Turning to look, she caught sight of red numbers on the digital clock: 2:31 A.M.

She stood, steadied herself, and moved like a sleepwalker toward the door. Another sound, a sharp click, outside in the hallway.

Her fingers closed around the doorknob, turned, pushed.

She stared out into dim green light and silence. Felt a presence. Looked right. Saw Sweetheart standing outside his door. He was dressed in a black silk robe. His hair was loose, gleaming black around his shoulders. His feet were bare, callused—*funny what one notices in odd moments.*

And he was staring at *her* bare feet. No, at the carpet. She followed his gaze and saw the package just inches from her toes. A box.

Sweetheart closed his door quietly. He crossed the short distance and knelt to examine the package.

"What is it?" Sylvia whispered.

He shook his head. "How lucky do you feel?" With great care, he balanced the box between his fingertips, carried it into her room, and set it very gently on the floor.

He called the front desk, engaged in a terse exchange, and hung up with a grunt. "About twenty minutes ago, it appeared on the bellman's stand—he was in the *loo.*"

"How was it delivered?"

"Adult male. Average. He wore a taxi driver's uniform. Bellman didn't know if he should bring it up tonight or wait until morning. He compromised, left it outside the door." Sweetheart moved quickly, efficiently, collecting what he needed; clean pillow case, scissors, tweezers, gloves.

"I keep thinking about the anthrax letters," Sylvia said.

"Don't breathe," Sweetheart shot back as he slid the scissors blade

into a fold of brown sack wrapping, and she knew he was only half
joking.

It was a videotape.

Typed on a square of plain white paper: OPERATION ALKAHEST.

"Alkahest . . . an alchemical term, relating to the holy grail for
alchemy," Sweetheart said slowly. "The philosopher's stone, the elixir—
the element that makes transmutation and immortality possible."

"Was Palmer working on another project at Porton Down?" Sylvia
asked faintly.

"Good question."

"This looks like the tapes we saw at BioPort." She brushed a
strand of hair from her eyes. Her pupils were dilated; her irises, normally a golden brown looked almost silver in the artificial light.

Without a word, Sweetheart slid the tape very gingerly into the
hotel's VCR and pressed play.

The image had been captured by a handheld camera; the film and
sound quality appeared identical to that of the tape they had seen earlier, the one labeled 16-32R. But the story that unfolded was ominously different.

A squirrel monkey, a tiny female with baleful eyes, stared back at
the lens. A small sign on the glass cage read: SABRINA.

Obviously healthy and familiar with the routine, Sabrina completed a series of neurological assessments demonstrating the animal's
ability to successfully perform coordination and cognition exercises.

The image blacked out, then jumped on-screen again—just as
Sabrina was exposed to aerosol, delivered automatically, as in the case
of the earlier video.

The clock in the corner of the screen showed 0713 hours; the date
was within the span of Palmer's Porton Down work, Project Nicander.

The image jumped again. The clock now showed that over
twenty-four hours had passed.

This time the monkey was disoriented, passive, unable to stand.

She stumbled, shivering, gazing up at the camera with glassy, unfocused eyes. Abruptly, she began to shake uncontrollably. She couldn't remain upright but slumped down on one side. Her mouth pulled back, teeth exposed.

Another cut: the glass cage was empty. The clock showed 1603 hours; no date.

It was impossible to discern whether the footage had been collected over hours, days, or weeks.

A flash of fur attacked glass. The monkey hurled herself at the enclosure repeatedly, until she stunned herself with one particularly vicious blow and lay gasping, head lolling, eyes wide and filled with terror. Her fur was bloody where she had torn away pieces of her own skin with her claws. She was moaning, chattering, now struggling to rise. In seconds she began the self-brutalizing behavior again.

"She's psychotic," Sylvia whispered. She forced herself not to turn away as the monkey slashed at her own face.

Just as abruptly as it had begun, the tape ended and the screen went to blue.

"My God, what was Palmer doing at Porton Down?" Sylvia said in a hoarse voice. "What kind of horror was she creating?"

Just before dawn in Los Alamos, Special Agent Darrel Hoopai caught the flash of movement near the Target's light blue Jaguar XK8 sports coupe. The Target appeared abruptly, a blond bull's-eye in his surveillance lens. She was dressed in her pajamas. Barefoot. Carrying a newspaper up to the front door of her Los Alamos house.

He bit off an expletive. *Where the hell did she come from?*

And more important: *Where the hell had she been?*

He notified his contact immediately. They held a brief conference. *Procedure:* surveillance had been uninterrupted; the Target had returned home at 2013 hours; she had dressed and prepared for bed at 2044 hours; she had turned off her bedroom light promptly at 0100 hours; at all times her Jaguar XK8 had remained in the driveway; all points were properly documented.

Policy: sit tight; maybe she had insomnia again; maybe she really did step out to take a walk or get the paper.

But why hadn't he seen her?

If she'd managed to sneak out a window, if she'd had a change of clothes stashed in another car, if that car was parked a block away . . .

S.A. Hoopai's belly churned. He shook his head.

How would she have arranged for a car?

He was stirring up trouble in his own mind.

He'd been watching very closely.

Yes, watching very closely.

And now he had the nagging feeling he'd just missed the home run of the season. The Target had made a move, and yours truly had missed it.

Alchemist . . . I wish you were here with me . . . I can't wait much longer so I comfort myself thinking of you and how we'll be together soon.

A dream last night: dead and dying everywhere, the aftermath of a biological holocaust, a ghost intoning, The alchemist devotes a lifetime to the study of impurity and imperfection, and the possibilities of transformation to purity, to perfection. The quest of transmutation—base metals to gold—was born in magic and mystery. Alchemy created chemistry as science.

Alchemist I understand what you were made of before heat and light, and I understand what you will become when you are ready to transform.

What a rare thing in this life to meet a kindred spirit. Do you understand what I am offering? Km.t. True partnership.

. . . have been rumors for years, Rikishi . . !

The LED letters ran across the tiny face of Sweetheart's Palm Pilot. Toshiyori had news for Strong Man.

Toshiyori had been characteristically brief in response to the encoded query, which translated to: *Operation Alkahest?*

Sweetheart cued: *More?*

He waited, scanning the London scene. Piccadilly Circus. The view of tacky flashing signs, street performers, and traffic was dulled by a light fog. Cars splashing water from puddles—and pedestrians dodging puddles and spray—flowed past him. But he was standing in another world, one governed by its own inviolable rules, where each "reality" could be cracked like the face of a mirror to reveal another "reality," and so on and so forth.

He gazed down at the letters flowing across the face of the hand-held device.

. . . fear of substance coming out of Sodom . . . string of incidents never reached press . . . no trace, no taste, don't breathe, see for yourself, chumeia 8732, reach for salvation, psalms 0797,099,01,102,3,3 . . .

With the use of a few keys, Sweetheart ran a search on the Web, pulling up the appropriate sites and articles according to the encoded directive. He put the pieces together.

If Operation Alkahest had existed—at BioPort or anywhere else— it represented a highly classified project dedicated to the development of a new form of biotoxin, one that would be odorless, tasteless, invisible, untraceable. According to military standards it was the best possible bioweapon: its route of target delivery could be cutaneous, gastrointestional, or inhalational; it didn't kill—instead, it maimed by destroying its victims' central nervous system and brain function. In the world of asymmetrical warfare, it was a heavenly weapon because it not only affected the sick, it also placed a huge burden on the healthy by demanding invaluable resources, breaking down morale, and ultimately tearing apart the social fabric.

In plain speak it simply meant that you had a better war when your enemies were maimed and psychotic than when they were dead. Dead was easy, maimed meant other living people acting as caretakers.

Sweetheart already knew the title of the operation referred to the alkahest, a mythical alchemical elixir—a philosopher's stone, the missing ingredient in the process of transmutation of elements into new elements by the alchemist; a mirror of atomic transmutation accomplished by the physicists. It was an obscene twist, elixir as death tool.

Sweetheart was about to pocket his Palm Pilot when he noticed a final string of letters.

. . . if rumor reality . . . avoid double cross . . . watch back, Rikishi . . .

Using a black umbrella as a cane, Sweetheart crossed the street to enter a plain high-rise. He passed tourists bound for Ripley's Believe It or Not and a girl selling chestnuts. The pungent smoky scent of roasting nuts made his mouth water.

On the eleventh floor, in a small corner office, he met with two gray-haired gentlemen in dark suits. They both sat across from him; his credentials were the only item on the polished walnut table. He said, "I appreciate your cooperation."

The taller, older man addressed Sweetheart's request with a tight smile.

The younger man intertwined his fingers behind his head and said, "We have no knowledge of any project of that name or designation."

"You know that I've been in contact with the FBI's legal attaché in London," Sweetheart said quietly. "You should understand that this investigation goes to a level beyond our Federal Bureau of Investigation. It is multijurisdictional; it involves at least three nations, including Great Britain and the United States. An MI-6 analyst was involved in the initial investigation—"

"If you're referring to Mr. Lang, we understand that he has been placed under restricted leave until further notice. Any files must be returned to our possession immediately."

"Files? How can that be, on a project that doesn't exist?"

"Mr. Lang has gained unauthorized access to classified documents."

"Gentlemen, let's begin this meeting again," Sweetheart said, his voice very soft. "Mr. Lang interests us." He set the videotape on the table. "This will interest you."

Sweetheart walked through the door of his suit at Claridge's and found Sylvia seated on the end of his bed. His skin formed goose bumps when he *heard* Christine Palmer say: ". . . years away, treatments might be found for Alzheimer's, epilepsy, stroke—a shopping list of neurologic—"

The sound stopped abruptly as Sylvia raised her hand, the remote clutched in her fingers. Palmer's image froze on-screen.

"What are you doing?" Sweetheart asked.

"Watching the BBC documentary you had stashed in your underwear. Trying to glean, to understand, to empathize, to *absorb*, all that profiling mumbo jumbo." She shrugged, not in the mood for a temperamental encounter. "Luke called about twenty minutes ago."

"You've made yourself at home."

"You were supposed to check in with him. He has something for your ears only. Believe me, I tried to pry it out of him, but that man's not only hunky, he's incorruptible." She reached for the bedside tray, which contained the last few bites of a scone and a cup of Keemun tea, very black, barely lukewarm. She was surrounded by boxes; files and folders were piled on the bed, on the floor at her feet.

"I see you helped yourself." He didn't look pleased. "Find anything interesting?"

"Four new and very thick files. Are they from Lang?"

"He had them sent over this morning—apparently they represent the bulk of his investigation."

"Where was I?"

"Sleeping."

"Why would Lang give them away?"

"Perhaps he realizes his days are numbered," Sweetheart murmured, crossing the room. "His days as they pertain to the investigation into Ms. Grayson's death."

"Did you confront him about the videotape?"

"I didn't see him. I haven't spoken to him." Sweetheart's face was smooth, blank paper. "The tape came from someone at BioPort—Cray, Jorgensen, Watley. Or it came from Paul Lang."

"Why wouldn't he just give it to us directly? Why all the subterfuge?"

"Paranoia."

"When are we seeing him again?"

"We aren't." Sweetheart glanced at his watch. "We have to be at Gatwick in four hours. You need to be packed and ready to go in forty-five minutes." His eyes were the color of steel and rust; they did not ask questions, they commanded.

She stared at him, seeing only that he was withholding—but *what?* "What is it? You found out something new. Where did you go this morning?"

"For a walk." His black hair, smoothed into a knot, was wet with rain. His lidded eyes were unfathomable.

"I was worried."

"I didn't think I'd be gone long," he said, *too* calm. He walked to the windows, pulled open the heavy drapes, and let gray, cold light into the room. "I stopped to have breakfast at a tea shop." He hadn't succeeded in banishing the edge of irritation from his tone. "All very *quaint*."

"I thought something happened." She shook her head, surprised to find that she had felt both angry and frightened. "After last night, the tape—"

"I decided to let you sleep, but I should've left you a note. I'm sorry." He shrugged off the apology, moving to the armchair opposite her, then poured himself a cup of tea in an empty water glass. His eyes stayed on Sylvia, his mind alert, his body apparently relaxed. Waiting.

Abruptly the image that had been frozen on-screen shuddered into motion: once again Christine Palmer's voice was audible, her face filled the screen. On camera—as in real life—she exuded charisma, acumen, and subtle sexuality. There was a restless quality to her movements, an edge that added tension to everything she did.

For the first time, Sylvia realized that Palmer's classic features were asymmetrical in one respect: her left eye was set just noticeably lower than her right.

According to Palmer, her team was honing in on neurotoxic substances isolated from sea snails and dinoflagellates. She faced the interviewer, explaining, "While these diseases cause suffering today, revolutionary treatments are within reach, especially with the promise of our research, along with the ongoing stem cell breakthroughs—"

Again Sylvia stopped the tape.

"She makes you believe her," Sweetheart said. "She's that charismatic."

"Please tell me you see through her," Sylvia countered. "She's lying. Not to the BBC, not to the viewer—she's lying to *herself.* Listen to the speech patterns on this next bit—*watch* her and *listen.*"

Palmer's image came to life, gazing at the BBC interviewer, then away, as she said, "The fact we could alleviate suffering in a profound way—*that's* what drives me to come to work each day."

Freeze-frame. Sylvia felt excited as she said, "Hear the clipped speech—she's cutting herself off. Watch her body language. She's turning away, hiding her mouth; that's the only time she physically evades the viewer during the entire interview. And watch her microexpressions . . . when she turns back, eyelids raised—anger— inner eyebrows raised—*distress.* She doesn't believe her own script."

Sweetheart took the remote from her hand. Without a word, he rewound, replayed the segment in slow motion. He let the tape play on.

The BBC narrator noted that previously isolated toxins from cobra venom were being used to treat immune disorders. Ditto toxins from scorpion venom, already in clinical trials for the treatment of certain brain tumors. Compounds from fer-de-lance venom were destined for use as antibiotics.

After a cut intended for commercial identification, the narrator delivered the standard cautionary segment: "Of course, there's a darker side to researching animal venom and other biotoxins. In the world of science it's known as 'NBC warfare'—nuclear, biological, chemical. And the use of biotoxins as weapons is nothing new. Poisoned arrows are mentioned in the Book of Job."

He concluded with enthusiastic predictions for the future of medical miracles as the camera pulled back to allow a view of Dr. Palmer in her laboratory, alone—no sign of Samantha Grayson, Dr. Harris Cray, or other project members.

"She's not like Adam Riker," Sylvia said slowly. "Riker had a single basic need, to control intimacy and relationship through power—that's what drove him to kill. Christine's more complex." She was so caught up in her train of thought, she didn't register the fact that she was using Palmer's first name, but she certainly would've been able to explain the process: the gap between profiler and target was narrowing.

"Christine's in conflict with her work. My God, how could she *not* be conflicted? Even if she's supposedly developing antidotes—and *cures*—at the same time her research creates new toxins, new poisons, new bioweapons. How could she not be conflicted?" Her eyes cut to Sweetheart. They were dark with fear. "I thought our job was profiling a serial poisoner."

"It is," he said sharply.

"But I find out we're dealing with toxins, bioweapons—"

"Sylvia."

"—that are so horrific, and so classified, that all we're getting are lies, which taint any profile we might try to create."

"Sylvia, stop." He moved to sit beside her. "You were right the first time. We are profiling a serial killer. Whatever went on at Porton Down or BioPort—whatever Project Nicander was about—that's not our business."

She stared at him. "We can't just ignore it."

"Yes, we can." His posture was rigid. "And we will."

.   .   .

On the way to the airport, the cabbie stopped in the heart of the district known as Covent Garden.

Bundled in an indigo slicker, Sylvia followed Sweetheart catty-corner to a narrow alley. Halfway down the alley, he came to a standstill in front of a heavily reinforced door. Water dripped off the overhead gutter, forming a puddle on the step. Sylvia read the faded sign printed on the wood: STAGE DOOR.

Surprisingly, when Sweetheart pushed on the lock bar, it opened. It was dark inside the theater. He led the way up a short flight of stairs, along a passage to a worm-eaten reception desk, where he carried on a brief, whispered conversation with a uniformed man. After some nodding and gesturing, he continued along the dim hallway in the general direction of voices and lights.

Sylvia caught her breath as they reached the wings, stage left, at the edge of the deepest-set scrim, where the world was dim and secretive. There they stood surrounded by shadowy figures: stagehands and actors awaiting cues.

Suddenly, a man said, "Let her come in."

A deep voice rose from the stage. "How now! What noise is that?"

Sylvia shrank back as a woman brushed past, leaving a faint trail of scent: cosmetics, orange peel, sweat. The actress stepped onstage, moving slowly, holding every eye. She was dressed in white and she moved with an odd grace. "They bore him barefac'd on the bier; hey non nonny . . ."

As Ophelia launched into her song of madness, Sylvia watched, mesmerized. Sweetheart had brought her to this Shakespearean tragedy just as the king, Laertes, and his doomed sister shared the stage. Ophelia gone mad after learning of her father's death by her lover's sword; Laertes wild with grief, hungering for revenge.

But it is the king who is guilty, Sylvia found herself thinking—*the murderous king with his poison.*

When the scene's final lines were delivered and the actress swept offstage and into the wings, Sweetheart followed. *"Hamlet?"* Sylvia whispered close on his heels. "Are you serious?"

"Hamlet," he said, knocking softly on the dressing room door, behind which Ophelia had disappeared. A voice called out, "It's open."

They entered the small musty room.

"I was expecting you." The voice drifted from behind a dressing screen. "Make yourselves at home, I'll be just a minute."

They sat. Sylvia was curious to meet the actress. She studied the dressing table, which was cluttered with jars of pancake, gum, spirits, powder, brushes, pencils. A creased rehearsal schedule had been taped to the mirror. A script lay open on a chair, a few lines underlined on the page.

Definitely not Shakespeare.

A man stepped out from behind the curtain. The blond wig had been removed, as had the bodice of his costume, but he was still wearing the flowing white skirt. He smiled, his teeth slightly yellow in contrast to the white pancake makeup and red lipstick.

Sylvia couldn't hide her surprise.

"Did you expect a fetching will-o'-the-wisp?" he asked. "This is a progressive production of *Hamlet,* darlin'."

"Dr. Sylvia Strange, meet the Honorable Sir Angus Blackmoore," Sweetheart said.

Sir Angus swept an imaginary hat from his head and bowed.

Sylvia sent her associate a dark look before turning her attention to the tall—and now, she saw, quite handsome—actor. "Sir Angus, it's a pleasure, but we're intruding in your dressing room—"

"Angus is fine." He produced a cigarillo from behind one ear. "Dressing *room* is a falsehood, a fabrication, a deceit, a downright lie. Dressing cupboard, dressing closet, dressing cubbyhole, dressing niche—but not room, *never* room."

Sylvia picked up a slender gold lighter from the table, flicked a flame, and held it to his cigarillo. Sweet, pungent smoke filled the air. "Thanks, ducks. This is all very telly-glam." His hands circled gracefully through the air, pushing smoke into swirls. "My cubbyhole. Your investigation of the deviant mind. My deviant mind. You've come to the right place." He faced them, hand on hip, heavily lined eyes black against the white pancake.

Sylvia knew she was staring; Sweetheart had told her only that they would be interviewing a longtime associate of Palmer.

Associate meaning what? Friend? Schoolmate? Relative?

"Chrissy and I were an item." Angus winked, enjoying Sylvia's surprise. "*Ssthientist* and *thes*pian," he lisped, sounding like Sylvester the cat. "*Sstho* romantic." Turning toward the mirror, he dipped a sponge in a jar of cold cream, then, starting at his forehead, he began to wipe it across his face. "In spite of the dress, luv, I don't fancy boys."

"It wasn't that," Sylvia sputtered. "Even if—I didn't—never mind." She sighed, and Sweetheart rolled his eyes.

Angus smiled. "I've been head over heels since childhood. We grew up together." He studied his image in the mirror, tugging at nooks and crannies with his sponge. "I knew her father—what an incredible man, more like a god, really. And I was close friends with Avery Winter, the *other* love of her life."

Sweetheart had hardly moved since entering the dressing room. Just through stillness, he seemed capable of reducing his size. He was paying close attention to the actor.

"Christine and Avery were engaged for centuries, promised to each other in nappies, I fear. But his cancer nixed the wedding. The big *C,* as you say across the ocean." The corners of his mouth drooped, and the face he made was a parody of Tragedy. "Christine wanted to marry anyway, but Avery refused. Out of pride and manli-

ness and honor—everything that I'm *not*. I was to be their best man.
So excruciatingly sad."

He discarded his sponge, reached for cotton balls and a bottle of astringent. The biting scent of alcohol filled the room. "And how deliciously *suspicious*. The two most influential men in Christine's life, dead within months of each other." He frowned. "Come to think of it, Avery croaked, and I moved to the head of the line. That doesn't look at all nice, now, does it?" But he seemed quite pleased with himself.

No one said anything for a few seconds, then Angus shrugged. "I never had a head for chemistry. Kicked out of public school. Good for nothing but actin' and fookin'. That's what Chrissy always told me."

"Are you in touch with Dr. Palmer—with Christine?" Sylvia asked.

"Haven't seen her since she left London. About six months?"

"Have you had any other sort of contact?" Sweetheart asked.

Angus nodded, smiling coyly. "She called me last night. Oh, yes, ostensibly to ask how I was doing, but I knew the real reason." He let them wait while he plucked a hair from his eyebrow. "She wanted to know if anyone was curious."

"Curious?"

"About *Christine*." Angus twisted his mouth into a frown. "I told her no one had been by to see me in ages." He pulled himself up straight in his chair. "Technically, I did not lie. But if she should happen to call again tonight, I'd have to say two Yanks had dropped in to visit."

"Will she call again?"

"That's not her usual style," Angus said. "Once every six weeks is her usual style. Unless you're the hunk of the month."

Sylvia blinked, skipping a beat. "She has regular lovers?"

Angus snorted. "Regular, irregular, obtuse, seduced; loose as a goose is our Christine. She meets a slew of them on the Internet, all very anonymous. I think her amours help her remember who she is." His voice was soft. "She needs them to remind herself she's mortal."

His eyes were on Sweetheart's back, but now he transferred his gaze to Sylvia. "'How all the other passions fleet to air, as doubtful thoughts, and rash-embrac'd despair and shuddering fear, and green-ey'd jealousy.'"

"Lear?" Sylvia guessed.

"Tsk, tsk." Angus wagged a finger.

"When you and Christine were lovers," Sweetheart asked quietly, "what project was she working on?"

"Chrissy and I have been doing the nasty for the past thirty years, here and there, off and on. But if you mean the finite period when we pretended we were serious, that spanned less than two years." He stared pointedly at Sweetheart, then made a moue with his mouth. "She was commuting to the Netherlands. Consulting all over the planet: Africa, the Americas, Asia, Japan. If I remember correctly, Japan was special to Chrissy."

This time Sylvia couldn't miss the emphasis, the breath, the beat.

But before she could comment, Angus had taken the floor again. "Back then she was doing what she always did," he said with dramatic flourishes, each gesture designed to draw attention to the man, the performer. He'd been an actor for so long, he probably wasn't even aware of his artifice. "She was researching some horrible, ugly creature and its nasty *juices.*"

"Neurotoxins?" Sylvia had one eye on Angus, the other on Sweetheart.

"Right."

"Was the work funded for the private sector, or was it government?"

"Both. Private, but the government had its finger in the pie." He frowned again. "Christine was disturbed by what the lab was doing with the fruit of her labors."

"Disturbed in what way?"

"Enraged, hysterical, guilt-ridden." He didn't speak for seconds.

Without the props of theatrical energy, his face belonged to another man, older, world-weary. "You see, they were always lying to her, and the work was—well, *'defensive,' 'offensive,'* one man's defense is another man's offense, as they say. It's all so confusing, isn't it?"

"What did she do?"

"You'll have to ask her that question."

"Did she ever spend time at a retreat or a hospital?" Sweetheart asked.

"Ah, the loony bin. No knickers left untwisted?" Angus smiled sadly. "It really wasn't much of a secret. After her father's death, and then Avery's so soon after, she needed time . . ." He stared morosely at his hands. "Christine went into retreat, and she came home better."

He seemed to withdraw then, his eyes wistful, his expression distant. "I still love that woman. I'll always love her. She's a marvelous actress, you know. Puts me to shame, she does. Dame Christine Palmer."

"What about trust?" Sylvia kept her eyes from Sweetheart. "Do you trust her?"

"I would trust her with my life."

Sweetheart suddenly stirred. "What sort of shape was Avery in at the end?"

"He wanted to die."

"Did he ask for Christine's help?"

"I don't see why not. After all, he *begged* me to put a pillow over his face, and I'm hopeless in that sort of situation."

"What about Christine? Do you believe she's capable of murder?"

"'But, soft! methinks I scent the morning air. Brief let me be. Sleeping within mine orchard, my custom always of the afternoon, upon my secure hour thy uncle stole, with juice of cursed hebona in a vial, and in the porches of mine ears did pour the leperous distilment . . .'" Sir Angus Blackmoore's voice faded as he placed his hand over his heart. "I'd never think of loving a woman who *wasn't* capable of murder."

"You mentioned Christine's other lovers," Sylvia began.

But Sir Angus cupped a hand to one ear and said, "Hark, I hear a curtain call!" Hastily, he settled the blond wig on his head and reached for the top to his costume.

Sylvia heard the door click as Sweetheart turned the knob, felt the swish of air as he pulled it slightly open. She reached out, touching the actor's arm. "It's clear you care about Christine—why are you willing to talk to us?"

"The sickness isn't my Chrissy. It's governments that cover up projects, that use their most brilliant minds, even knowing those minds are breakable. The sickness is bureaucracy, where no one person takes responsibility—where no one person is guilty of anything—because it is the government or the corporation that decides." He turned toward the mirror. "Do you know you have a lovely and very transparent face?"

He held up both hands, cupping air, framing Sylvia's reflection. "'Your face, my thane, is as a book where men may read strange matters.' A little *Macbeth* for Dr. Strange."

They were late, the last passengers to make their way through intense security checks and board flight 6312, departing Gatwick at 4:15 P.M. Wednesday, arriving Albuquerque via Atlanta at 11:14 P.M. *Wednesday*.

Fourteen hours and twenty-six minutes of flight time.

When the plane had leveled out at cruising altitude, Sylvia carefully placed her hands in her lap as she turned toward Sweetheart. His eyes were cold and gray, marked by a constant change of color, like the ocean between storms.

"You have an interesting habit, Sweetheart." Her voice was soft, implying casual intimacy. "You don't turn away when you're lying. The more you withhold the truth, the more confrontational you become. You're actually the opposite of Palmer. I find that intriguing." She pulled a magazine from the seat-back fabric slot and began to thumb aimlessly through pages. She bit her lip, spent several moments collecting herself, then began to speak again, very quietly. "I keep being amazed by the fact you treat me as if I'm blind. Is it possible you didn't think I'd figure it out?"

"I don't know what you're talking about." But he couldn't quite mask the unease that narrowed his eyes.

The magazine slipped from her lap to the floor. She ignored it and said, "You fed me that bullshit: 'We're only here to profile Christine—forget anything and everything else—we focus on her, on the murders, on the profile.' Oops, only one problem—that's *not* what you're doing. You're after something else. This case doesn't stop with Dr. Palmer. She's part of something much bigger—and even more dangerous."

"Keep your voice down." Several passengers glanced over, then away, refusing to stare openly.

"Luke made one mistake when he called this morning," Sylvia said in a whisper. "He was *polite*—he *feigned* interest when I mentioned some questions about Palmer's profile. He had information for you, but that information had nothing to do with Christine Palmer. What the hell are you working on, Sweetheart?"

Sylvia pulled her laptop from beneath the seat. She booted up, worrying the corner of a fingernail while the program rolled across the screen. She waited for the blinking cursor, and when she had it, she typed:

you're tracking a spy—someone dealing in illegal bioweapons—sam g / p lang / dr cray / palmer??—you're like the scientist in iraq who stops publishing in journals when his work becomes classified and everyone knows but nobody says—always look for the one who's not talking—you got too quiet—tell luke he screwed up

Neither of them spoke for the next hour. The plane was dim, and most passengers were sleeping off their dinner, an airplane meal of pork tenderloin or chicken fettuccine, or they were watching the flickering movie screens mounted from the ceiling every fifth row.

She e-mailed Matt, telling him she couldn't wait to see him, trying to communicate how much she'd truly missed him. Then she closed her eyes and tried transporting herself to the tiny and heavenly beach in Costa Rica where they'd vacationed together a month earlier . . .

She drifted in and out of memory, almost falling into sleep, alternately drowsing or tracking the black velvet world outside the jet, her own face reflected faintly in the thick, scratched pane.

Finally, Sweetheart touched her arm, and she turned to look at him. Her eyes weren't filled with anger, as he'd expected, but with sadness.

"I'm sorry," he said softly. "I've lived this way for such a long time—my life divided, separated, information compartmentalized—it may not be right, but I accept it's the way things are. I forget that it can hurt the people around me."

He faltered, then took another breath. "My work, the secrecy, the intelligence, it bleeds over into my other life." He looked down at his hands. "I grew up with secrets. They filled all the spaces when I was a child. The truth is, I don't know how to live any other way."

Sylvia reached out to take hold of his hand. When he studied her face, all he could see was that same overwhelming sadness.

She leaned her head against his shoulder, almost like a child, and then she whispered, "That's a dangerous way to live. I'm afraid for you. I'm afraid for me."

It wasn't until they were debarking at Houston that she saw the shock of red hair belonging to Dr. Harris Cray. It took her several seconds to put name to face—BioPort and Porton Down seemed like another lifetime.

The molecular toxicologist had been seated on the aisle about fifteen rows back. He nodded when he saw that he'd been recognized.

Outside the jetway, as they were leaving the gate, he walked up to them.

"I'm taking over for Dr. Thomas," he said. "I'll be working with Christine, with Dr. Palmer, on the project at LANL." He shrugged. "I was the obvious choice. But it's always interesting how things turn out, isn't it?"

The flight from Houston to Albuquerque was smooth, uneventful, but Sylvia slept fitfully, and her dreams had her tossing and turning through cloudless skies.

As the plane entered the airspace over New Mexico, she was dreaming about a poisoner who wore a long beaded dress and a mask of *la Tragédie*. The poisoner held out an offering, a goblet of wine. Sylvia tried to push the goblet away, but the poisoner was strong and the wine spilled. A drop touched Sylvia's cheek. It burned, sizzling a hole in her skin. She cried out.

When the poisoner stepped back, laughing, the mask fell away, and Sylvia saw she had been fooled by a man—but as she watched, the face changed from Paul Lang to Harris Cray.

Sylvia crept into Serena's bedroom just after 1 A.M. on Thursday, (9 A.M. London time). Her foster daughter stirred, stretching under the covers, rubbing her eyes.

"Hi."

"Hey, sleepyhead." Sylvia snuggled next to Serena. "I missed you."

"You, too. I'm a little bit mad at you."

"Because I went to London?"

"Because I was scared something bad would happen."

"I'm back safe and sound. I'm sorry I frightened you, baby. I didn't mean to."

"Sometimes your work is scary."

"What frightens you about it?"

"You go after people who are evil." Serena frowned. "Like that man who killed his family."

"Adam Riker?" The story had made national headlines, but Serena, like most kids her age, didn't make a habit of watching CNN.

Sylvia was surprised; her foster daughter had never mentioned the case before. "What do you know about Riker?" she asked.

"He killed lots and lots of people and you worked with the police to catch him."

"And the police did catch him. Now he can't hurt anybody else."

"He's dead," Serena said softly. "But so is his family." She sighed. "He killed his own kids . . . and he killed his wife, too, didn't he?"

"Yes." Sylvia closed her eyes, trying not to remember too much.

"What if he'd tried to kill you, too?" Serena's voice was so soft Sylvia had to strain to hear the words.

"Oh, honey, he never had the chance to get close to me." Sylvia squeezed Serena, lightly kissing her forehead. "You should remember something important—I know how to do my job. I don't put myself in danger. I'm very careful."

"Promise?" Serena asked. Her eyelids were drooping over her luminous eyes, and her breathing had deepened to guide her into sleep.

"I promise."

Fifteen minutes later, when Matt looked in on them, they were both asleep. He adjusted the covers, trying not to disturb them, but Sylvia's eyes opened, and she smiled tentatively, yawning.

"Are you mad at me, too?" she whispered.

"I got over it," he said, brushing his fingers against her cheek. His hair was mussed, his eyes were sleepy, his flannel pajamas were creased. "Then I just missed you."

"I missed you, too. *God, did I miss you.* I tried calling you again yesterday—last night, New Mexico time—but I got the machine . . ."

He held a finger to his lips.

She slipped out of Serena's bed, adjusting the covers before she followed Matt into the hallway. "I didn't want to leave you four messages, repeating myself." She paused, her mind beginning to expand to possibilities. "Did you work late?"

"My meetings ran long." He started up the stairs. "I stayed overnight in Albuquerque."

She trailed him into the bedroom. "Meetings with . . . ?" She heard him sigh, then he turned toward her. The room was dark, but moonlight fell through the skylight and she could see his face clearly as he said, "Lucia Hernandez called in some of her chits—people who owed her favors."

"Don't you mean Lucia called in her brother-in-law's chits? It helps to have a sister married to a senator."

"Whatever," he said. "Lucia was kind enough to set up a dinner—one that helped make funding for the new project more than a pipe dream. It looks like we'll be able to expand special operations, create the new command center to coordinate law enforcement, emergency responders, HazMat teams . . ." He stopped, and his eyes grew wide. "You're not jealous?"

"Of course not."

"Good. Because that would be ridiculous."

"But Lucia Hernandez isn't just any business associate—she's smart and she's beautiful."

"You're right." He took her arm. "Damn it, Sylvia, I'm going to marry you next week—I love you—I've been trying to marry you for years—I can't wait to have our child."

"I'm *not* jealous."

"Where are you going?"

"I need a shower." Sylvia was already walking into the bathroom, shutting the door behind her. She opened the shower tap and stepped into water that was only lukewarm. Through the clear curtain she saw him come in and position himself against the wall, arms crossed, staring at her. "I hate it when you walk away and I'm talking to you."

"Sorry." She selected a bottle from the shower rack and squirted shampoo into her palm. "I'm exhausted, my muscles ache, and I need to wash off all that recycled air—all those airplane cooties—"

"Cooties?"

"—so I can go to bed. Don't start an argument, please."

"I'm not starting an argument." His voice registered fear. But he shrugged it off, saying, "Take your shower. I love you. I missed you. I'm just glad you're back."

"Me, too." She lathered her hair, squinting as soap burned her eyes.

"I want to hear more about your trip."

"Tomorrow. I'll tell you all about it."

He didn't go away. He stood watching her—and then he started unbuttoning his pajamas.

"What do you think you're doing?"

"Getting in." He kicked off his pants before following her into the shower. "Turn around, I'll soap your back."

She pressed her face against the tile and sighed with pleasure when the loofah roughed her back, her butt. "Ooh, that's good . . ."

Familiar pressure against her thigh. She turned to kiss him and he responded, moving his mouth onto hers, murmuring, "See what happens when you go away?"

When they came up for air, she took his face in her hands and asked, "Does that mean I'm forgiven?"

"I'm afraid not. A trip to London without your fiancé requires severe punishment."

"What kind of punishment?"

"This kind of punishment . . ."

"Oh. Good."

. . .

Matt made it to bed before she did. She finished smoothing moistur-
izer on her skin, then gave her teeth another brush, even flossed. She
expected to find him asleep, probably snoring. But he was wide
awake, seated on the side of the bed, her black leather purse in his lap.
"Why did you lie to me?"

Not quite registering, she shook her head.

He held up the pink plastic packet of contraceptive pills. "You're
still taking these."

"Yes."

"Fuck." He said it softly, ominously—a man who almost never
used profanity. "I can't believe it. Shit."

"Matt . . ."

"Hush." He held up one hand. His expression changed, altered by
emotions—pain, sadness, fear.

She started to say something—couldn't think what—and her
mouth opened but nothing came out. She just shook her head.

"I thought we'd agreed," he said. "In there, just now, I thought:
Maybe it's happening right now. Maybe we're creating a life."

"I know I should have—" She felt herself cringing. "I thought I
was ready but—I can't help it if I need more time."

"You're right. You can't help it if you need time. But I deserve the
truth." He threw the purse, the pills, on the floor and stood. As he
walked past her, he whispered, "Jesus, Sylvia."

1:45 A.M. Thursday.

"I ran those names you gave me through MOSAIK."

"And?" Sweetheart prodded. He was sitting in the dark, in his room
at the Eldorado Hotel. A bone-dry desert wind slapped the windows.

"Dr. Cray is clean. Which makes me suspicious." Luke's voice—traveling eight hundred miles via satellites and scrambled signals—was soft. "Why is it these guys are usually vulnerable? *Natura humanas.*"

"Dig deeper."

"Always do." Luke asked about the weather in Santa Fe, complained about the smog in L.A. They made small talk.

Finally, Sweetheart asked, "What have you got on Lang?"

"Something you'll like," Luke said, audibly stifling a yawn. "Mr. Lang has credit problems. His girlfriend definitely hankered after the finer things. Their relationship—or the fact Lang tried to borrow money—caused family problems, including a skirmish with a relative. Lang's in debt."

Sweetheart whistled when Luke mentioned an amount.

"You asked me to check on the times Samantha Grayson missed work," Luke said. "Apparently she wasn't sick—or at least not sick enough to stay home in bed." He paused, and the small space was filled by the clicking of a keyboard asking questions and the intimate electronic answers of a powerful computer. "She racked up frequent-flyer miles with trips to Amsterdam, Athens, Hong Kong, the Seychelles—apparently she liked to dive, do the scuba thing."

"I didn't know people did the scuba thing in Amsterdam," Sweetheart said dryly.

"Or Hong Kong. But they do in the Seychelles. I hear the water's hot there. So she was in hot water." Luke gave a small laugh. "By the way, Paul Lang never got to go along for the ride."

"I doubt he really knew what she was up to."

"The trips were arranged by a travel agency—World Tours. It's since gone out of business. Apparently World Tours, Inc., was connected to World Enterprises, and their enterprises included a chain of hotels and escort services. World Enterprises has a corporate address in Hong Kong."

"We keep ending up back at the Chinese connection," Sweetheart said. "Who paid for Grayson's trips?"

"She never paid for the flights or the hotels. But her credit cards—make that *seven* cards, with a total balance of twenty-eight thousand dollars—are heavy on clothes, jewelry, and luxury items."

"Porton Down's internal security didn't pick up on it? That level of debt should've sent up a gigantic red flag."

"Nobody would pick up on it without the tip you gave me from your source—four of the cards are under Samuel Grayson's name. Her father. He died in nineteen ninety-eight."

"So she just kept the cards going," Sweetheart said, "and paid the bills."

"Electronic transfer from an account in her father's name. Actually, she made a large payment about eight weeks before she died. Thirteen thousand dollars. The money didn't come from her salary."

"Let me guess. World Enterprises paid for her services as a travel agent."

"World Enterprises paid for her services as *something*. She was a party girl."

"And perhaps a courier." Sweetheart took a deep breath, held it for a few seconds, and exhaled slowly. "Was she carrying money, goods, or information?"

"Good question. I'll keep looking. Hey, Professor," Luke said faintly. "Give my regards to Dr. Strange. Tell her I plan to kiss the bride."

Sweetheart grunted. He heard Luke ask, "By the way, what are you getting them for a wedding present?" In lieu of an answer, he disconnected.

He weighed this information with the other bit he had received tonight.

Toshiyori had written:

*Answer to your request must be negative. Secrecy imperative. Regret if this
endangers your friends. Stakes are great.*

For the next three hours Sweetheart sat in shadow, letting his mind
flow like water but always keeping a fixed point to return to—flow, return, flow, return—like breath, like sumo practice, a meditation.

He traveled the globe in stillness. Visions of Hong Kong hovered
in his consciousness, and geography was particular, not haphazard.

The sound of the voice that came to him was hushed and melodi-
ous, and one he rarely allowed himself to imagine. A lullaby his
mother used to sing to him in the morning just before dawn, when
she returned home.

He remembered a sea of blue with waves that tickled his skin; per-
fume; his mother's dress somehow permanently etched in his consciousness; blue, her favorite color, the blue of the mountains as
afternoon clouds draped the sun and the air was heavy and ripe, the
blue of peacock feathers and fish just beneath the glassy surface of salt
water.

From there the imagined scene shifted between Hong Kong and
Hawaii.

His life on two islands—but the history was gone along with his
mother, her lovers, his father. As always, on the rare occasions he
allowed these shattered excuses of memory to emerge from his sub-
conscious, he wondered, *Why am I still here?*

Another vision, much more recent, much less fractured, floated
into his consciousness: two bodies, intertwined.

Japan. Rain falling against paper.

Soft voices and the smell of vinegar.

He was surprised by the pain and anger.

The longing.

And something else, another emotion, sharp, the color of pure jade.

These emotions were not familiar.

They didn't please him.

They disturbed his equanimity.

Paul Lang stared at the compact black carrying case. When he opened it, he smelled the sharp, tangy scent of something chemical. The vials fit perfectly in neat slots. The Velcro sheath kept them snug, the thick lining protecting them from breakage. Some of the slots were empty. A few still contained vials.

Samantha always kept the case with her toiletries. It held her medicines, she'd said. He'd believed her. But after her death, he'd found it at the very top of the bathroom shelves. She'd tucked it behind a box of first-aid odds and ends. Perhaps she'd tossed it up there hurriedly when he'd surprised her one day.

He could only guess.

His hands shook, his fingers trembled, as he lifted the largest vial. The seal was broken. When he held it to the light, he saw almost-microscopic dust. It could've been anything. *Anything*.

These days, he'd begun to imagine opening the vial and inhaling the contents. Alternately, he thought of putting the vial into his pocket and walking to the tube, sitting on the train, crushing the vial beneath his foot. *Waiting*.

These days he imagined many things.

But tonight he slid the vial back into its slot; he tamped down the Velcro; he closed the case. He packed it with the few clothes and the passport he was taking on the trip. To America. To New Mexico. He would gain eight hours and arrive by 6 P.M. Thursday evening.

He'd learned the hard way to detect betrayal. The American profilers had lied to him. They weren't going to bring Christine Palmer to justice. She was going to get away with murder—just like she always did—unless he did something about it.

He had his own plan, his own way to make contact.

He zipped his garment bag, logged off his laptop, and shut it down.

He stared at the clock. He had an hour to rest. He didn't choose the bed. Instead, he found the exact spot on the floor where Samantha had died, and he lay down, pulling his knees to his chin. Finally, he closed his eyes.

PART III

Lex Cornelia

redrider: did you miss me?

alchemist: yes

redrider: can't know what that means to me

alchemist: I know

redrider: want to offer a token of my esteem

alchemist: not necessary

redrider: I insist / will tell you where and when

alchemist: dangerous

redrider: trust me

alchemist: you could ruin everything

redrider: have faith

alchemist: don't cross boundaries

redrider: sooner or later we must move to next level

. . . . .

redrider: we have to trust each other

. . . . .

redrider: no turning back

Special Agent Darrel Hoopai had been around the block and back again. He knew *hinky* when he felt it. And he could definitely feel it this Thursday morning when he rolled out of bed at 6:03 A.M. and Jessie, his very pregnant wife, said, "What's wrong, honey, you've got that look."

"What look?"

"The look you get when something's bugging you."

Hoopai imagined that *look* had been creeping up on him for the past twenty-four hours, ever since Christine Palmer had turned up in his nightscopes. Damn, he prided himself on the fact that he didn't leave holes in his surveillance. And then he had to go and leave a whopper, a black hole, an unknown. It might be a forty-five-second hole; it might be a forty-five-minute hole; it might be a seventy-five-minute hole. A lot of things could happen in a span of seventy-five minutes.

In his mind Hoopai now visualized all five doors, hence five avenues of egress from the Target's residence (not counting windows).

The basement door was sheltered—Hoopai decided that if he were going to slip out of that house, he would've used the basement door.

If the situation allowed—surveillance positions, no unforseen circumstances, no surprise visitors—it might be possible to exit the residence unobserved.

He had to admit it to himself. No surveillance was perfect. There were always holes. But seventy-five-minutes holes . . .

The Target could drive to Santa Fe and back.

She could drive to the airport.

She could drive off a cliff.

That was why Hoopai decided to run a check of all vehicles parked within a five-block radius of the Target's house. The search turned up three vehicles with expired plates. One of those—a battered and apparently abandoned Toyota Tercel—was registered to a resident of the town of Española.

When questioned by Special Agent Hoopai, the previous owner remembered, "A lady bought it off me—a few months back, but I don't remember exactly. I parked it out near the highway with those other cars and trucks—no law, is there?"

S.A. Hoopai asked if the man remembered the lady's name.

The man shrugged, then brightened. "But she was a looker."

Jeff Hess, Hoopai's special agent in charge, agreed they would leave the vehicle where it was, along with the global positioning device they placed strategically on the auto body. If the vehicle was used—by the Target or anybody else—they would receive the notification and the tracking signal.

Special Agent Hoopai wasn't all that satisfied with the arrangement. "Why do I have the feeling that car ain't going nowhere fast?" he asked his coagent, S.A. Weaver.

"You mean, it's *going* nowhere fast," Weaver said.

"That's what I said."

"You said *ain't*. Ain't going nowhere means going somewhere."

They left it at that.

He could feel it—something was going to happen—and not nec-essarily something that would make him or his fellow agents happy.

This *cop* hunch left him bad-tempered. Nervous.

And then there was the fact that another scientist—a carrot-top named Harris Cray—had shown up to replace Dr. Thomas. And now Dr. Cray and Dr. Palmer were all chummy and playing squash and hanging out in her baby-blue Jag.

In addition, there was a good chance the profiling team's cover was blown. A very good chance. Now *everybody* and their cousin knew there'd been an inquiry in England.

S.A. Hoopai didn't like getting kicked around by a target, espe-cially one who was a serial killer. Poisoning. He stared at his eggs when he sat down to breakfast. He lifted his fork, cut into a yolk, watched the yellow pool spread, set his fork down again. Not hungry.

"What?" Jessie asked, setting orange juice on the table. She placed her palms on her full belly, fingers spread, as if holding the world.

"What, *what?*"

"You've got that look again."

Sun through the skylight lulled Sylvia from a melatonin sleep just after 7 A.M. In contrast to cold and wet London, desert sky and dry air shocked her system, giving everything she touched a static charge.

She felt hollow. Last night's scene with Matt replayed itself in her mind. Conflicting needs asserted themselves. She wanted to find him and explain, but he'd left for work while she was still asleep. She wanted to hide in bed, never come out again, never see another person.

She was still lingering beneath the sheets when Serena brought her a cup of coffee. Strong. Good. It went down with a jolt, and halfway into her second cup she registered the caffeine kickoff.

Matt had left behind a note that Serena now produced: *Syl, mark the Harveys and Justine Carver wedding confirmed. Your mom wants the guest room all four nights. Nine days to go. Love M.*

The hollow feeling returned. Apparently their wedding was still *on*.

The groom hadn't walked out on the bride.

She wouldn't have blamed him if he had. At the moment she hated herself.

When she emerged from the shower, Serena met her at the door for a fashion consultation. She was holding a sweater in each hand. "Red or purple?"

"Purple, definitely, you'll look adorable." Smiling, Sylvia ran her towel over her wet hair. "New sweater?"

"My dad got it for me."

"Did he pick it out?" Sylvia asked, watching the smile grow on Serena's face.

"I picked it out for him to pick out."

"Good plan."

"When are you going to pick up your wedding dress? They finished the alterations two weeks ago. Mrs. Trujillo called twice. And Rosie's getting a little panicked, I think."

"You're right." Sylvia looked surprised. "I'll drop by today."

"This is important, Sylvia." Serena placed her hands on her hips and tipped her head to one side; the posture made her look eleven going on twenty. "I need to see it on you."

"I want you to see it on me, too, make sure it fits. I absolutely need your approval on this." Sylvia turned toward the mirror and found herself looking past the damp woman in the blue plaid bathrobe straight into Serena's huge brown eyes. "What?"

"You're getting married next Saturday."

Another pang. She ignored it for the sake of her foster daughter.

"I have the feeling you've got something to say." Sylvia pivoted, resting her butt against the vanity, crossing her arms. "Shoot."

"Well . . ." Two bright red roses had appeared in Serena's cheeks; she blurted it out: "Are you and Matt going to have a baby?"

Sylvia felt the wave wash over her—not tidal, but a decent-sized sneaker wave—and she was praying she looked calm and cool at the same instant she could still taste the birth control pill she'd swallowed just five minutes earlier.

"We're thinking about it," she said, feeling the lump in her throat. "Why are you asking, honey?"

"Sometimes that's why people get married, because the wife gets . . ."

"I'm not pregnant, Serena. Not yet." Sylvia perched on the edge of the tub, guiding Serena to sit beside her and wrapping an arm around her foster daughter's shoulders. "Matt and I think we're going to try to have a baby." She saw the concern on Serena's face and asked, "Why do you look so worried?"

"I want you to have a baby." Serena brightened. "It would be like having a little sister or brother." There was the slightest hesitation. "Wouldn't it?"

"It would." Sylvia searched Serena's face, trying to read the rainbow of emotions visible in the eyes, the mouth, the set of the chin. She saw uncertainty, eagerness, a little bit of fear, and strength.

"You know, if we do have a baby, we'll love you just as much as we do now. You'll always be my eldest daughter, wise and beautiful. I love you so much. That will never, ever change."

"But you're not really my real mom."

"No, but you and I are connected as much as any mother and daughter. Just in a different way. We're connected through fate and love."

"*Destino,*" Serena said slowly.

"Destiny." Sylvia nodded.

"Sometimes I dream about her . . ."

"Your mother?" Sylvia prodded ever so gently. "She comes to you in your dreams?"

Serena nodded. "She always tells me she misses me and she's sad she had to go away to heaven and leave me behind, but she's very very proud of me." Serena looked up, her eyes wide with wonder. "She calls me her *angelita*."

"Her little angel."

Serena set her shoulders back and said, "I hope that you and Matt have a little angel, Sylvia."

Sylvia caught her breath—something about the yearning in those young eyes. She felt her eyes begin to tear.

And then the moment was over, broken by Serena's matter-of-fact voice saying, "Okay," as she reached down to button her purple sweater. "My field trip is this weekend."

"And tomorrow night I'm talking at your school, I know," Sylvia said, noticing how grown-up her foster daughter looked. The school had planned a two-day field trip to the observatory at White Sands. "Do you want to stay at your dad's tomorrow night?" She stood, moving back to the vanity, where she picked up a yellow comb. "That way you're closer to school and the buses on Saturday morning."

"And he can pick me up at the auditorium after your speech."

"It's settled, then." Something clicked in Sylvia's brain. "Shouldn't you be in school?" she asked slowly.

"Yes."

"Who's driving you?"

Grinning, Serena pointed a finger at Sylvia.

"Oh. Oops."

Hurriedly, Sylvia gathered sunscreen and lipstick, but she stopped in her tracks when she felt—*felt* as clearly as a tap on the shoulder, although Serena hadn't moved a muscle—one last question. She swung around and held out her hands.

"Do you ever wish you were my real mom?" Serena blurted out.

"Yes," Sylvia said, nodding. "Oh, yes."

"Me, too. I wish that sometimes."

. . . .

Sylvia made it across town to the school on upper Canyon in twenty-six minutes, which meant Serena was only thirty minutes late. The return trip took two hours because the truck needed gas, and then Sylvia stopped by the feed store for a forty-pound bag of dog food and twenty pounds of birdseed. She even dashed into the grocery store, where her mind made it three items down the mental list (milk, toilet paper, miso soup) before her cell phone rang.

"This is Sylvia."

Silence. A distant humming noise. Wrong number or bad connection.

She was about to slide her phone into its case when it rang again. *"What?"*

"Exactly. *What* color azaleas do you want by the altar? Pink, lavender, white, or assorted?"

"Oh, fuck. Assorted."

"That's what I thought. Fuck assorted. It's so nice to hear your voice," Rosie Sanchez added with mock sweetness.

"It's great to hear your voice. I wasn't sure you were still speaking to me after I ran out on you. Oh, Rosie, I'm such a mess."

"I can tell, *jita*. Are you suffering from PMS, jet lag, or panic?"

"Assorted."

Rosie laughed. "Can I help?"

"Mmm . . . did you and Ray fight before your wedding?"

"Like cats and dogs. Where are you? Can you meet for coffee?"

"I just dropped Serena off at school. I'm running a few errands before I settle in to work. I need to focus—"

"Work? You're getting married in a few days, *jita*. What's going on?"

"London was problematic—I've got this profile to finish, then I'll be able to concentrate."

"I mean, what's going on with the wedding plans?" Rosie snorted.

"You're going to be one of those women who's on the cell phone when they wheel her into the delivery room and she's in labor, screaming, *Just let me file this report!*"

"I know, I know." Sylvia sighed, aware of the fact that Rosie had unwittingly hit upon the dangerous topic of childbearing. Psychic connections. She said, "Two more days of work and then I'm done. I am. *Really!*"

"I didn't say anything."

"I tell you what, order me a bouquet while you're at it—and something for my hair. A—what do they call it—a halo?"

"A floral garland," Rosie said, clucking her tongue. "Sylvia, is there something wrong?"

"I think I ruined everything. I told Matt the worst lie."

"You lied? About what? *Jita*—not another man!"

"Of course not." Sylvia almost laughed. "Oh, damn, I forgot to pick up the wedding dress. I love you, I'll call you—*bye.*"

She hung the dress in her bedroom closet. She pulled it out again and tried it on. She stood in front of the full-length mirror, studying her reflection. The silky fabric was the palest shade of lilac, almost white in certain lights. The neck was scooped, the waist long, lean, and flattering, the knee-length skirt bias cut with graceful flow. It was a terrific dress—and it made her look terrific, according to Bessie Trujillo, the seamstress who'd done the alteration. Sylvia needed Serena's approval and Rosie's. She swung around, watching the skirt swirl. There was surprising and seductive comfort in the ritual of a wedding. She slipped out of the dress, still staring at herself as she stood naked in the bedroom.

First you use work to escape marriage, then you use marriage to escape work—then you can't make up your mind about one of the most important questions in life: children. Way to go, Sylvia.

"I just want to forget about life for a few hours," she told her reflection.

She let the dogs out into the yard, giving them each a rawhide bone, then pulled the shades, turned off the ringer on the house phone, and set her cell phone on vibrate. She brewed a large pot of Assam tea, made wheat toast, and rummaged through the cupboard for jam. Finally she found a package of Reese's peanut butter cups hidden in the cookie jar.

Now she was ready to focus.

She sat down at her computer to begin the preparation.

Profiling, the wild, questionable, flashy little sister of criminal investigation. Pure profiling, the painstaking approach developed by the FBI, consisted of overlapping stages: data collection (police and autopsy reports and crime scene photos); an attempt to classify the crime based on available data; reconstruction of the crime; and finally, the basic hypothesis, the attempt to define the psychological and physical, behavioral, and demographical identity of the offender.

She had a stack of notes on Christine Palmer. She had video. She had hours of tape stored in her brain. Now came the task of putting raw data into some order, creating some hypothesis that law enforcement could actually use. And it had to be ready by 9 A.M. sharp the next morning, when the feds were scheduled for briefing.

She was concentrating, settling deeply into her work, so that she almost didn't register the faint vibrational hum of the phone as the call came in. When she recognized the incoming number, she picked up.

"Where are you?" Edmond Sweetheart asked.

"Thinking about an asp." She'd understood the question to mean, where was she in the evolution of the profile, was she making progress?

"Ass, or *asp*? As in Cleopatra?"

"Cleopatra, exactly." She walked past her desk, ignoring the blinking cursor and the text-filled screen, to gaze out the window. Three of Mrs. Calidro's cows had found their way into her lower pasture. They were grazing on fall grass and the last of the summer's wildflowers. Closer to the house, a flicker had settled on a dying branch of the old piñon near the road. The bird fluttered to another branch, and the gorgeous sunset flame of its wings and breast brightened the gray day.

"The queen's alchemists were busy," Sylvia said softly. "Cleopatra had them in the royal kitchen, whipping up concoctions of henbane and belladonna."

"*Atropa belladonna* and *Hyoscyamus niger.*"

"She tested the poisons on her slaves, but the pain they suffered frightened her." The flicker took off from the piñon, leaving a trail of fire against cloud with each wing stroke. Sylvia watched until the bird was out of sight, then said, "So she tried strychnine—"

"*Strychnos nux vomica,*" Sweetheart murmured.

"—on Egyptian prisoners, but the convulsions were horrible and the corpses were ugly." Sylvia was quiet for a moment before she followed her train of thought. "But the venom of the asp was a different story."

She released the catch and opened the window just enough to feel the sharp bite of cold in the air; she closed and locked the window again.

"Of course, Cleopatra tested death by asp on her human guinea pigs," she said. "And those test subjects turned out to be the *lucky* ones: they died quickly, with little time for pain, looking presentable."

Sylvia walked to the love seat, where she stretched out and closed her eyes, resting her cheek against the handset. "The queen was no altruist, she didn't test poisons for the sake of increasing the body of alchemical knowledge. She had an end goal in sight, a selfish goal: a quick, painless, almost pleasant death. She wanted a *good* suicide— and from all historical accounts, that's exactly what she got."

Sylvia opened her eyes, propping herself on one arm, gazing at the encyclopedia of poisons that lay open atop a pile of books.

"Science is about testing hypotheses; the research is geared toward proving or disproving. The poisoner is a researcher, too; the poisoner has an end goal." She was comforted by the seashell sound of her breathing near the mouthpiece.

"Choose your poison," Sweetheart said.

"If you're Dr. Christine Palmer and you've chosen exotic, virtually invisible neurotoxins . . . where does that lead you in the end, to what goal?"

"Did she use her father and lover as guinea pigs?"

"Perhaps. Or perhaps one of her goals was a painless death, an end to their suffering." Sylvia frowned, rubbing her forehead with the palm of her hand. She felt the first hint of a headache. "There's got to be a relationship between Palmer's individual murders—the poisonings over the years—and her work in laboratories, her scientific research. I don't mean the obvious—access, accessibility of toxins—I mean a psychological relationship." She sighed, frustrated by her lack of clarity.

"You're working with missing pieces."

"I know what I'm missing: what is the exact nature of her research—at BioPort, at the Dutch labs, at LANL?"

"You want missing pieces," he said. "At Porton Down, Project Nicander focused on neurotoxicologic aspects of the microorganisms—responses to toxins in tissue cultures and animal models, preclinical trials. At Los Alamos, within the scope of Project Mithradates, the research has been geared toward molecular genetic studies, genetic identification and characterization of toxins from two or three of the rogue species. The BLS-three labs are there for a reason—cultures and toxin samples have been generated at LANL *infrequently*, but we know that lethal toxins are handled and stored on-site."

"Right. Go on."

"The Dutch labs had the task of examining the mechanisms that support toxin expression by the dinoflagellates. The research has been ongoing."

"Who's funding such a massive series of projects?"

"*Who isn't?* The British and U.S. military have participated in their respective government projects. So has the national and international private sector."

She let the information sink in—some of it was new, some of it they'd already discussed. Then she said, "I'm still missing the common denominator when it comes to her victims. I don't mean the obvious fact that they were researchers, scientists, peers. There's a deeper connection. They interconnect, I know they do, and they're not what the published papers and the lab spokespersons say they are."

She waited, restless, balancing the odd sensation that Sweetheart was about to reveal some additional and crucial bit of information—she sensed that he was caught in a struggle—but the moment passed. If he had information, he was keeping it to himself.

She shook off her frustration and began to move again: to the bookshelves, where she ran her fingers across the spines of countless volumes on philosophy and psychology and history, to the window. Just in time to see the silver Mercedes pull up in her driveway.

The driver's door opened and Edmond Sweetheart climbed out. A cord dangled from his ear, the only sign he was speaking into a telephone.

"I had no idea you lived in the wilderness," he said, only half joking. She could barely see his lips moving as she heard the words through the speaker.

"Now that you're here," she said, "you might as well come in."

. . .

"You like wood," Sweetheart said, setting the steaming mug of green tea on the Craftsman side table. They had settled in the living room, where the wide windows offered a view of the road, the pasture, and distant calderas.

"Yes."

"And stone."

"Yes."

"Your father and mother?" he studied the black-and-white photograph in the small pewter frame on the table.

"They were on their honeymoon."

"Ah," he said, nodding, as if this fact explained much more than a detail of the photograph.

"Did you come to talk about interior decorating?" she asked flatly.

"The clash of old and new—it is a clash, not a blend—I like that. It tells me about you. I've been curious about you, Sylvia." As he spoke, he was taking everything in—cataloguing her possessions, the titles of her books and CDs, the vintage film collection, Matt's collection of monochromes, and of course the furniture and decorative aesthetics—and at the same time, he was speaking, just beginning to unravel a thread that would inevitably lead him into the recitation of a narrative. He turned to look into her eyes. "You're a clash as well, not a blend. That's why you're struggling when it comes to melding your two worlds, work and family."

She remained silent, watching him, knowing he would make his point.

"Let's take a walk," he said somewhat abruptly.

She frowned, studying his face. "I'll get my jacket."

Outside, as they walked down the path, Rocko and Nikki galloping ahead, he began to speak slowly. "You asked for the missing pieces," he said. "I can't help you as much as I'd like. What is ultimately revealed or kept secret—" His gaze took in the acreage, the ridge back, the endless sky, but he wasn't seeing them, not fully. He said, "I can't choose freely."

"Then who chooses?" Sylvia whistled for Nikki, who was almost out of earshot, but she was watching Sweetheart.

He looked at her, his eyebrows arching slightly, but he waited long enough to speak so that she knew he wouldn't answer the question. Instead, he said, "MI-6 has lost track of Paul Lang."

"Excuse me?"

"Their surveillance failed," Sweetheart said brusquely. "But we *think* he boarded a flight to the states."

"Is he in New Mexico?"

"Almost certainly."

"What does that mean—to us, to the project? How will it affect us? Did he contact you?"

Sweetheart turned around, heading back toward the Mercedes. As she followed, he handed her a palm-sized digital base unit. "Press the green button."

She did, raising the small speaker to her ear. Paul Lang's voice—calm and conversational—was clearly audible: *"Did I wake you?"*

"Lang," Sweetheart had confirmed.

"One of these days I may be in your neighborhood. Thought it would be rude not to call."

"I appreciate the courtesy. MI-6, the feds, everybody's looking for you."

"Tell them I just want to set things right."

Thick clouds rolled in by 7 P.M. Thursday; the sky turned dark and a wind kicked up leaves. Sweetheart had been gone for hours. Sylvia woke to find herself curled up on the couch in her study with Rocko in her lap and Nikki warming her feet. The stacks of pages and books on the floor had grown. To walk was to navigate an obstacle course.

She still had a lot of ground to cover on the profile.

She took a break at eight to go to the gym. She needed to work up a sweat and clear her head, and it was too late to run under the ominously dark skies. The combination of jet lag and the faint, anxious hum under her heartbeat left her needing fresh air and the chance to stretch her muscles, even briefly.

By 8:30 P.M., when she signed in at the front desk of the gym, a light rain had begun to fall. Inside the facility, the air, as always, held the strong scent of chlorine and the faint smell of mildew. A mist was visible above the pool's turquoise water, and above the pool, on the high ceiling, lights shimmered in reflection. In the Jacuzzi, two plump middle-aged women were talking to an elderly man. The child care center looked quiet. As she entered the women's locker room, she glanced vaguely at the bulletin board, where posters advertised CPR and spinning classes, and business cards had been left for various services—massage, house-sitting, memberships to share.

The locker room was deserted. She chose her usual locker near the door, number thirty-one, tossing her purse and coat inside. She changed quickly into workout clothes, noticing from the sound of voices in the bathroom that at least one or two women were still using the facilities.

In the workout area, a man and two teenage girls were covering countless miles on aerobic machines, while a handful of people were lifting free weights on the far side of the room. Sylvia stepped up to the first in a series of circuit trainers. She wrapped her fingers around the thick metal bar and began to stretch.

While her muscles loosened, her mind worked. She reviewed conversations with Rosie, with Serena, and a phone call from her mother, Bonnie, a week earlier. She and her mother weren't close, yet they'd managed to renew ties after years of semiestrangement. Bonnie would attend the wedding. On the phone, neither of them had said a word about Sylvia's father. He'd disappeared so many years ago, and neither of them knew if Daniel Strange was dead or alive. He remained a liminal figure, neither existing nor not existing.

Her mind moved from thoughts of her own father to thoughts of Christine Palmer—and her father, Fielding Palmer.

She found herself drawn back to the puzzle of character—that combination of traits at the core of each human being, long-lasting, indelible, consistent through life, but always acted upon by environment. She imagined character as a massive rock deep in the ocean, indestructible, unmovable, yet worn away and shaped by wave after wave.

One father, a man from poor but tenacious roots, a man who ran away from life . . . the other father, brilliant, gifted, a man who qualified as royalty in the world of science. Two men who couldn't be more different—except that each left a trail, each marked his daughter's life in a profound, indelible way.

She ran on the treadmill, picking up pace, reaching full stride. Forty-five minutes of blessed numbness. When she lay back on the floor and closed her eyes, lengthening her muscles, her mind floated.

The question presented itself: could she have helped her father take his own life if he was suffering? If so, at what cost?

She didn't know the answer.

The music, which had been playing softly in the background, abruptly went silent. A hint that the staff was getting ready to close. Sylvia opened her eyes, then sat up slowly to check the clock. She had another ten minutes before they would get really serious about locking doors.

When she reentered the locker room, she heard the sound of a shower. Good. A deserted locker room always felt eerie, and the gray-cast sky, the rain, had created an encompassing darkness that seemed to penetrate the building. She grabbed her towel from her locker, and then she slid the combination lock through the hasp with a click.

The water ran hot, tingling her skin, awakening cells. She rinsed her hair before shifting the hot water to cold, surrendering to the resulting sensory crash.

When she stepped out of the shower, she wrapped herself quickly in her towel.

She had the sense that someone had just left the room. She stood still, listening, but there was nothing to be heard—only the routine quiet of a deserted locker room. She hurried out to locker number thirty-one.

Everything was in place. She shook her head, feeling paranoid. Still, when she opened the locker and saw that her possessions were all there, including her wallet, she breathed a sigh of relief. Okay, she was being jumpy, but considering the material she'd been living with . . .

There was no attendant at the counter when she exited the health club. Outside it was dark, misty, and the lights above the parking lot shone down on two dozen vehicles, most of which belonged to diners at the adjacent restaurant. She started toward her truck.

Her mind was still caught up in her work, reviewing first impressions, analyzing data, searching for stray facts, and most important, for those bits of information that refused to meld smoothly with the rest of the picture. She'd been preoccupied for several days now—this occupation of another dimension was always part of the profiling process—and she felt only half present in the world. Even during her workout, much of her progress was dictated by muscle memory instead of in-the-moment awareness.

But now, suddenly, after dark, in an almost deserted parking lot, she felt dashed into the present as if time were a wave and she had just hit shore. She didn't get the chance to wonder what had sucked her back from the world of rumination. As she approached her truck, she heard footsteps.

"Dr. Strange?"

She turned to find herself only a few feet from Christine Palmer. The reaction was visceral—a shiver passed through her and the hair stood up on the back of her neck. "Dr. Palmer."

"I startled you."

"I'm surprised you recognized me."

"I have an eye for faces."

Sylvia shrugged. She'd begun to take in details: Palmer was wearing street clothes; she had a cream-colored leather bag slung over her left shoulder; her hair appeared slightly damp, and it was pulled back from her face in a style that would look severe on a less attractive woman. So it had been Palmer in the locker room while she was showering.

Sylvia said, "I didn't know you belong—"

"I'm not a member, but I use the racquetball courts now and then."

"Did you play today?"

"Actually, we did." Palmer inclined her head toward a light blue convertible Jaguar, a drop-dead sports model (very new from the looks of it) parked directly beneath a twelve-foot light standard. It took Sylvia a moment to see that a red-haired man was standing beside the passenger door of the Jag. Dr. Harris Cray seemed to be turning up everywhere. He was dressed in sweats and athletic shoes. "But it was more of a warm-up than a match," Palmer added.

"Who won?"

"I make a habit of winning." Palmer smiled, backing away. "I have an advantage over Harris—he's still adjusting to the altitude after England. He's come to replace Dr. Thomas on the project. But you know that." She turned, tossing the words over her shoulder as she began to walk slowly toward her car. "I believe you two met at BioPort."

Sylvia failed to reply—what could she say? She watched in surprise as Dr. Cray raised his arm in a greeting.

She unlocked her truck and climbed inside. She waited, watching as Palmer pulled out of the lot. The Jaguar—definitely *new*—caught the light and glimmered expensively as it rolled silently past. Still Sylvia didn't move. About thirty seconds after Palmer had disappeared, a dark gray Lincoln pulled out from another row.

"Hello, FBI," Sylvia said softly. She locked her doors—then checked them again before driving home.

The news traveled like wildfire.

It covered four thousand miles—from New Mexico to Washington, D.C., and back. By 11:30 P.M. Thursday evening, the director of LANL had heard a disturbing story of harassment in his own laboratory against a world-renowned toxicologist—harassment that just might involve the FBI.

The director decided to look into the situation immediately.

The decision had a ripple effect, a warning coming down from on high: *Lay off Dr. Christine Palmer.*

alchemist:	let's get one thing straight
redrider:	yes
alchemist:	from now on I make the moves
redrider:	yes
alchemist:	you have endangered yourself / me
redrider:	have faith
alchemist:	they're closing in
redrider:	of course
alchemist:	have you planned ahead?
redrider:	don't insult me
alchemist:	escape plan?
redrider:	I know you want out too
alchemist:	yes
redrider:	one question / no! / I *demand* answer / will you trust me?

. . . . .

redrider:	*trust me*
alchemist:	yes

On Friday morning at 5:18 A.M., Special Agent Darrel Hoopai gulped breath and began the three-mile ascent of the mountain. He was following the Target. Jogging. Scrambling to keep pace with the skinny, pasty white, knock-kneed runner just ahead. Hoopai's calves were burning. He could already feel a blister forming on his left heel.

A cyclist passed him up; so did a young kid with million-dollar running shoes that flashed on and off like miniature traffic signals. Without breaking a sweat, the kid breezed by the skinny, pasty-white, knock-kneed runner, then he passed a couple in matching Lycra, and now he was gaining on the Target.

Breathless—his throat raw—Hoopai swore silently; another minute and he'd be eating the Target's dust. Sleep deprivation, that was the problem, he thought as he forced one foot in front of the other; his leg muscles felt as if they were made of lead. The Target went to bed too late and got up too damn early. Who functioned on four hours' sleep, anyway? It was weird, people who could live on a schedule that would leave ninety-nine percent of the population sleep-deprived. Something biochemical had to be going on with people like that.

At least he was doing better than Weaver, who couldn't skip his way out of a paper bag. Hoopai'd always wondered how a guy as klutzy as Weaver ever made it through the academy in the first place. Probably because he was a monster when it came to numbers. Still, all trainees had to pass the basics.

Thinking about Weaver seemed to conjure up the agent; Hoopai heard the faint radio-transmitted voice in his earphone, and he huffed back his status update.

Hoopai was a slow-end runner bordering on jogger—he managed to do a couple of miles on the track or at the gym almost every day, but his triathlete days were a blur in a distant past.

The Target was burning up ground.

Hoopai's heartbeat quickened—the poor muscle was about to explode—when the Target disappeared over a rise.

He'd give her points—she was in shape. She could take the mountain with the best of the early-morning Olympiad wannabes. LANL had its share of these guys. Dawn or dusk, lunch hour and coffee breaks, weather permitting, they were out doing the fitness thing: cycling, hiking, running, skiing.

He was familiar with her morning routine; she liked to start the day with a kickboxing or yoga class. She'd run once before—on the second day of surveillance, two days after Doug Thomas, the molecular toxicologist on the Target's project, slammed his car into a truck. Hoopai remembered they'd scrambled to keep up the surveillance without breaking cover.

His shoe caught on a wedge of asphalt. He stumbled, caught himself, and kept going. Another cyclist passed him, and another—a peloton, a school of wheels, went swimming by in their skimpy outfits.

The day Doug Thomas died, Palmer had passed through LANL security at 4:15 A.M., and she'd been at work in her lab by the crack of dawn. (*The thing about poison—you can be thirty miles or three hundred miles away when your victim dies.*)

Hoopai crested the rise and took a deep breath, ready and relieved to head downhill for the next thirty yards—when he realized he'd lost her. The Target. She was nowhere in sight. He slowed, cursed under his breath, picked up pace again, and scanned the area, which was wooded, rocky, and filled with hiding places.

Hoopai had a grandfather who'd been a Navajo code talker. His grandmother, still alive, was a healer. They'd taught him how to track stray goats and sheep that strayed from the herd. He swore at himself for not paying attention—this was a stupid mistake.

Then he saw her. Sitting on a hillock beneath a huge ponderosa pine. A cell phone was pressed to her ear. S.A. Hoopai's eyes were good—twenty-twenty—and he'd swear she was smiling.

Through gritted teeth, he whispered harshly into his transmitter. "The Target has spotted the Hawk. Time for a drive-by."

Hoopai kept jogging—he had no choice—up the next hill, finally slowing when he knew for sure the Target wasn't following him, finally turning around.

An eighth of a mile back down the hill, he ran straight into the lab's physical security guys with their M-16s and their pretty white jeep.

"Palmer caught the agent jogging on her heels—she called security." Sweetheart watched from the passenger seat as Sylvia took the 502 hill in fourth gear. "On top of that," he said, "word came from LANL's director, who's wondering if there are security issues surrounding senior lab staff that need to be addressed. Now LANL's given the feds an ultimatum: come up with something definitive, or back off Christine Palmer. We're skating on thin ice."

"She's playing with us." Sylvia was riding the gas, pushing the engine, ignoring signals to downshift.

"We don't know if the FBI agent blew his cover or not," Sweetheart continued over the grind of the engine. "Palmer called lab security and reported a man behaving suspiciously."

"What's to know? He blew his cover, and she's using her political connections to fight back."

"Either way, the feds are down to the wire." For the past thirty minutes, Sweetheart had made a point of ignoring Sylvia's volatile mood, her razor-sharp edge, but the task was becoming more difficult.

"She *knows* she's being watched." Sylvia jerked the truck into the left lane to pass a slow Subaru. "It's stupid and dangerous to assume she doesn't."

"I'm not assuming anything. Do you want to back off and shift the damn truck, Sylvia?"

She took a breath, downshifted, and murmured, "Sorry about that."

He grunted, accepting her apology. Then he said, "After Wen Ho Lee, Hannsen, McVeigh, everyone's touchy. This isn't the FBI's golden moment. In the case of Doug Thomas, there's no official homicide investigation, and no one's ready to accuse Palmer of murder. The lab's caught between a rock and a hard place. LANL would have their throats cut in civil court if they did anything that stained the reputation of a respected scientist who turned out to be innocent; and they'd lose their heads if someone ended up getting hurt by a scientist working on LANL property, one of their own. Basically, they've been looking the other way when it comes to federal surveillance. But now they're balking."

"They don't want to touch her because she's too valuable," Sylvia said harshly. "No one can duplicate her research." Her gaze crossed the white volcanic cliffs with their sculpted swirls, their caves, their breathtaking angles favored as nesting sites by birds of prey.

"To give them their due," Sweetheart said, "there's not enough evidence to support probable cause with Palmer."

"I never said there was." She honked her horn at a flatbed truck that had been weaving across lanes for the past mile. The truck bed was dangerously overstacked with cedar and piñon logs. "I'm not blind, I can see LANL's point." She honked again.

Sweetheart had called her early that morning, rousing her from sleep. She was still exhausted and off balance—in less than forty-eight hours they'd traveled from desert to London cityscape and back to desert. But it was more than geography that had her spinning internally.

She was still trying to distinguish the various stratum—geo, psycho, social—of this investigation. The assignment of profiling a serial poisoner—with all its historical intricacies of inquiry—was difficult enough; but they'd pulled back the first layer to find whispers of Palmer's involvement in a secret bioweapons project. Now all information regarding that project had to be ignored; the scope of their job was profiling a serial killer. Period. End of discussion.

Talk about compartmentalization.

She honked again, kept her palm pressed down.

The driver of the pickup flipped her the bird.

She flipped him back—then glanced at Sweetheart. "Does Christine Palmer know that Paul Lang might be in the area?"

"Not unless he told her himself—the feds got held up on the phone tap."

Sylvia groaned. "If he's planning to take personal revenge for Samantha Grayson's death, he won't call Palmer first."

"Lang's a wild card, but we've got Palmer under surveillance—at least for a few more hours."

With a swift look at her passenger, she asked, "What are you telling me?"

"We've run out of time," Sweetheart said tersely. "It's all or nothing. We need to give the agents, the investigators, whatever we've dug up on Palmer. Hard data, wild theories, anything they might be able to use."

"To use?" Her mind struggled to register.

"At most they've got thirty-six hours to flush her out."

"How?"

"Bait."

The meeting took place at the Hilltop Motel, smack-dab in the heart of downtown Los Alamos. The two-story building was distinguished by its faux-château style.

Sylvia followed Sweetheart from the parking lot, up a flight of stairs, along a paneled hall. Sweetheart tapped on the door of 217, which opened almost immediately. Sylvia was introduced to special agents Simmons, Weaver, and Hoopai (the one Palmer had tagged, the one with the Navajo cheekbones) and their supervisor, Special Agent in Charge Jeff Hess (who bore a faint resemblance to Cary Grant). She'd already met Drew Dexter, LANL's deputy division director of internal safety and security. Judging from the expression on his face, he looked as if he disapproved of the gathering. Not a total surprise, considering he was representing the lab.

When everyone was settled, Agent Jeff Hess addressed the group. "Let's get going, people. We're glad you all could make it. We're here this morning to consolidate information and come up with a strategy. We've reached a crossroads in the investigation—it's time to produce results or back off.

"First, I'd like a quick review of the facts pertaining to Dr. Douglas Thomas's death," Hess added. "LANL's deputy director of internal security"—he nodded at Drew Dexter, not so subtly sharing territory—"has offered to bring us up to date."

Dexter cleared his throat, and then his soft Louisiana accent filled the room. "Before we get to Dr. Thomas, I need to quickly address the issue of surveillance. The lab is weighing employee safety—the protection of personnel—from various perspectives, with multiple considerations, most of which are not easily understood by nonscientists." He paused, his glance sweeping the faces. "I don't think I need to add, we've got very clear legal directives in this matter."

But they didn't, Sylvia thought—that was part of the trouble. And he'd just insulted a room full of federal agents. *Way to go, Drew.*

"With that said," Dexter continued, "Doug Thomas's blood and tissue work came back from Lawrence Livermore's forensic path lab, showing contamination by an unidentified strain of neurotoxin. The symptoms are consistent with toxins being studied by Palmer's project group." Dexter pushed back in the cheap plastic chair so that he was supported by two metal legs. "We still don't have a definite vehicle for contamination—we don't know if the pathway was ingestion, topical, aerosol, all of which are possibilities." He shifted weight and the chair's front legs audibly touched ground.

"Which fits Palmer's pattern," Sweetheart said after a brief silence.

Jeff Hess nodded to Sweetheart and Strange. "This is our profiling team. They've been working with behavioral sciences in Virginia, and they're going to give us a preliminary profile on the Target—with the aim of aiding any interrogation situation that arises. Along the way we're going to look for ways to *facilitate* that happening."

In other words, to find ways to push Palmer's buttons, to impel her to action, Sylvia thought, hearing Sweetheart's introduction.

"It's going to be a cram session," Sweetheart said, shooting Sylvia a quick glance. "You'll need to take notes, give us feedback, and you'll probably want to keep the coffee pot brewing. Let's get started. Dr. Strange?"

"Before we talk about your target, I'm going to brief you on the basic profiling data that's available on poisoners." Sylvia was ready with the summary handout she'd prepared over the past twenty-four hours. The investigators leafed through the pages as she began to speak.

"You're holding an outline of the data we'll cover. We plan to move quickly, so ask questions when they come up. We'll do our best to provide answers."

She scanned their faces, and when she was sure they were along for the ride, she said, "Let's begin with the fact that Christine Palmer edited *The Handbook on Criminal Poisoning and Forensic Toxicology.* Most of you are familiar with that landmark text from your academy training."

Heads bobbed—point taken.

"Well, Palmer wrote the book, as they say. The literature on poisoners is surprisingly sparse," she continued. "Westveer, Trestrail, and Pinizzotto authored one of the few peer-reviewed papers on poisoners. They looked at available data from the Uniform Crime Report—issues of gender, race, class of poison (chemical or narcotic), homicide rate by population, and circumstance. They analyzed just under three hundred criminal poisonings."

To keep her thoughts flowing, she began to pace a short track in front of the sliding glass door that gave access to the balcony. Outside, visible through a small space between blinds, the blue-and-white Truchas Peaks spiked the turquoise sky. Whipped-cream clouds hovered just above the peaks.

"A third of their cases fall under the category 'victim related to offender'—either within the family or outside, as in acquaintance, friend, sexual partner. Two-thirds of the study cases are categorized as 'victim-offender relationship *unknown*.'"

She stopped moving and faced them to deliver the first major proviso: "The study included *only* those cases in which the investigating agency determined poison as the COD. The problem's obvious, right, guys? Nobody knows how many homicidal poisonings *don't* make the books. Somebody—investigator, medical examiner, coroner, family member—looks at the corpse and says 'disease,' 'natural causes.'" She shrugged. "It's a safe bet a number of poisoners are getting away with murder."

And so the basic cram session began.

As she moved through the statistical data, including information on categories created by gender and racial breakdowns, nobody seemed surprised to hear that the poisoners in the study were predominately white, or that offenders stayed within racial boundaries—white killing white, so on and so forth.

"What about age data and victimology?" S.A. Hoopai asked.

"Victims ranged from less than a week old to seventy-five-plus years."

"Age and known offender data?"

"Two offenders were under age fourteen, seven were older than seventy-five, most were between the ages of twenty and thirty-four."

"Keep in mind," Sweetheart interjected, "we're covering only *known* offenders."

"Let's talk circumstances." Sylvia snapped her fingers and said, "Fifty-one of the poisoning homicides in the study were related to the drug trade, two were related to rapes, and five to other sex crimes." The stats rolled off her tongue, interrupted by questions here and there.

Special Agent Simmons raised her hand to shoulder height. "Any data on victim gender in lovers' triangles?" she asked.

Sylvia nodded. "We've got some general stats. Wives—with or without the help of their lovers—poisoned husbands three times more often than husbands poisoned wives."

"Well, yeah." Hoopai drew out the phrase with a shrug. "Men just shoot their wives."

Agent Simmons raised one eyebrow. "Wives poison the husbands because it's slow and painful. She feeds him his favorite dish laced with arsenic and asks, 'Did you get enough to eat, hon? Want seconds?'"

Everybody laughed—to neutralize the mood, to forget they were analyzing the ways people kill the same people they'd once professed to love.

When they'd refocused, Sylvia said, "You handed me the perfect segue, S.A. Simmons. I'm sure some of you have picked up on similarities between bombers and poisoners. Delay between death action and actual death. A fascination with technology and science, be it wiring devices or toxic mixtures. The collection of paraphernalia. And finally—especially in cases of product tampering, like the Tylenol deaths back in the nineteen eighties—no need for proximity with death. But that last point is the exception."

Sylvia stood, arms at her side, late-morning sun casting shadows across her shoulders. "Which brings us to the crucial point," she said, studying the faces of the investigators.

"Ultimately, poison is different from other crimes. It's never committed in the heat of passion. It takes cunning, intentional deception, planning—and often the ability to administer the toxic dose repeatedly, over a period of time, with complete disregard for the suffering of the victim. Intelligence and the ability to detach and compartmentalize are qualities that Christine Palmer has in spades."

She took a deep breath, glancing at her wristwatch. "If there aren't any questions, let's break for lunch. See you back here at one o'clock."

. . .

Sylvia filled her time with a run along the back roads of Los Alamos. She knew that Palmer was at her lab—under surveillance—so there was little danger of another accidental encounter.

She cut uphill, breathing deeply, taking perverse pleasure in the sharp pain in her side. It was one way to wake herself up again, to clear her mind, to prepare for the next portion of the day. To blot out conscious thought, she kept her eyes on the charred hills, the burn areas that were unavoidable evidence of the Cerro Grande fire, evidence that would last for decades and, if you looked closely enough, centuries. The blackened trees jutted from the earth like crude spikes. Erosion had left deep veins in the soil. But here and there, new growth was already evident.

The last mile of the run was a study in regeneration. Internally, Sylvia tried to wear off her sharp edge. She was only hours from walking away; she'd gotten her wish, a big case, and now she couldn't wait to finish.

By one o'clock, she was back in uniform: Levi's, boots, a silk pullover sweater, a hasty touch-up with powder and lipstick. She was also ready to take up where they'd left off.

When everyone was settled again—fast-food cups on the table, jackets off, sunglasses stowed—Sylvia faced them. Behind her, a six-by-six-foot expanse of bare wall.

"I want you to close your eyes for a moment and consider this description of the stereotypical poisoner," she said. "She's connected with the medical profession or the sciences. She's a loner, with above-average intelligence, educated, nonconfrontational. She has a cowardly temperament. She's a daydreamer and a game player. She's vain, avaricious, and remorseless. An underachiever. She's probably childish, immature, one of those people who never grew up. To top the list off, she feels *entitled*. If you stand in her way, be careful what you order for lunch."

As they laughed, Sweetheart quietly clicked on his laptop, and a visual instantly filled the wall: a life-size image of Dr. Christine Palmer. From here on, it was his show.

"Now take a good look," Sweetheart said, "and meet the Target. How well does she match the stereotype?" He let them study the projection, a photojournalist's portrait of Dr. Palmer in the field. Intelligent, focused, striking—charismatic even on film.

"She is connected to the sciences, *yes*. She's also highly educated, extremely intelligent, but she's not your average loner. Palmer is single, sexually active, and she's had a series of heterosexual relationships. She also maintains an international social network. A hundred people will vouch for her genius, her loyalty to the profession, her willingness to undertake research that carries personal risk."

He tapped a key on his laptop and the image changed: another photo of Palmer, this time on horseback.

"Is she a daydreamer and a game player? *Yes*." Sweetheart closed his eyes, as if picturing her face. "But perhaps no more so than others in her profession. She is ambitious, analytical, highly intelligent—and her research is theoretical as well as practical. So, yes, she knows how to daydream. If she didn't, she wouldn't have received so many awards for her research."

Click. Christine Palmer on-site in Africa during one of the worst Ebola outbreaks.

He said, "The target is clearly *not* an underachiever. Her work is her world. Remorseless? Perhaps. But take a good look at this photograph—clearly, she's been willing to put herself at risk, apparently to help others." He paused. "So . . . how are you going to begin to understand her? And how the hell do you talk to her?"

The investigators were leaning forward in their seats, paying very close attention.

"We all know the basics of interrogation—power, appeal, persuasion—but in this case, they ain't gonna cut it, not without a whole lot of finesse, because Christine Palmer doesn't recognize your power, she's not afraid of you." He paused, drawing an even closer focus. "We're talking about someone who has a hundred ways to kill at her fingertips. She knows the power of life and death."

"So she's got some sort of God complex?" Drew Dexter said with a derisive snort. "So she's untouchable?"

"Not a God complex." Sweetheart shook his head. "We're not talking about a psychological concept—we're talking about the *actual* ability to kill without detection. She's done it six, ten, fifteen times already. And she's walked away."

"That's not just a self-perception of power," Sylvia interjected. "Christine Palmer has empirical evidence that she can get away with murder."

Sweetheart nodded, saying, "So when you're face-to-face with her, when you're conducting an interview, your job won't be to *psych* her out, your job won't be to confront her illusions or deal with her delusions—Palmer isn't crazy." Sweetheart's eyebrows arched. He made eye contact with every person in the room before he continued. "You'll have to stand your ground. Don't let her take control of the interrogation. Because if she does, it's over."

S.A. Simmons spoke up. "So we've got to be smarter than she is— but make her think she's in control."

"She *is* in control," Sylvia said sharply. "Don't forget that for a minute."

"And don't try to challenge her intellect," Sweetheart said. "She's smarter than you—she's smarter than anybody in this room."

"By the same token, she's more narcissistic than anybody in this room," Sylvia said. "So challenge her ego. But do it honestly. If you try to outmaneuver her—if you try to pull a hustle—she'll catch you in the act, and she'll dismiss you completely."

"So where's her jugular?" S.A.C. Hess asked softly.

It was the perfect lead-in.

"You've all heard the expression *Curiosity killed the cat.*" Sylvia's lips curled up in a mean little smile. "If you want to find Palmer's weak spot, pique her curiosity. Ask for her expertise."

She was standing near the rheostat, and she dimmed the lights. "Imagine a day when you wake up with a slight headache. Within the next hour or so, you know you're getting the flu. You try to remember who you've been in contact with lately who was sick. A coworker? Your accountant? Your neighbor's child? But your thoughts are scattered, you have trouble concentrating."

She moved slowly around their chairs, her voice barely above a whisper. "Soon your nausea is accompanied by intense abdominal cramps and diarrhea—you don't make it to the bathroom in time, and you mess yourself. Your feet and hands begin to itch. You ache all over. It's agony to move a muscle. Breathing becomes difficult. You're coughing, but it's a dry cough. You're restless, you can't sleep, you can't find a comfortable position. Your head feels as if it will explode . . . you're starting to get scared."

Sylvia had reached the back of the room, and she stood behind the investigators. "Your heart is racing, beating irregularly, which scares you more. Over the next few hours the fear comes and goes—at times you're just worried, at other times you're terrified." She kept her tone even, hypnotic. "Minutes or hours pass, you're not sure how much time goes by because you've lost your normal temporal sense—in fact, all your normal sensory perceptions are gone. You know you're too weak to move. You know this isn't right. You try to find the telephone to call for help. Your legs aren't working, your vision is blurred. Even if you find the phone, you can't remember how to use it or who to call. Your fingers are too stiff to dial. Eventually, the fear dissipates. You don't care that your blood pressure is dropping, your circulation is collapsing. You're paralyzed, but you know—even with the confusion, the light-headedness, the disorientation and dizziness—you *know* you might be dying. Still, there is an intense lethargy. A waking sleep. A paralysis of the mind and body. You're unable to move a muscle to save your own life." She paused, letting the pictures fill their minds.

"This is it, welcome to the world of neurotoxins," she whispered finally. "This is what happens when your body is exposed to any of a number of neurotoxins that can be found in LANL's BLS-three safety level containment laboratories—neurotoxins that Christine Palmer works with on a daily basis. And she's fascinated by them. She collects data, facts, details. She's obsessed with symptoms."

Sylvia closed her own eyes, picturing Samantha Grayson's features in death. When she spoke, her voice was again a whisper. "Now, think about the scientist—a woman whose life is dedicated to developing antidotes. Think about what has to be going on in her head to inflict this horror on another human being."

Sylvia stepped out onto the motel veranda. The air was cool, and there was the slightest breeze. In the distance, the scars on Santa Fe Baldy were visible, while the Truchas Peaks shone like blue-and-white teats.

She felt something that rarely bothered her—a craving for a cigarette. The candy bar she stashed in her purse for just this type of emergency made her feel better; the sight of her birth control pills made her feel worse.

She ate the candy without pleasure and took one more look at the view.

With her eyes on the mountain, she stepped back into the room and the stale air of a half-dozen individuals. The mood was somber and subdued. It was Special Agent Hoopai who raised the final, most pertinent question.

"After everything we've heard"—he shook his head—"The Target holds the cards. How do we get to her?"

There was silence. All eyes turned toward the profilers.

"You get to her through me," Sylvia said.

Sweetheart took an audible breath, but it was Hess who explained. "Dr. Strange has agreed to participate in a special operation. Christine Palmer is on alert, she's suspicious, this much is obvious. Dr. Strange called Palmer's office earlier today and left a message requesting a meeting. Ostensibly to discuss victim symptomology in contamination cases." Hess tipped his head. "With all that's occurred, this request can only be seen by the Target as a *challenge*."

"What if she doesn't bite?" Special Agent Hoopai asked.

The timing couldn't have been more perfect if they'd been onstage following cues. Sylvia's cell phone rang. It was Christine Palmer, saying *yes*.

Sylvia reached Cristo Rey School with fewer than three minutes to spare. It was a fitting end to three long days: she was exhausted, standing in front of a packed auditorium of sixth-, seventh-, and eighth-graders—and her mind had gone blank.

Time to forget serial poisoners, forget governments manufacturing biotoxins in the name of defensive research.

The chatter of teenagers and parents reached a deafening crescendo. They were restless. Sylvia opened her mouth, but her throat felt so dry she was afraid she would choke. She was saved by the sight of Serena smiling radiantly, emerging from the wings with a small plastic pitcher and a glass.

"Whoops," her foster daughter whispered into her ear, "we forgot your ice water."

Those words brought Sylvia back to the present. Gratefully, she swallowed the water, setting the glass on the podium, clearing her throat.

Sylvia began to speak. "Last month, a tragedy occurred: a Santa Fe seventh-grader died from an overdose of heroin . . ."

It was no accident that Sweetheart hitched a ride down the hill with Drew Dexter. It was the perfect opportunity to touch base and feel out the security division deputy director, test the pulse of the lab. It was Dexter who'd suggested the detour to Saints and Sinners, a local tavern on the outskirts of the town of Española. Dexter had taken a shortcut through pueblo land to reach the destination.

And now Sweetheart let his gaze travel around the single room of the bar. A half-dozen customers were talking to their beer or the bartender. Apparently it was going to be a slow night; only the diehards were hanging on to their stools or the long, polished wooden bar top.

Dexter sat back until the chair was balanced on two legs, and then he webbed his fingers together behind his cropped silver-blond hair. The deputy director of security looked tired, rough-shaven, rumpled.

He said, "I'll be glad when we move on from this case. These are the ones I always hated when I did criminal investigation. Palmer could walk away now and you'd have nothing to stop her."

Sweetheart nodded. "Where will you be tomorrow?"

"As far away from you and the feds as possible. The lab wants complete dissociation from any effort to entrap Palmer. Where I'm concerned, the lab gets what it wants."

But there was something, Sweetheart could see that, so he just waited.

When Dexter was ready, he said, "A man matching Paul Lang's description tried to enter a secure area of LANL today. We caught him on the security cameras. But he disappeared before we could get him." He slid an envelope across the table.

Sweetheart opened the flap and peered discreetly inside at the surveillance photo. "So we know he's here. But why?"

"Isn't that obvious? The feds and the Brits have him on a 'watch' list because they're worried about one of their own gone ballistic."

"I never liked 'obvious,'" Sweetheart said.

The bartender delivered two Newcastles. He took Sweetheart's $20 bill with him when he left.

Dexter frowned. "Less obvious . . . Lang has a contact at the lab. Maybe even Palmer."

Sweetheart's eyes narrowed. He was considering how much to confide in Dexter. He chose the middle road. "You know Doug Thomas owed child support, credit cards, the usual."

Dexter nodded grudgingly. "Something like that."

"But you don't know about the offshore accounts," Sweetheart said, matching Dexter's low tones. "Not until we tell you where to look."

Dexter just raised his eyebrows.

"There was a deposit the day before he died." Sweetheart etched the number on the table with his finger: *$50,000*. He watched his companion take in the dollar signs and digits. "The bank was told to expect another deposit within a week—for a similar amount."

Dexter's face darkened and he swallowed anger with his beer. "Bastard was a traitor." He wiped his mouth roughly. "A traitor and a profiteer."

"Selling what?"

"Information or product." Dexter paused. "Or something even more valuable."

"A recipe for production."

"But I doubt Thomas had access to the big picture. That's

Palmer's domain." Dexter stared at his glass as if he might find what they were seeking. "I'm betting he sold a sample of the product itself."

"Why haven't we heard that something's out there?"

"Maybe both our sources need updating," Dexter said. Then he smiled. "Or maybe it's not out there."

Sweetheart's eyebrows rose again. "Thomas got the deposit, he did his part of the deal—"

"And then he died," Dexter finished.

"Before the product was delivered to the buyer."

"So who has it?" Dexter frowned. "Dr. Palmer?"

"Or maybe Paul Lang didn't come to take his revenge on Palmer, maybe he took over as courier—maybe he came to pick up the delivery he never got."

The steps are simple.

First, choose. Which toxin will be most appropriate? Which is at hand? Is there some lesson to be learned, some question to be answered by choosing one over the other? If possible, always choose a teacher.

Second, study. Observe, be patient, acquire knowledge of the adversary's world: lifestyle, habits, preferences, territory, traits. Opportunities abound.

Third, implement. The elixir must be secreted in a location that will remain undetected and undetectable by the adversary. A distillation in a bottle of favorite shampoo; just one example.

Fourth, beware. And be wary. This is when danger is highest, perhaps the one and only moment of connection.

Fifth, finalize. Remove all evidence, clean house, tie up loose ends.

Sixth, wait. Hours, days, weeks, months. Wait for the adversary to self-administer a toxic dose.

Seventh, watch. Sit back and enjoy the show.

Sylvia woke before dawn with butterflies in her stomach. A dull headache had disturbed her sleep and left her feeling disoriented, and she had to force herself out of bed. She retrieved a sweatsuit from the dryer, double-tied the laces on her trail runners, and took off for the ridge with both dogs in tow. Rocko was slow but steady; Nikki, the three-legged wonder dog, was faster than most animals with four.

Between the two of them, the dogs kept her at a steady pace, but the thirty-minute run did little to clear mental cobwebs or make her feel easier about her imminent rendezvous with Christine Palmer.

She finished cooling down with stretches on the deck, paying special attention to the ache in her thighs and the tightness in both Achilles'.

The air was soft and crisp. The sun had splashed papaya colors all across the sky. A slight breeze rustled the branches of cottonwoods, elms, aspens, and locusts, scattering the turning leaves, sending them spiraling to the ground. A perfect fall morning, but Sylvia couldn't enjoy it. She was feeling more and more on edge, and slightly queasy. The colors seemed too bright, the breeze too cool.

When she entered the kitchen, the aroma of brewing beans almost gave her a contact caffeine high. Matt was pouring cream into his mug. Sylvia watched him fill hers with coffee so brown it looked black; a curl of steam wafted from the surface in slow motion.

He was dressed in Levi's (buttoned but not yet zipped), no shirt, no shoes; his short salt-and-pepper hair was fresh out of bed, ruffled every which way. All in all, he was easy on the eyes.

She kissed him, accepted the mug, and sipped the coffee. They'd settled into an uneasy peace—a truce—until she was through with this day, this case.

"Rosie called while you were running," he said. "She's threatening to camp in the driveway if you don't call her back. She wants me to issue a B.O.L.O."

She managed a halfway smile. "I'll call her later."

He went to work feeding hungry dogs. Two ceramic bowls—one small, one large—were partially filled with kibble. He topped the meals off with scraps saved from people meals. The dogs, familiar with the routine, waited patiently side by side, licking their chops. It took them less than twenty seconds to devour their respective breakfasts.

Sylvia and Matt settled at the kitchen table. A wall of glass offered a view of the deck, the garden, and the acreage beyond, where volcanic rock formations were decorated with prickly pear, cholla, and chamiso. The wall might as well have been between them.

She nibbled plain rye toast. Her stomach was jumpy, and she hoped a light meal would settle it. She found herself massaging her temples, trying to work out the dull pain.

Matt watched her, giving her time to gather herself. Wordlessly, she thanked him for his instincts, for his awareness of her rhythms. She knew she wasn't always easy to be around.

After a silence, she wiped the crumbs from her chin and said, "I'd better shower. Get going."

"You sure you want to do this?"

"No." Her smile belonged to a skittish, worried ten-year-old. Wrapping her arms around herself, taking a deep breath, she eased the internal swell of anxiety. "But I will. I've got to meet with Palmer."

"Why? What do you expect to learn that you don't already know?"

"I'll be doing exactly what Christine Palmer's doing—I'll be *testing* and I'll be *fishing* for information. I'll try to give the surveillance team the chance to get a read on her—how much she suspects, if she's about to make a move. At the same time, I'll see what she gives me to work with—because the key to the profile is Palmer herself. And we've run out of time." Sylvia took a breath. "It's this or nothing, Matt. What would you do?"

"I'd go," he said slowly. He toyed with a slice of crust from her plate. "If she knows it's a setup—and you and I both believe she does—you'll be sitting two feet away from a killer who feels cornered. That makes you the bait."

"Maybe." Sylvia acknowledged the point with a nod. "But Palmer's too smart to do anything obvious, and I'll be surrounded by federal agents: one inside the restaurant, Sweetheart and two agents in the van, another agent—"

"You don't have to tell me about surveillance procedure," Matt said quietly.

She frowned, then blinked; even the strong coffee hadn't cleared her head. "I thought it would make you feel better to know the specifics."

"It would make me feel better if you didn't go at all."

"That's not an option." She gave a small shrug, her attention on him. For the past year he'd been away from the streets, from basic cop work, to focus on the politics of law enforcement—fund-raising for programs, acting as liason with the governor's office. He was the man who got things done.

But she knew the promotion had come at a cost. He missed the action, the adrenaline, the primal human *immediacy* of his true job. He was still a criminal investigator, a damn good one, and—she knew—restless to get back into the action. She asked, "Do you want in on this?"

"Damn straight I want in. But too many cooks spoil the soup, too many cops screw up surveillance." He stood abruptly, carrying plates to the sink, then setting them down hard enough to make noise.

Sylvia twisted her mouth, covering her ears with her hands. "You don't have to take it out on the dishes."

Stalling, he moved some things around, gave the dogs water, refilled his mug and hers before he spoke again. "If I believed I'd be any help—not just a hindrance—I'd be there." He shook his head, placing his hands on her shoulders. "Be careful, Syl," he said. "Forget everything else—we'll work it all out later. I love you." His voice was plain, stripped of machismo; he sounded like a man worried about the woman he loved.

The Tesuque Village Market was quiet. It was a weekday, too late for the drive-time commuters, too early for the poets and the unemployed. The local hangout, an old low-slung adobe, was situated on a lightly trafficked corner. The occasional car or motorcycle cruised past the market, which was dwarfed beneath the overhanging branches of huge cottonwoods and Chinese elms.

Sylvia had arrived fifteen minutes early in order to select a predetermined table on the patio—a corner table that offered a peripheral view of the road and the light gray surveillance van roughly eighty feet away, but no eye contact with any federal agents (they couldn't risk Palmer reading inadvertent signs of recognition in Sylvia's body language).

A glass of iced tea and a small fruit plate were arranged on the table in front of her, along with the folder that contained a journal article on the issue of contamination in research labs—the reading material, the food selection, the location of the table, and the proximity of the agents were all part of a prearranged plan with a theme of no surprises.

Sylvia was wearing a wire—permission reluctantly granted after the feds filed a 475 with the U.S. attorney's office. It itched. She resisted the urge to scratch as she pulled the article from the folder and began to read, or more accurately, to make a pretense of reading.

Ninety minutes earlier, she'd made contact with Sweetheart and the agents. As they wired her, they'd gone over the scenario and her agenda: talk to Palmer, listen, encourage intimacy—and be very, very careful.

"What do you want me to do if she offers me something—a book, papers, folders? Supposedly we're meeting to discuss exposure to toxins and symptomology. I don't want to tip her off by acting spooked."

"If she offers you something you can't refuse, handle it with care." Sweetheart watched Sylvia, his eyes narrowing with concern. "Let Palmer leave the table first. That way we can bag the evidence. Nobody's expecting an attempted homicide, but it pays to be careful. Remember, the South Africans tried to assassinate their target with a poisoned umbrella—the Russians succeeded forty years earlier."

"A poisoned umbrella. Great. Pray it doesn't rain."

The surveillance team was in contact with Special Agent Weaver, who was monitoring the target; he let them know the instant she left the Nest.

They'd agreed that Sylvia would proceed to the restaurant on her own, avoiding cell phone, radio, or visual contact with the surveillance team. The only agent she would see during the meeting would be S.A. Simmons—in jogging gear and sporting a ponytail—who would seat herself behind Sylvia at a neighboring table.

They'd discussed several additional contingency plans, and then the morning briefing had ended with Sweetheart pulling Sylvia aside for one last question, one last chance to back out. "Are you going to be okay with all this?"

"I'm fine." But the words were sharp, so she made an effort to soften them. "It will all go fine."

So far, it hadn't.

Not from the first moment, when Palmer leaned down to offer Sylvia a peck on the cheek. Not only had the toxicologist broken social boundaries and invaded Sylvia's personal boundary, but she'd also put her on the defensive by forcing her into a clumsy process of evasion. To avoid contact, Sylvia had opted to play the part of a harassed, disorganized psychologist: she'd dodged the kiss, ignored the proffered hand, launched into distracting chatter about her "morning from hell."

To make matters worse, Palmer had staked out her territory by choosing the adjacent table, offering an excuse: "You don't mind if we change, do you? I've had this quirk since childhood—I don't like my back to the road."

Sylvia—after complying with the request—now sat in a chair that offered no view of the surveillance van but was in a direct sight line with Special Agent Simmons. She had to twist awkwardly in the chair to keep her eyes off the federal agent.

"I brought you a present," Palmer said, holding up a two-inch stack of reading material. Although she leaned back easily in her chair, her gaze was attentive, her eyes bright. "A basic primer on incidents and issues of contamination in the workplace. I'm entrusting it to you, Dr. Strange. As a rule I don't lend material." She held the stack in midair, offering it to Sylvia, refusing to set it down.

"I appreciate your generosity." Sylvia waited several seconds—then, just as she was about to accept the toxicologist's gift, Palmer placed the stack on the table.

"Tell me about your morning from hell."

"My morning from—?" Sylvia shrugged, uncomfortable with the feeling that Palmer had her under a microscope. "Oh, just the usual—too many things to do, woke up on the wrong side of the bed."

"That doesn't sound fun," Palmer murmured. She glanced at their waitress, who had appeared with a coffeepot and an order pad. "Just coffee," she said.

"Cream?"

"Black."

As the waitress left the table, Palmer returned her attention to Sylvia. "If you're always overscheduled, perhaps you need to make some changes in your life."

"Good point. They make a great breakfast burrito here, by the way."

"My day starts at four-thirty. I eat early."

"You get up before five every day? That's impressive." Sylvia shifted her gaze past S.A. Simmons and back to Palmer. The wire under her shirt was digging into her skin; she was conscious of the ongoing audio surveillance. She also had to pee, which wasn't part of the plan. "What time do you go to bed?"

"One A.M."

"On the dot?"

"Actually, yes." Palmer's eyes were wide, unblinking. "I learned long ago that I function best on a strict regimen—always less than five hours' sleep."

Why did Sylvia have the distinct impression that Christine Palmer was expecting something she wasn't getting? She said, "I've known some highly creative people who thrive on very little sleep."

"That's reassuring." Palmer leaned forward, reaching across the table to press her palm to Sylvia's forehead. "You're flushed. And you're warm."

Sylvia flinched, pulling away. "I managed to squeeze in a run this morning." She could feel the spot where Palmer had touched her skin. "I'm probably still revved."

"How's the project going?" Palmer asked abruptly.

"The project . . ." Sylvia took her time. "You mean Dr. Thomas, the psychological autopsy?"

"That must be what I mean," Palmer said, her expression speculative. "You're still involved?"

"Absolutely." There it was again, the feeling that somehow she'd disappointed Palmer. "I'm still gathering data."

"From what I hear, you've been thorough."

"I like to think so." Sylvia pictured Dr. Harris Cray standing next to Palmer's Jaguar; the minute he arrived from London, he must've given his new project director an earful. "Case histories, symptomology data, interviews with project members—this meeting with you, for instance—it's all part of the basic process of gathering, then culling."

"What about research into other incidents of contamination?" Palmer asked slowly. "I assume that interests you as well."

"Of course." The exchange was loaded but oblique. Sylvia wondered if Palmer would probe more aggressively, overtly—without stating as much, they'd just covered the trip to Porton Down and the investigation into Samantha Grayson's death.

But Palmer switched gears again. "How can I be helpful?"

Sylvia realized she was staring. "I'm sorry?"

"What would make it easier for you to piece together what happened to Doug Thomas? I want to help."

"I need to understand more about his work," Sylvia said slowly. "You could tell me about the project."

"How technical do you want me to get?"

"Start with medium. I'll let you know if you need to go less or more."

Palmer nodded. "A lot of what we do is DNA isolation, gene

amplification. For instance, when there are close groupings of taxonomic families, we analyze the similarities; some genes are more highly consistent, or well-conserved, than others. If there are strong similarities between family A and family B, we extract the DNA, attach primers to the site for a specific gene, make multiple copies—"

"Try the simple version."

"That *was* the simple version." Palmer offered a cool smile. "Do you like to cook?"

"I make a mean enchilada. My meatballs are decent."

"Cooking is one of my passions. If I wasn't doing what I do now, I'd be a chef." Palmer picked up a knife from the place setting and used it as a miniature pointer to illustrate key points on the tabletop as she spoke.

She said, "Basically, PCR—polymerase chain reaction—is cooking. Except everything's done on a small scale. Most of the work is invisible to the naked eye. We put a few drops, one-hundredth of a milliliter, in a tube; we put in the basic template, an enzyme, a few other chemicals, equal parts DNA, and our two primers. We put all that into a machine and—we *cook*. It's all about breaking the DNA apart because amplification happens in single strands."

As Palmer caught sight of the waitress, she raised her hand, signaling for more coffee. "Does what I said make any sense?"

Sylvia nodded. "It's interesting."

"I'm glad. Most people tune out when I try to explain. I've learned to limit my interactions."

"That's too bad."

"Is it?" Palmer shrugged, then stretched back casually in the chair. Her gaze settled on the woman with the ponytail who was dressed in running gear; she refocused on two busboys as they swept bright orange and yellow leaves from the steps; finally, her eyes followed the waitress, who arrived, two-fisted, with a pot of coffee and a pitcher of iced tea.

When Sylvia tasted tea from the newly refilled glass, it was so cold it felt hot against her throat. She reminded herself to stay away from liquid until the meeting was finished; she kept her mind off the Chinese courtesan who died of a burst bladder three or four thousand years ago.

Christine Palmer drank some of her coffee, then set the mug on the table and reached into her jacket pocket to produce a small paper packet. She opened the packet and tipped it over her coffee until a stream of white power spilled out.

Sylvia's eyes widened.

"Clarity formula," Palmer said. "A homeopathic remedy. It actually helps me stay focused. Considering your morning, maybe you should try it." She dipped her spoon into the cup and stirred.

A nervous laugh escaped Sylvia's mouth. She watched the dark swirling liquid as it created a tiny vortex. "I've had my share of Santa Fe remedies. I've tried accupuncture, herbs, even magnets."

"Magnets?" Palmer sounded amused. "For what?"

"Headaches—and the answer is *no*. As far as I could tell, the magnets didn't help."

"Are they migraines?"

"Yes." A shiver crawled from the back of Sylvia's neck along her scalp.

"I used to get them when I was on the pill," Palmer said. "I went off, the headaches stopped."

"You were lucky."

"I was smart." Palmer lifted her cup and sipped. "You definitely need to make changes in your life."

"Did you see that?" Special Agent Hoopai asked, surprised. "The Target just spiked her own coffee."

"I saw it." Sweetheart stared at the monitors; cameras were part of the van's standard equipment. At the moment they were picking up

Sylvia and Palmer, and the wire was transmitting audio: Palmer was further explaining DNA amplification.

"What's in that packet?" Hoopai mumbled.

Sweetheart's eyes narrowed. As he studied Palmer's face in the center monitor, he felt as if he were looking at someone he'd known in another life—but the sense of detachment he'd expected did not materialize internally.

He kept his breathing normal, slowing it slightly to match his heartbeat, allowing his mind to process data. He pictured the files in his mind, scanning mentally through facts, dates, statements from witnesses.

She never touches anything from a pharmacy, no drugs, not even aspirin.

She's too smart to try anything so obvious, he thought. *Still . . .* gyoji matta. *Keep your eyes open, Sylvia.*

"What's she up to?" Hoopai wondered aloud.

Clearly, Sylvia was wondering the same thing. Her glance swept the patio, taking in Special Agent Simmons and two elderly men in dungarees who were now waiting for the hostess, and then she returned her attention to Christine Palmer.

"Careful." Sweetheart found himself breathing. "Palmer hasn't done anything yet. Don't break out of the gate—not yet. Just stay calm." His whispered words were meant both for Sylvia and for himself.

"Are you allowed to talk about the types of organisms you're dealing with?" Sylvia asked.

"I can talk around the restrictions," Palmer said. "Do you know the history at LANL? Up until the past few years, the labs were scaled back to biosafety levels one and two. The biosafety standards were established by the CDC and the WHO." Palmer paused. "If you read *The Hot Zone,* or if you know about Ebola and hantaviruses, you know about BSL-four—where the most dangerous pathogens are handled under strict safety precautions. In two thousand two, the threat reduction unit at LANL received post–September eleventh fresh-air funding. With the anthrax killings, biosciences hit the limelight. Several labs were upgraded and equipped to handle BSL-three pathogens."

Palmer took several sips of coffee before she continued. "Remember, in DNA amplification, there's no need to have an active organism in the lab. We're dealing with material that's already been isolated—material for several months' work might look like a tray of ice cubes." Palmer paused, ignoring the waitress who glided past their table.

When they were alone again, she continued in a lower tone. "Have you been reading about the outbreaks of red tide—I'm using the term loosely because these are not red tides in the strictest sense—off the coast of Cancun, Costa Rica?"

"Wasn't there one a couple of weeks ago off Corpus Christi?"

Palmer nodded. "All those coastal waters have something in common. They're warm and they're polluted. And now, let's say, they've got something else in common: a rogue organism seems to be killing fish and making people sick." Palmer cupped her chin in the palms of her hands. With her smooth, perfectly blond hair, her delicate features, her blue-green eyes, she looked like an exotic angel.

She said, "My specialty is neurotoxins. I've done years of research on dinoflagellates. I'm here, close to the site of the outbreaks. If a neurotoxin needs to be isolated, I'm the one to do it."

Sylvia frowned. "That would be a whole different process than the DNA amplification, wouldn't it?"

"It's much more primitive lab work—a simple extraction process to collect toxin, characterize it, and begin to formulate tox screens, even a serum."

"How do you do that?"

"To isolate toxins, we *mash*, we strain, we extract—we're back to cooking metaphors. So it makes sense to fly out fresh samples of whole animals to LANL."

"*Whole* animals?" Sylvia said slowly. "What exactly does that mean?"

"We can't reproduce living organisms from DNA fragments— whole animals are living organisms. Anthrax spores, bacteria, microorganisms. That way I can have blooms of these organisms in the lab for both procedures: DNA and toxin isolation."

"How dangerous are the organisms?"

"I'm speaking in hypotheticals, you understand. One is virtually harmless."

"What about a bloom?" Sylvia tapped her fingers against the table-top.

"Very dangerous. Once you've extracted the toxin, a tiny amount could contaminate the lab."

"Was Dr. Thomas working on extraction?"

Sitting back, crossing her legs, Palmer raised her eyebrows and wagged a finger as if to say the question was too specific to answer. "I did some homework on you. You're famous."

Sylvia frowned. "You've got the wrong Dr. Strange."

"I don't think so." Palmer smiled, but it was a small, calculated curve of the lips. "You've gotten a lot of press for someone who works for the New Mexico Health Department—didn't you say that's who you're with?"

"I've worked with many different agencies on a contractual basis." For an instant, Sylvia saw Paul Lang's face as the MI-6 analyst said, *You know Christine Palmer the same way you know a cobra when you see it.*

Palmer cupped her chin with one hand. "Who were you working with on the Adam Riker case?"

Sylvia felt the cold spreading out from deep in her belly. She reached for her tea, but she didn't raise the glass from the table. "I was asked to consult with law enforcement."

"Local law enforcement?"

"Yes."

"But if I remember, it was a federal case."

"You followed the Riker case?"

"It made the international papers." Palmer's mouth hardened around her words. "A big story. A federal case."

"That's right."

"So you were working with the FBI."

"Answer the question, Brown Eyes." Special Agent Hoopai kept his eyes on the monitor, his knee vibrating, his short-twitch muscles working overtime. He watched Dr. Strange just *sitting* there at the table. "C'mon, c'mon. I don't feel like a hero today, Doc."

"She'll handle it," Sweetheart said sharply.

"Palmer's walking all over her."

"It's under *control*." Sweetheart kept his eyes on Sylvia. He could tell she was shaky, off-kilter. In sumo, it would be said she was *shini-tari,* losing ground, perhaps unable to recover.

The tiny surveillance microphone was picking up background noises, and there was slight static in the transmission, but both men clearly heard Christine Palmer rephrase her most recent statement as a question: "Were you working with the FBI on the Riker case, Dr. Strange?"

Oshidashi, *Sylvia, push out.*

On the monitor, Sylvia blinked, and she tipped her head slightly as if returning from some distant place. "My contacts were with local law enforcement," she said, and her voice held a nice edge of impatience that rang true inside the van.

Yes, thank you.

But Sylvia was still a million miles away—remembering the day they caught Adam Riker. The FBI profilers had warned law enforcement that Riker would react violently if cornered. The profilers were concerned primarily with suicidal ideation.

They hadn't really wanted input from a local psychologist, but Sylvia had begun to get a sense of Adam and what made him tick. Even in her dreams she was on a first-name basis with the serial poisoner. Local law enforcement had taken her seriously when she warned them not to go after Riker if his family was around. Somehow the feds didn't get the message. When two agents arrived on his doorstep, he gave himself up peacefully enough—with the request that his pregnant wife and four children might finish their breakfast undisturbed. Within thirty minutes, the arresting officers had six new corpses—five of them under the age of twelve.

The scenario had replayed itself within an instant in her mind—and now she felt herself pulled back to real time by the sound of Christine Palmer's voice asking, "Are you all right?"

Again she flashed on the comment from Paul Lang. *You know Christine Palmer the way you know a cobra . . .*

Snakes and serial killers both strike when they're cornered.

Palmer was losing patience with the charade, the meeting. Sylvia could feel the other woman's restless energy. It was time to make the move they'd discussed in the surveillance briefing that same morning: *If the moment arises, leave the table, give Palmer the chance to do something stupid. It's a long shot, but at this point we've got nothing to lose.*

Sylvia blinked, looking slightly embarrassed. She crossed her legs, then uncrossed them. "Have you ever heard the story about the Chinese courtesan—it was a few thousand years ago—but she died of a ruptured bladder because back then courtesans weren't allowed to excuse themselves when the emperor was speaking." She stood, smiling apologetically, actually feeling a bit woozy. "Will you excuse me? Too much tea. I'll be right back."

Hoopai sucked in his breath. *Brown Eyes just left the table.*

Sweetheart focused completely on the monitor. Alone, Palmer seemed casually interested in the street scene. Just beyond the patio, a group of children was playing under a massive cottonwood; a stray dog wandered into the street.

Visible beyond Palmer, Special Agent Simmons kept her eyes carefully from Palmer's table—but her body language had shifted almost imperceptibly; she'd tightened down a notch.

Christine Palmer picked up her coffee, drained the cup, and set it down just a few inches from Sylvia's glass.

"She's not going to try anything," Hoopai whispered. "She wouldn't . . ."

Words ran through Sweetheart's brain—the Dutch researcher describing the aftermath of Palmer's poisoning attempts: *She kept asking me how I was feeling . . . kept pushing for details . . . Was I sick to my stomach, was I dizzy? Which symptoms came first?*

Palmer's movements were so casual, none of the agents reacted when she reached into her pocket.

It was the lack of movement that caught Sweetheart's attention. "What's this, what's going on here?" he murmured.

Palmer had just pulled out a small packet from her pocket.

"Can you get a read, do you have clear sight lines?" Sweetheart asked—a query to the second surveillance vehicle, parked twenty feet away.

They heard Special Agent Weaver's voice through the transmitter: "It's paper—no, foil," the agent said. "Looks homemade—now she's keeping it out of view, too cautious, too careful—but she's unfolding the top."

"I don't believe it," Sweetheart said sharply.

Hoopai grunted. "See for yourself, she's opened it up."

"She hasn't done anything yet," Sweetheart snapped. "Hold position."

"Hold position," Hoopai repeated into the transmitter.

Clearly visible on the monitor, Palmer's glance swept the patio, taking in Special Agent Simmons and a trio of cyclists who were waiting for the hostess.

"Oh God, we're getting perfect video on this," Hoopai breathed. *Sweet Jesus.*

"It's too perfect," Sweetheart said. Every fiber in his body was reacting in alarm. "She's trying to flush us out—it's too damn obvious."

"You said she's narcissistic. What if she's so arrogant she thinks she can get away with anything?" Hoopai countered.

At that moment, Palmer moved her hand, simultaneously tipping the packet, a minimal gesture, so the contents—this time a very small amount of light gray powder—spilled into the glass of iced tea; Sylvia's glass.

"Holy shit," Hoopai breathed. "She went for it. I don't believe this."

"*Don't* believe it," Sweetheart said. Time seemed to slow into an almost lazy motion—Sweetheart, probably everybody on the team, thinking, *This is ridiculous. No one's that stupid. Come on, she didn't— what if she did?*

"How are we going to call it?"

"Let her walk away," Sweetheart whispered. "Analyze the glass."

Hoopai's eyes stayed on the monitor. "If we let her walk, we lose our chance to get her into an interrogation room!"

"We've got her on film," Sweetheart said. "If the screen shows toxin—"

"What if it's a trace and it disappears before the lab can screen? Then we lose her, we can't pull her in—*damn.*"

Palmer was already reaching past the glass as if she'd meant to pick up the salt shaker in the first place.

"What are we doing?" The question, an urgent hiss via transmitter, was originating from Special Agent Weaver in the second van.

"We don't do anything," Sweetheart said. "She's playing with us."

"We don't know she *didn't* put something bad in there. Are you going to risk it?"

"Hold off until the last minute," Sweetheart said. "I'm telling you it's too damn obvious."

"I can't take that risk," Hoopai said.

"Don't be *stupid.* Hold off sixty seconds, let's see what—"

"I'm in charge of this surveillance op—"

"Hold off, damn it!" Sweetheart commanded.

Sylvia stepped out of the restaurant, heading straight for Palmer and the contaminated glass. She reached the table and sat. "Where were we—" She broke off in surprise.

A woman had materialized next to her at the table: Special Agent Simmons.

Sylvia saw Christine Palmer take in Simmons and then turn toward the street and the two approaching federal agents, both wearing blue caps and jackets complete with the FBI insignia.

Gut instinct—they're making the wrong move, Sylvia thought.

Palmer looked back at Sylvia. Her face registered both disappointment and triumph—her eyes sparked with something more furtive, but she showed absolutely no sign of surprise. No sign of fear.

"No," Sylvia whispered. "This is a mistake—"

Palmer raised her hands, reaching out, as if offering to take on some burden.

But Special Agent Simmons was already at Christine Palmer's side, ready and willing to protect evidence. Calm, cool, and collected, she said, "FBI. Keep your hands on the table, Dr. Palmer."

The FBI was responsible for transporting Christine Palmer to the U.S. marshal's office at the federal courthouse in Albuquerque. Jeff Hess, the special agent in charge, would supervise the interrogation sessions and he would make sure Palmer was afforded due process. Sylvia and Sweetheart would be able to observe via remote video.

In Tesuque, S.A. Hoopai, Sweetheart, and Sylvia were lagging behind the transport vehicle by ten minutes.

Hoopai felt good—they'd *caught* Palmer, damn it. He felt vindicated. "Take a breath," he encouraged Sylvia, removing the surveillance wire from her rib cage.

She was standing in front of the van, her back to the market, and she swore as he ripped the tape smartly from her skin. "Jesus, you had me taped up for seven-to-ten-day ground delivery." She rubbed at the red patches. "I *itch*."

"A lot of people are allergic," the federal agent soothed. He had a rugged, tanned face, and his teeth showed very white when he smiled.

"To the tape or to the wire?" Sylvia asked wryly.

She tried to feign some sense of achievement. Instead, what she felt was increasing alarm. It was all wrong—the setup, the arrest.

"Finished with me? Thanks, Hoopai," she said, as she tugged down her cotton shirt and straightened her shoulders. She heard Sweetheart's voice—was he talking to himself? She turned to see him standing about ten feet from the van.

"Walk me to my truck," she said when she reached his side.

Much to her relief, he cooperated, steadying her as they covered ground. He didn't speak—he was just as trapped in his thoughts as she was in hers. She was grateful for the silence because it gave her time to process the very recent chain of events. If the rather crude poisoning attempt had caught her completely off guard, the actual arrest had been surprisingly discreet: Christine Palmer offered no resistance. She'd been cooperative and, most unpredictably, passive.

Sylvia couldn't shake the bad feeling that something had gone very wrong. She knew Sweetheart felt the same way—that much was obvious in his demeanor, in his ominous silence.

"Palmer expected it," Sylvia finally said, willing herself to voice her thoughts. "We played right into her hands."

"The evidence will reach Virginia in a matter of hours—top priority. We'll have the preliminary results tomorrow, and we'll use them against Palmer." Sweetheart murmured something else under his breath—something that sounded like *gohei*. He ignored Sylvia's questioning glance and said, "For better or worse, this investigation's out in the open."

They'd reached the narrow parking lot on the north side of Tesuque Village Market, and he waited while Sylvia dug in her pockets, searching for the keys to her truck. "Will you question her?" she asked as her fingers closed around metal.

"Question her?" he repeated, his voice oddly flat.

Sweetheart had stayed out of sight during the arrest process. There had been no reason to reveal his presence, his involvement—in fact, there was a distinct advantage if a suspect *wasn't* aware that a profiler was advising her interrogators.

He seemed to pull himself from a trance to say, "Not unless the investigators reach an impasse."

Sylvia nodded. She found his expression a curious mix of aggravation, impatience, disquiet, and nonattendance. Sweetheart wasn't completely present (that fact bothered Sylvia) and she spoke sharply: "Will Palmer break, or hold?"

When he didn't respond immediately, she felt the whisper of her own dark mood. She shrugged as if to shake off the melancholy. She said, "She'll have the best lawyers money and a high profile can buy. Think about Hatfill, his lawyers, his front page headlines. I'm sure the dream team's on its way. And we played right into her hands." She felt queasy, and her fingers trembled as she unlocked her truck.

Over Sweetheart's broad, muscled shoulder she could see Special Agent Hoopai across the road stepping into the van. The door slammed shut, the sound carried. She shuddered slightly, on overload, hyperaware of sensory information.

"There was nothing to do but arrest her," Sweetheart said.

But he didn't look happy. He looked *remorseful,* which couldn't be right.

"I'm sorry I got you into this," he said in a low voice.

"You didn't." She shook her head. "I knew what was at stake." She worked up a thin smile. "And besides, the Target's in custody. The job's done—at least for now." She was thinking she had to call Matt, tell him she was fine.

But she didn't feel fine. She felt numb.

She forced herself to follow Sweetheart, Hoopai, and the surveillance van on the sixty-mile drive to the federal courthouse in Albuquerque. The normally easy drive felt long and tedious. Sylvia couldn't relax.

Repeatedly her truck fell far behind the van—but when she sped up, her foot dogged the accelerator, and more than once she caught herself doing close to a hundred.

Once they reached Albuquerque, both vehicles dodged road construction and snarled traffic. They were forced to detour to reach their destination. Major interstate construction had inspired tributary projects. Red cones and flagmen added to her bad mood. So did the weather: the city air was warm and hazy, and a dusty wind had picked up from the southwest.

The federal courthouse was located at the core of downtown. The U.S. marshal's office was on the second floor.

In an adjacent office, Sylvia found Sweetheart and Hoopai already watching the monitors. Video cameras mounted inside the U.S. marshal's office were transmitting images of the scene: chairs were casually arranged, and Palmer was seated across from S.A.C. Hess and S.A. Simmons. No desks, no harsh lights, no third degree.

"There's something you should know," Sweetheart said, reaching out to grip Sylvia's arm as she stood beside him. His pupils were tiny dark orbs between almost closed lids. "She's waived the right to have an attorney present. She's willing to talk. She says she has nothing to hide."

The first round of questioning lasted two hours. Palmer remained calm and collected; if anything, she appeared bored by the proceedings. She denied that she had poisoned anyone. The agents persisted.

"We caught you on camera, Christine," Hess said. "You were pouring it into her drink."

Christine Palmer smiled innocently at the special agent in charge. "It?"

"What was in the packet?"

"Nux vomica, among other homeopathics. You should try it—great for upset stomach, headache, nausea." She smiled again, glancing around the room, letting her gaze rest on one of the unobtrusively mounted video cameras. "Ask Dr. Strange to come in here. I'd like to hear it from her—is she really so paranoid that she believes I'd try to poison her with a homeopathic remedy? She should get her facts straight."

Sylvia moved closer to the monitor. The sound coming from the marshal's office was thin, with a faint and artificial echo. On the screen, she could see her own ghostly reflection superimposed over Palmer's face—as if she were ephemeral, a haunting spirit.

"Nobody's going to ask you to confront her," Sweetheart said quietly.

Sylvia turned away from the monitor to stare at him. She knew this was the point in the proceedings where she should be fully present, observing body language and speech patterns, watching for ways to get to Palmer, looking for leverage—but it all seemed meaningless. She felt they'd already been defeated.

"I can't stay here." Suddenly overwhelmed, she clutched her bag and bolted to the door. "I'm not helping anybody."

Tearing his gaze from the monitors, Sweetheart followed her. "Let's go outside," he said. "Get some air."

"You stay," she began.

"No. Where are you parked?"

He escorted her through the courthouse toward the back exit, where prisoners arrived and the holding cells were located. The hall smelled of alcohol and urine; two officers ushering a young tattooed man in an orange jumpsuit passed them. The prisoner kept his chin low, eyes downcast, shuffling feet and ankle chains.

Outside, Sylvia stood on concrete warmed by late autumn sunlight. The glare was almost unbearable. She felt Sweetheart's arm around her shoulder and heard his voice coming from far away, asking if she was okay.

Of course. But her tongue felt stiff, not interested in pushing the lie from her mouth. "After all that, we blew it." She shook her head. "Palmer's treating this like it's a joke—and she's *right.*"

"I'll get someone to drive you home."

"No. I'm feeling better. The air is helping. I was just upset and tense—and I'm disappointed—but that doesn't matter now. You need to get back inside, do your best to make sure she doesn't walk." She saw the sense of urgency on his face; he was torn, needing to make sure she was safe, needing to watch the interrogation sessions. And she was beginning to feel more grounded, more clearheaded, as if she'd shaken off whatever had spooked her inside the courthouse. "What will they do with her now?"

"Hold her, probably until Monday morning, although it's not going to look good to a judge. We'll have preliminary results from the tox screens by then. Even if we have nothing solid, the best lawyer wouldn't have an easy go of it, getting her out before then, finding a federal judge who'll take time away from weekend worship on the golf course."

Sylvia shaded her eyes with her hand. "The sample's clean. I know it. You do, too." She bit the edge of her lip. "When the feds closed in—" She fell silent for a moment, searching for words. "Palmer looked *satisfied.*"

"Give our guys a chance," Sweetheart said. "They're good at their job."

"Right. So is Palmer." She stood, gazing east toward the Sandia Mountains. Sun highlighted the bruised peaks. "I'll try to come back this evening."

"No." Already, he was turning to walk back toward the building. "You've done your job. You've more than held up your side of the bargain. You gave me the profile. You gave us this opportunity. I can take it from here."

· · · ·

The rest of the day passed in a blur.

When she pulled into her property, she saw Matt's car. He was finishing his packing for an overnight trip to Las Cruces, the last in a series of meetings.

He took one look at her and said, "I'll cancel."

But she convinced him to go. "I'm going to make myself a bowl of soup and go to bed."

"On top of planning for the wedding, you still haven't caught up from London."

It's more than that, she thought. *I could sleep for a week. It's this case, it's exhausting me.* The Riker case had done the same thing.

It was almost ten o'clock when Sweetheart finally called. He kept it short: "Palmer's still in custody. She's sticking to her story."

On Sunday, Sylvia woke early with a full-on migraine.

She skipped her morning run; the dogs eyed her dolefully, but her head hurt so badly she couldn't even muster guilt.

She stared at the food on the shelves, then closed the cupboards. She'd burned her mouth on a cup of scalding coffee. The burn wasn't going away. The thought of food made her weak.

There were messages on the machine. Rosie wanted to know if the rental company was going to deliver chairs and tables for the wedding on Friday or Saturday—oh, and did she want the cinnamon or the spruce tablecloths for the caterers—and *oh,* did she need the rings picked up? Matt called several times, asking her to call and check in because he was worried. Sweetheart tersely requested a callback.

She didn't bother to respond.

Instead, she called in the refill for her migraine medicine, found her purse and keys, and began the drive across town to the pharmacy.

By the time she reached the drugstore, the pain from the headache was making her sick to her stomach. The migraine was affecting her eyes; this time the aura was much brighter than usual.

She took the back road home. She'd planned to stop for fresh fruit, milk, and bread at the market, but the headache was intensifying. She hadn't even covered two miles and the back of her neck was numb, her fingers were tingling. The sensation was eerie. She shook off a stab of fear.

I'm fine, just a touch of flu.

She could almost believe it until she reached the intersection of Cerrillos and Rodeo. Just ahead, the traffic light shifted to yellow. The image doubled, then tripled. She cut her eyes from the road and stared down at her feet.

The brake, use the brake.

But her body didn't respond, and the truck went plowing through the intersection just after the light turned red. Three lanes of oncoming traffic skidded to a halt. A car turning left swerved to avoid a collision. Horns blared.

She accelerated.

Burning mouth, nausea, vomiting, diarrhea—all symptoms easily explained without thought of exotic neurotoxins. The flu was going around—variations of stomach and digestive tract ailments, headaches, sensitivity to light and sound.

As she drove, she struggled to see—the world was covered in gray dust or the most delicate netting. She blinked, removing her sunglasses, wiping the lenses.

The driver behind her honked. She saw that the speedometer needle had dropped to fifteen miles per hour.

She seemed to be floating away from the car, the road.

Disorientation, feeling light-headed, floating sensations, disembodiment.

Then, abruptly, she came crashing back into her body.

The world was moving a million miles a minute. She gasped, clamping her fingers on the wheel, her foot on the accelerator. She caught fragments of signs, road marks—but she was traveling so fast she didn't recognize the places and streets she'd passed countless times.

This is exactly what happened to the others.

But the thought raced through her mind before she could catch it—and even begin to comprehend what it meant.

Her pulse sped up, then slowed. She took deep breaths. She tried to ignore her pounding heart—the big muscle was contracting so intensely that each beat *hurt.*

Again, the world shifted. It slipped back into normal.

If I was poisoned, my muscles would be paralyzed, and I wouldn't be able to breathe.

She saw her road up ahead. Just in time. She slowed, braking for the turn, and executed it perfectly. She felt so relieved to be herself again, she began to cry.

"I'm okay, I'm okay," she whispered again and again. The rearview mirror caught her reflection, and she chided herself: *How stupid, you scared yourself half to death.*

One by one, she passed the familiar houses of her neighbors in La Cieneguilla.

Turning on to the dirt road that led to her property, the truck bounced over the cattle guard. She inhaled, but her lungs couldn't seem to expand.

Black pupils spread like ink, darkening the hazel of her irises.

The same blackness seemed to cover the world.

She began to laugh—finding it odd, yes, but unable to stop. Her head fell back against the seat.

.   .   .

Time passed in great crashing waves of bright lights, blinding color, deafening noises, excruciating physical sensation—only to slow to a grinding halt, a freeze-frame. Then it began again, this time in slow motion.

A physicist's dream: dense matter where there had been no previous resistance; liquids that should have been solids.

Sylvia was aware of unfamiliar voices. At first she thought she was surrounded by people. It occurred to her to ask for help. But that demanded effort, and she let herself surrender to inertia. After a while, she realized the voices came from inside her own brain.

She was strapped inside her truck. She managed to free herself somehow, to push down on some kind of lever—felt herself fall. After that she lost track of everything but the voices.

When she listened to the part of her mind still attached to sanity, she was aware of the drift, of the madness that blurred the rest of her thoughts and perceptions.

At one point she did cry out for help. But the next instant, the awareness of the utter futility of her efforts was as chilling as anything she had ever experienced in her life.

Mercifully, this black hole of existential oblivion also passed.

Abruptly, she found herself crawling over a rough, rocking field. The night was bright with stars; she could see lights glowing in the distance. She was cold, shivering, but her muscles burned. Agonizing pain.

A day has passed . . .

Frenetic activity alternated with paralysis.

She lay clutching earth, somewhere in the world, dizzy from a spinning planet, unable to move. Thoughts flew by like night birds. A few landed long enough to register: *This is a poison world. I've touched poison. No one should have to fight this hard to stay on a planet.*

And finally, she closed her eyes to give in to the cool hand of death.

It came as she'd always known it would, like falling off a bridge, like flying, that first moment of *This can't be happening, not to me, not now, I'm not ready.*

But it was familiar, not unexpected, something she'd imagined countless times in life. Until only the sadness was unbearable. How much she'd miss them all, the people she loved, the child she'd never have. Bitter sadness.

Don't let me die alone.

But the letting go was easier than anything she'd ever known.

PART IV

Chambre Ardente

CHAPTER
23

Alchemist, I can't reach you but I try anyway. is this dying????? night sweats, the monsters come to me. they won't get away with this—keeping you from me. last night a dream—dead and dying everywhere. holocaust a ghost screaming. the alchemist devotes a lifetime to the study of impurity and imperfection and the possibilities of transformation—trans—for—ma—tion—to purity to perfection!!!! the quest of transmutation base metals to gold alchemy created chemistry as science. the transmutation of radioactive elements is no more, no less, than alchemy—through death, the Alchemist has discovered the elixir, the grand magistery, the alkahest. Death is the final gift—in the dream a million boys in uniform lined up their eyes blind, bloody foam drips from the corners of their mouths some are crippled others are crying and one reaches out for the Alchemist. he screams I understand what the Alchemist was made of before heat and light and I know what the Alchemist will become in the end. suffering brings understanding, enlightenment, a transmutation of the soul—help me help me help me help me help me help me help me help me help

me...

....

....

Paul Lang stared at the stain on the ceiling of his motel room. The color of weak coffee, it vaguely resembled the shape of Indonesia, islands on a sagging plaster sea. It was the second-best view in the dingy room.

The best view was a small patch of very blue sky visible in the frame of the bathroom window. Desert sky. Española sky.

He was twenty miles from Los Alamos, twenty miles from Santa Fe, twenty miles from Christine Palmer, twenty miles from Edmond Sweetheart. But no one was going to look for him in this back-road grease trap frequented by junkies and slags. All he needed was another day to finish the task he'd set for himself.

He'd already driven up the hill to the lab, but cameras and security had dictated that he return when the event would be less public. The plan had been set. Lang didn't like the directive he'd been given, but this wasn't the moment to be choosy.

A door slammed outside; a woman gave a shrill laugh, then yelped; a man said something in Spanish; a car engine roared to life, settling into a deep throb.

Lang gazed at the watch on his wrist—the gold hands showed that it was midafternoon in the American Southwest. A few more hours. That was all.

He breathed deeply, then expelled air with a shuddering sigh. His eyes returned to Indonesia's shadow on the ceiling.

He'd been working toward this end for a very long time.

Dr. Harris Cray set the phone down in its cradle and stared blindly at the data on his computer screen:

. . . relevant toxin samples for the core facility. These samples will be the source for neuropsychologic studies, genetic identification and characterization, molecular genetic studies; monoclonal and axenic cultures, toxin induction and biosynthesis . . .

It was late. He still wasn't adjusted to this new circadian cycle.

He was tired and his eyes ached.

And now he was also frightened.

He paused, squeezing his eyes shut, trying to still the trembling in his fingers. The news about Palmer's detention had come as a shock. How dare they lay a hand on her? How dare they violate her territory and throw everything off track when they were *so* close? This wasn't what he'd planned after all these years.

The FBI had sealed off her office, her lab—they were trespassing, touching what wasn't theirs to touch, interfering with things they couldn't understand. The lab director himself had been down here surpervising the inventory of their section. Every vial, every slide, every fragment of DNA was being accounted for—and suspicion was so thick you could taste it.

He pulled himself up sharply.

He couldn't afford to fall into emotional quicksand. His surprise, his rage, over Christine was nothing compared to the news he'd just heard. He had to get out of here—he had to move quickly—and yet he felt paralyzed.

He shook his head abruptly. He was not a man given to internal reflection. The realm of his emotions might as well have been a remote plateau in Mongolia.

He heard voices down the hall, someone leaving.

None of it mattered, he told himself. The important work was already completed.

He stood quickly, already scanning a mental checklist of items he would need to gather—*now or never*—before he made his exit.

And for an instant, in the shadow cast across the monitor, he caught sight of his own reflection.

Christine Palmer waited with her back straight, her chin high, her shoulders set. She didn't move. On the video monitor in the adjacent room, where an FBI agent monitored her at all times, it seemed as if the film had stopped. The agent actually began to check the system—but then he saw her blink.

Eerie, the agent thought. To be that self-contained was uncanny.

Now he heard voices as the door behind him opened, and he turned to see S.A. Hess enter the room. Hess, who was returning from a break of almost an hour, stepped over to the monitor and gazed at it silently for long seconds.

"What's she been up to?"

"This." The agent nodded toward the monitor. "And she asked for some paper and a pencil earlier. Said she wanted to make some notes."

"Where are they?" Hess asked.

The agent tipped his head, indicating the room she now occupied.

As if on command, Palmer slid her hands into her lap and began to shred a small sheet of paper.

An instant later, when Jeff Hess entered the U.S. marshal's office, Palmer greeted him pleasantly, as if she was relaxed and comfortable.

Apparently she was.

When he took the torn paper and gazed down at the words, she caught him in the light of her gray-blue eyes and said, "I'm glad you're here. I want to talk about a security breach . . ."

Paul Lang turned the car in to the vacant lot. Trash and old tires were strewn among overgrown weeds. The sun through thunderclouds cast cool shadows on the parched land.

He drove with his head and arm out the car window, watching for gulleys and machinery debris that might do serious damage to tires. The gas station—the dusty CLOSED sign visible in the window—featured a public telephone. He hoped it was functional; vandals had left their mark on the concrete embankment behind the station, as well as on various abandoned vehicles that had needed repairs long ago.

He pulled up next to the battered phone booth and set the brake. The phone was still attached to the wire—good sign—and there was an audible dial tone when he held the receiver to his ear.

He pulled a small black book from his pocket, opening it to a dog-eared page, dialing the number of the cell phone. As it began to ring, he watched an airborne convention of ravens. At least two dozen of the birds were circling, almost like buzzards. He wondered vaguely what they were up to, why they were flying in such complicated spirals.

The ringing stopped abruptly as someone picked up.

"We're on," Lang said.

"It was stupid to call."

Lang smiled; his mouth tasted bitter. "You called me, remember? You set it all in motion."

"You know what I— Just stay on schedule."

"Nothing's changed?" Lang was gazing off in the distance where a car and a much larger truck were both cresting the hill. He watched as the car pulled around the truck and flashed its lights. The truck responded, accelerating with a quick flick of headlights, a road game.

"Nothing's changed."

The car sped past the station. The truck was still a few lengths behind, and when it finally rumbled past, the driver let loose his horn.

Lang said, "I just wanted to make sure we're on the same page: it's all in place, moving forward."

Drew Dexter, deputy director of security, sat behind his desk at LANL. The pencil between the fingers of his left hand was tapping out a staccato beat. His mind wandered around thoughts of Dr. Christine Palmer. He'd been notified that she was in custody.

He glanced at his watch—almost twenty-four hours now since the arrest.

Rumors were circulating about the psychologist, about Dr. Strange, a poisoning . . .

Dexter shifted in his chair, bringing pencil to paper.

A classified document lay next to the notebook. It concerned a series of medical experiments performed on soldiers years earlier.

As he began to write, he wondered if he should give Edmond Sweetheart a call. He wondered how much of this information it was advisable to share.

He didn't like this restless feeling in his gut. There were moments in security and enforcement when everything could turn on a dime. This felt like one of those moments. He picked up the phone to contact lab security. It was time to know exactly what each unit was up to—it was time to be extremely alert.

Paul Lang waited on a side street, out of range of the light cast by an overhead streetlamp, in sight of the crossroads where he was supposed to meet his contact. In the distance, the traffic signal changed from green to yellow to red and back to green at hypnotic intervals.

He sat behind the wheel of the car in silence as fevered thoughts raced through his head. Samantha had been haunting his dreams, his waking hours, when he failed to stay alert. Her presence left him restless, edgy, as if he hadn't eaten for weeks and was driven by hunger. In this case, his hunger was revenge. But not an obvious type of revenge, because Christine Palmer wasn't an obvious woman.

As the image of Palmer's face filled his mind, Lang's breath quickened. He closed his eyes, then opened them again abruptly, shivering. The night sky was cloud-covered, the thin moon invisible. The air, faintly chill, smelled of smoke.

He'd kept track of the minutes, the hours. If punctual, his contact should be here within the next six minutes. He closed his eyes again, letting his head fall forward and his neck release. His hands shook constantly these days. His stomach hurt. His head ached. Enough to make a man think he was dying. An intense wave of self-pity washed over him. Samantha had been his life, his love—now that she was gone, he was left with the only other obsession he'd ever known in his life: Christine Palmer.

He sat up straight as a car entered the intersection ahead and turned in his direction. It traveled slowly, headlights bright, until it was fifty feet away; then it pulled to the curb, slowing to a stop. While Paul Lang watched, the car door opened and a shadow stepped out carrying a briefcase.

His contact had shown up after all.

The walls gave off a glow so sharp it burned through skin. She saw vague shapes. She assumed they were human. They shone with a phosphorescence that obscured edges and sharp features.

She tried to free herself from the light, the glare, but when she struggled, it only grew brighter until it threatened to shatter consciousness.

This time the light was slightly less intense.

There was a new problem. Her body was stored in ice. No one could survive temperatures like this. Fine. She was dead.

But still her muscles shook, her entire body vibrated with cold. Her brain caught fire.

Someone said her name.

She opened her eyes.

Blackness everywhere; shimmer of light.

You should learn to mind your own business.

She saw the face, recognized the voice—Adam Riker. He was surrounded by his dead family. They watched her accusingly. But Riker spoke only to her—he said, *It didn't have to turn out this way.*

She cried out, falling back into darkness.

A woman came to visit. A golden goddess. Must be an old friend, she thought. Someone from years ago, perhaps Yale or MIT.

Had she gone to MIT? She didn't think so. And what about Yale? She wasn't sure. She was frightened by her own uncertainty.

"It's fine," the woman said.

"I can't remember your name." Sylvia smiled, trying to cover embarrassment, explaining that she'd been under the weather lately. *Out of sorts.*

"A touch of flu? There's lot's of that going around."

"It's the hospital food," she said, trying to sit up, shocked by the pain that shot down her spine. *Beware the white gowns.*

The woman shook her head, smiling. "I never share my food with strangers." She reached into the pocket of her coat—it had somehow turned from gold to pale lavender—and pulled out a snake. She held it up, letting it bite her face.

"I have protection," the woman said.

The world tipped, righted itself, then tipped again.

She saw the small, dark-haired person seated in a chair next to the bed.

"Serena," she whispered.

Serena reached out her arms and draped herself gently over Sylvia.

The room seem to flood with light, but this time the brightness was soothing. Healing.

. . .

A nurse was changing bags on the IV. Sylvia opened her mouth, try-ing unsuccessfully to say Hello.

"Hey . . ." The nurse gazed at her speculatively. "Welcome back."

Where am I? She thought she asked the question, but she wasn't sure. The nurse answered either way.

"You're still in isolation, honey."

Sylvia looked around. Her bed was surrounded by plastic curtains. She could hear voices, although she couldn't see anyone but the nurse. "How long have I been here?"

"Your doctor will explain all that."

"I want to see my family."

"No one's allowed in here but medical staff," the nurse said, readying a blood pressure cuff.

"Why change the rules now?" Sylvia's throat ached even when she whispered. "I've had visitors before."

The nurse shook her head, sharp eyes assessing. "No, you haven't, honey," she said softly. "But a lot of people have been worried about you."

The doctor appeared, a woman with ebony skin and bright red lips. She studied the charts and smiled. "Feeling better?"

"I'm hungry."

"That's a good sign. I'm Dr. Casey."

"What happened?"

"What do you remember?"

"Not much. It's all—frag—mixed up." She took time to collect herself. "Poison?"

"Your symptoms were consistent with a powerful neurotoxin."

"Which toxin?"

"I'm sorry. We don't know. Not yet."

"How long—have I?"

"You've been here eight days."

"I missed my wedding."

They came in shifts.

The team of doctors would only allow brief visits.

When Matt and Serena walked into the room, Sylvia saw the fear on their faces. "Was I that sick?" she asked, and her own fear was like a weight behind her ribs.

Serena watched her with somber black-brown eyes. She hesitated, then said, "Matt thought you were dead."

"You found me?" Sylvia asked.

He took her hand in his. "When I couldn't reach you by phone, I came back early."

"I'm sorry." The edges of the room softened. She felt herself drifting away, felt a fleeting surge of emotion, but that passed, and she was left with a weariness that went clear to the bone.

"Matt saved your life," Serena said softly.

"I love you both so much," Sylvia whispered. "Didn't want to hurt you."

And then she slept.

She woke an hour later, panicky, with no idea where she was, why she was there—barely hanging on to *who* she was.

It took the nurses fifteen minutes to calm her down.

Matt walked in thirty minutes later.

He lay beside her on the bed.

Finally, Sylvia whispered, "When am I going to get better? Each time I wake up, it's like starting all over again. I have to fill in the blanks. And some of them . . . I still can't figure out." She took a deep breath;

she was like a frightened child working hard to convince a grown-up that a risky course of action made perfect sense. "Maybe if I went home, if I was in my own home, my own bed, maybe I'd be okay."

"They want to be sure . . ." Matt trailed off, and he couldn't completely mask the stricken expression on his face.

"Sure I'm not damaged? If they keep sticking pins and needles into me, I'll never get well." She tried to sound natural, tried to lighten the mood.

"They can't guarantee they've isolated the compound, the toxin that made you sick. They sent samples to the forensic lab at Lawrence Livermore. They can make some good guesses—those guys are some of the best—but they can't say for certain."

Sylvia struggled to organize her thoughts, to discipline her still-fractured memory—one of the side effects of the toxin.

"How did Christine Palmer do it? Did I touch something? During the surveillance? The pages she passed to me?"

"Everything came back clean, Sylvia." Matt shook his head. "The FBI sent a team to search your house, your car, anything that could possibly be used to transmit. They went back to the restaurant, they went to your office. They've sampled shampoo, toothpaste, hairbrush, any possible vehicle of transmission."

"Nothing?"

"No trace."

The numbness traveled from her feet up her legs. The room began to shimmer. She was floating above her own body.

Matt's voice, distant and small, a collapsing point of energy, giving an order: "Get the doctor. *Now.*"

Rosie and Ray Sanchez came the next day, when Sylvia was well enough to be cranky.

"When do I get out of here?"

"Soon enough, *jita*." Rosie clucked and fussed and behaved in a manner that was equally cranky. Ray stood like a tree that had somehow planted itself in ICU at the UNM hospital.

"This room is better," he said, eyeing it critically.

"Better than what?"

"Better than that Plexiglas cell they locked you inside—"

"Raymond." Rosie shot him a stormy look.

Ray looked at Sylvia and shrugged. "What do I know?" he mumbled.

"Why are you being hard on Ray?"

"I'm hard on him because I love him," Rosie said. "And because he's my husband with a big mouth."

Sylvia frowned. "What did you mean, Plexiglas cell?"

"You don't remember at all?" Rosie asked. She was fluffing up a pillow, punching it so fiercely Sylvia was afraid the stuffing would explode. "At first they weren't sure if you were contagious, so they kept you in the extra-extra-isolation chamber, or whatever the hell they call it, pardon my French. I call it lockdown."

Rosie had spent more years than she cared to admit as an investigator at the penitentiary of New Mexico. She knew *lockdown* when she saw it.

"You spent a week in that thing," she snapped, angry at the world. Her spike heels clicked sharply against the tile floor.

Ray was fidgeting with the curtains, fighting with cords. He said, "This room's much better. You can see the Sandias if you push your nose into the corner of the window."

"Great," Sylvia said, smiling sleepily. Her energy was evaporating again. "Something to look forward to," she murmured.

Rosie took her hand. "One step at a time. Abuelita sends her love. She wants to come and smudge the place, get rid of *los demonios*."

"I wish she *would* smudge for demons," Sylvia said, her eyes closing. "They won't go away."

"According to Dr. Casey, I'm showing classic signs of acute exposure to a neurotoxin." Sylvia frowned at Matt. "Paresthes—paresthesia, cold-hot reversal, vertigo, orthostatic hy—po—tension. I'm stabilized, out of immediate danger," she said, ignoring the fact she was tripping over words. "That's the good news. The bad news is they don't know the orgic—organic character of the toxin, its chemical profile, can't begin to guess about my long-term prognosis." She took a deep breath. "Damage to kidneys, liver, CMS—I mean CNS—immune system. DNA. Reproductive organs—Could there be permanent genetic damage? They don't have the answers."

"That's unacceptable."

"That's what I said. I told the doc to find me someone who *could* give me answers. Guess what?"

Matt shook his head.

"More good news. The leading expert on exotic toxins is in the neighborhood: Dr. Christine Palmer."

The next best thing, the consultant from Lawrence Livermore via phone conferencing: "We're limited in our ability to screen and identify the full spectrum of cultures, especially exotic cultures. Currently, identification requires in vitro propagation, morphological identification through light and electron scanning microscopy."

Sylvia tried to follow the stream of words, but she found the task nearly impossible; this was a language she no longer spoke.

"We do have field detection assays for blood analysis for some toxins, others require standard bioassay of the organism itself for toxicity.

If we use a primitive method of identification—specifically via symptoms exhibited—we find that victims of ciguatoxin and maitotoxin, for instance, exhibit—"

"Ciguatoxin is from fish," Dr. Casey interjected.

"—malaise, nausea, numbness and tingling, abdominal cramps, diarrhea, itching, ataxia, blurred vision . . ."

The list was endless.

The flat, matter-of-fact recitation continued: "If the toxin was an aminoperhydroquinazoline compound . . . similar to that of saxitoxin . . . used in nerve gas experiments . . . produced by tetrodotoxin, and the origin is pufferfish . . . numbness occurs first in the face and extremeties, then the feeling of floating and lightness, then vomiting and diarrhea, and finally, cyanosis, hypotension, convulsions, and possibly cardiac arrest."

He hardly slowed to breathe. "These are symptoms that occur when the toxin is in its base form, but we're open to the possibility that Dr. Strange was exposed to a compound, a toxin that is a newly developed, intentional *mutant,* if you will."

Silence. Finally, Dr. Casey asked, "If that's the case, what are the ramifications? What can we expect for her prognosis?"

"That's a good question," the consultant said through the speaker. "We'll be tracking the doctor's progress with great interest."

She was about to jump out of her skin.

They told her these "feelings of restless irritability" were a neurological symptom, the aftermath of the poison.

She was threatening to take hostages; she'd warned them she'd sue if they didn't let her out.

"Anger"; another symptom.

She was depressed by another day passing since she'd returned to the world of the living. Add them up, she'd lost nine days of her life.

"Mood swings," they said. Symptom.

She cursed them silently—unable to remember their names half the time—she didn't need them to tell her that memory holes were yet another (perhaps the *worst*) symptom.

"Get me out of here."

Nobody listened.

But Sweetheart finally appeared at her door.

"I was wondering when you'd show up." Sylvia kept her eyes on him, saw the tension in the way he held himself. "Were you waiting for the funeral?" He didn't respond, and after the silence stretched, she shrugged. "Well, you missed it. I was buried last week."

He sat in a chair at the foot of the bed. His face was smooth as the surface of a lake; his eyes were black stones. "I thought I'd lost you, Sylvia."

She shifted her gaze to the hard shadows on the wall. "You were right."

"It's my fault. I never should have left you vulnerable." He said it calmly, without drama, but the words hung in the air between them. "I take full responsibility for what's happened."

She struggled for language, unable to respond, knowing she'd wanted to hear him say those words, but now feeling uneasy, detached.

He searched for words he was free to speak. "If it makes any difference, this case goes deeper than Palmer." He stopped, then started. "There are issues . . ."

"I don't care about your issues," she said softly.

"That's understandable. I spoke with your doctors, with Dr. Casey." He paused. "I'm sorry for all you've been through."

"You're sorry." Her anger was evaporating. "I don't know what I am. I keep trying to find words."

"Maybe they'll come with time."

She studied his face. "My world has changed. No going back."

He reached for her hand, but she pulled away. Numb. A part of her gone dead.

"I owe you," he said.

"You owe me what you've always owed me: the truth."

He looked at her now, his face naked in a way she'd never seen before, his expression one of deep remorse. "You're right. I owe you the truth at the very least."

Sweetheart returned less than an hour later accompanied by Darrel Hoopai. The special agent clutched a bouquet of wilted daisies.

"This isn't a social call," Sylvia said slowly.

"Not a social call," Sweetheart confirmed. Hoopai pulled the door shut and stationed himself directly in front of it.

Sylvia closed her eyes, took a breath. Preparation. For whatever news they were here to deliver.

"We've got a situation," Sweetheart said. "Sensitive information disappeared from B-30."

"Palmer stole something?"

"Not Palmer." Sweetheart shook his head. "But her hard drive disappeared."

"Disappeared?"

"Do you remember during the Cerro Grande fire? A drive with classified information disappeared for three weeks, then turned up again."

"Behind the Xerox machine," Sylvia said. "I thought all computer drives, all disks with classified information, are locked up, kept in a vault."

"That's exactly right, Dr. Strange."

Sylvia looked up to see Drew Dexter, LANL's deputy director of security, standing in the doorway.

"May I come in?" He stepped into the room and closed the door. "In this particular case, we're not sure how long the hard drive was missing. Serial numbers are checked periodically. And theoretically, all members of a team working with classified information are supposed to make sure drives and disks are safely locked up. In practice, that doesn't always happen. Our best guess is that someone planned to remove the drive from the lab, and they couldn't get it past security, so they copied some or all of the contents." Dexter frowned. He looked like a man doing his best to contain strong emotions. "Perhaps at that point they panicked and hid the drive instead of trying to cover their tracks. It was found behind a copy machine. Déjà vu all over again. There was information on that drive that would be dangerous in the wrong hands."

"What's this got to do with me?"

"We need your help."

"No." The anger was chemical. A reaction in her blood just the same as if someone had jabbed a needle into her vein. Adrenaline. Stress cortisols. A simple increase in blood pressure. "Go talk to Palmer."

"We have. We are."

Sylvia saw the cue in Sweetheart's eyes. "You've got to be kidding," she whispered.

S.A. Hoopai said it out loud: "Palmer's on our side."

CHAPTER

26

"Palmer's the one who clued us in," Hoopai said softly.

The chronology, according to the feds:

"Palmer was in custody. By Monday morning lawyers were banging at the doors—reporters were going to be next. It was moot anyway, since tox reports came back clean. The packet contained nux vomica, just like Palmer said. Leaving investigators with their pants down. No grounds to hold her."

But leaving *Palmer* with the perfect oppertunity to hold a press conference à la bioweapons expert Steven Hatfill back in 2002, when the FBI was looking for the perpetrator of the "anthrax letters." She and her lawyers could claim the FBI was waging a smear campaign—through innuendo, harassment, and speculation—because they were desperate to come up with evidence.

Instead, she'd chosen to cooperate.

Sweetheart took over. "From the moment she was in custody, the FBI closed off her office, her lab, and took inventory. That's when we found the that the drive had been missing from B-30. Assume it was copied. It contains a vital manufacturing process—partially encrypted, but one that could be deciphered over time by a diligent party."

"You said Christine Palmer clued you in." Sylvia frowned. "I'm confused. If she was in custody, how did she know about the hard drive?"

It was Dexter who finally responded. "Dr. Palmer warned us about a possible security breach. A theft. A toxin sample may be missing as well."

"My God," Sylvia whispered. "If a toxin's missing—"

Sweetheart cut her off. "We don't know that—not absolutely."

"It's virtually impossible to maintain an accurate inventory of biological substances." Drew Dexter's soft Louisiana accent filled the room. "That was the main issue back in two thousand one and two. Anthrax. The Ames strain. You can't keep track of every milliliter. A new inventory procedure has been implemented on the Hill. Hopefully it will provide us with answers." He looked away. "But for the moment, LANL's treating this as an internal investigation."

Sweetheart kept his eyes on Sylvia. "LANL has to function on the credo of *Don't let the bad guys know if something's on the open market.*"

"They can't withhold that kind of information." Sylvia stared at Dexter.

"We can and we will," he said sharply. "Until we know exactly what is or is *not* missing."

"People's lives are at stake."

"We don't know that," Dexter said.

"Sylvia." Sweetheart moved closer to the bed. "I understand what you're feeling. Think. We can't afford to cause a panic."

Finally she nodded. "Christine Palmer must have taken it—somehow she got it out—reported it missing—"

"We don't think so," Dexter said. "It's possible that before his death Doug Thomas smuggled out a sample."

"Doug Thomas?" Sylvia searched her mind and the fact fell into place: Dr. Thomas, Palmer's colleague at LANL, the man she'd murdered. "Wouldn't lab security have stopped him?"

"Unfortunately, not necessarily," Dexter said. "We can't check every fountain pen, every pill bottle."

"It would be risky," Hoopai said. "But Dr. Thomas needed money, he was willing to take risks."

Sylvia closed her eyes; her thoughts were jumbled, kept slipping out of place. A visual flash: Christine Palmer and a red-haired man. Opening her eyes, she said, "There was another doctor."

Sweetheart's voice, slow and measured, explaining to a child: "Harris Cray. We have security surveillance of Dr. Cray leaving the lab Friday—midmorning—while you were meeting with Christine Palmer at Tesuque Village Market. He carried a briefcase."

"What does he say about the hard drive?"

Hoopai stepped in this time. "Cray's disappeared."

"Jesus," Sylvia said. "I'm afraid to ask about Lang."

"Lang's another story. We found the motel in Española where he stayed. He checked out last Saturday morning. Nobody's seen him since"

"It all has a pleasing symmetry," Sylvia said bitterly. "You're minus a hazardous material, top-secret information, an MI-6 investigator, and a scientist with top-secret clearance. They've got a one-week lead at the very least. There's no way that information hasn't already changed hands to the North Koreans, the Iraqis, the mafia—a dozen other nations or private entities in the market for bio-weapons."

"It's possible."

"Possible?"

"But we have intelligence that says Lang's still in the country—that a sale hasn't occurred. Not yet."

"What's this have to do with Christine Palmer?"

"She claims to have relevant information."

"And you believe her?" Sylvia asked harshly. "She's a serial murderer."

No one spoke until Sylvia asked: "When did Palmer come forward?"

"While she was in custody. She says she was given the information earlier, but she didn't believe it came from a credible source."

"Who is her source?" Sylvia was barely able to control her anger.

"She's not volunteering that information."

"Why the hell can't you order her to hand it over? If she refuses, charge her with obstruction of justice."

"As it stands, she could already cause trouble for the feds," Sweetheart said.

Hoopai shook his head. "You're forgetting: legally she's not guilty of anything."

Dexter said, "She's offering to cooperate."

It was Sweetheart who filled in the blank. "She wants something in return."

Sylvia stared at the three men. "She wants *me*."

"God damn it, no one can force you to do this, Sylvia." It was twenty minutes later and Matt was glaring at Sweetheart.

The two men had placed themselves on opposite sides of the hospital bed, but even that was too close for comfort. Matt was pumped and adrenalized, Sweetheart guarded, ready to defend himself if it came to that.

Sylvia closed the travel bag. "Matt, it's okay," she said, trying to reach him through his protective rage. *I need you and I'm okay. Both at the same time. Do you hear me, babe?*

He broke eye contact with Sweetheart, took another step toward Sylvia, and reached for her hand. She breathed a sigh of relief. There would be no fistfight, no brawl in the isolation ward of the hospital. His fingers twined through her own, and she gripped his just as hard as she could.

She heard Sweetheart saying, "The doctors are releasing you in the next hour—with conditions. We have to monitor you, make sure nothing new turns up—"

She cut Sweetheart off: "I need time alone with Matt."

He nodded but telegraphed impatience as he left the room. His footsteps echoed down the hall, then the door hissed shut.

Matt sat on the bed, visibly struggling to recover his composure. Sylvia caught the transitory emotions on his face—fear, rage, desolation. She felt a rush of anxiety. She was losing him.

Bad moment.

Perhaps Matt sensed her struggle, because when she opened her eyes again, he'd regained control. He smiled—not a perfect imitation but a decent one—and said, "You're right, it's okay. *We're okay.*"

She nodded, grateful that he put her needs before his own, right here, right now. She wasn't sure how much strength she possessed. "Let's talk about it rationally," she said in a voice that didn't sound rational to her own ears.

Matt nodded. But he sat mute, looking so obviously distressed she almost smiled. Finally he said, "You first."

"Let's break it down into basics," she said carefully. "What exactly are they asking me to do?"

"They want you to work with this woman—this psycho—after she tried to kill you. They want you to interact with Palmer, they want you to kiss her ass if need be, until they get what they're after."

Matt made a visible effort to defuse himself. He let out the air he'd trapped in his lungs. "I don't want you in the same city as Palmer, much less the same room. She's sick. She's cold-blooded. She'll try again until she gets it right." He shook his head, and his voice was low and hard. "For what she did to you, I'll kill her myself."

Sylvia nodded, even found enough air to speak. "Nobody can force me to work with her—with Palmer. I need to know what's inside me. The doctors don't know. But Christine Palmer does. She chose it. She administered it. And then she waited to watch me die."

She shook her head, blinking back tears. "What if this poison never leaves my body? What if it's part of my DNA? Some toxins do that. They lie dormant until—until they're passed on to your children—"

She couldn't finish. The worst question had to be asked. "Can you forgive me?" she finally whispered. "I lied to you. And now we may never have the chance . . ."

"Hush." Matt brushed his fingers against her cheek. "There's nothing to forgive. I love you."

When they were ready, Sylvia asked to see Sweetheart. Alone.

He entered the room a minute later. She said, "Before I go any further, I need answers."

"When you came to my house, you said you were filling in missing pieces. You told me about the umbrella project that included LANL, Porton Down, the Dutch labs. You told me it was funded by the private sector and by various governments. There were military applications."

Sweetheart nodded slowly.

"What does the military want to gain from the research?"

He looked at her; his eyebrows arching slightly. "It's a dangerous game to play—in order to develop defenses against a weapon, you must first *possess* that weapon."

"Go on."

"When you have a comprehensive, interwoven umbrella project such as this one, you are incorporating a half-dozen projects at various research facilities. These projects will be supported by central administrative and clinical oversight; and the culture, bioassay, and production of toxin will guarantee available product for the research. Now that product—in this case, specific neurotoxins—will find its way from lab to lab."

"And the researchers will move from lab to lab as well."

"Yes."

"And spies—anyone interested in selling the toxins or the manufacturing processes—will move without suspicion." She stared at him, realizing her suspicions had been justified. "You didn't go after a serial poisoner, you were chasing a spy. How long?"

"Over four years ago I became aware that a mole was buried deeper than Aldrich Ames. When Robert Hanssen surfaced, we thought we'd caught our man. We weren't that lucky. The spy was still out there."

"Christine Palmer?"

"I had reasons to believe Palmer might be the mole; there was a pattern when it came to the information that was passed. It centered around Palmer's projects."

"A black market in bioweapons."

Sweetheart nodded. "The buyers are remarkably consistent: independent terrorist groups and the same hungry governments—Iraq, Iran, Libya, North Korea, China, India . . ."

"A small, incestuous world," Sylvia whispered. "Let me get this straight—my brain isn't working too well. A serial poisoner working on top-secret projects, with highly sensitive and lethal neurotoxins, is also spying for enemy governments—"

"No."

"Somebody else was stealing the toxins." She nodded once, slowly. "Samantha Grayson and Doug Thomas." Another lightbulb went off. "Christine Palmer murdered them both. She murdered spies."

"The meeting is set for three this afternoon, which gives us two hours. Tit for tat. Palmer will trade information for information—" Sweetheart bit off his words as a nurse entered the room.

Sylvia waited while the nurse pumped the final gusts of air into the blood pressure cuff. The last time she'd have to go through this, at least for awhile. It was all part of the process of getting discharged.

The good news: her vital signs had stabilized, for the most part. The bad news: the symptoms were chronic, ephermeral, durable. No telling how long they'd continue to manifest—weeks, months, years? *Yes, no, maybe.*

She sighed. The nurse released the cuff and said, "You're almost out, honey. Be patient."

As soon as the woman left the room, Sylvia confronted Sweetheart. "Let's get the parameters straight. First, my foster daughter gets protection. She's out of the picture completely; she'll stay with her father. If Palmer makes even a passing reference to Serena, the bet is off, I won't play."

"Understood." Sweetheart nodded.

"Second, the investigation into how she administered the poison is ongoing—ditto *what* toxin she used. I want answers. That's the only reason I'm doing this."

Another nod.

"At every meeting I want her searched—for hypos, aerosols, implements, *anything* even remotely out of the ordinary."

"That's a given."

"At no time will I be left alone with her. I won't do that, so don't expect me to."

"Right. But know that the FBI's presence will be kept to a minimum. This isn't an official investigation, Sylvia. It can't be. For the sake of security, all meetings have to be covert. We can't have a battalion of federal agents—"

"I understand."

Sweetheart's gaze swept her face. He was assessing, measuring, gauging her emotional and mental reserves, praying she had enough of both. He was also watching her like a hawk for any appearance of symptoms—he couldn't know if she was functional enough to do the job. "You know what she wants from you . . ."

"What else? She wants the dirty details. She's just dying to know why her poison didn't work. She wants to know why the hell I'm still alive."

Edmond Sweetheart was standing in the concrete heart of Albuquerque outside the University Hospital. All around him, white buildings reflected sun beneath a sky so blue it hurt his eyes. He thought about a man he'd been pursuing for years. A mole in place for more than a decade; a spy whose handlers were most probably the Chinese. A man who continued to slip through his fingers.

Sweetheart stared down at the LED letters scrolling across the tiny green face of the Palm unit. This was the answer to his question asked minutes earlier: *What information are you picking up, Toshiyori?*

The response came over a scrambled signal from the other side of the country:

—word out that someone has a product, is looking for a buyer, deep pockets— the usual suspects are interested—the Iraqis look good—a minor disturbance at the Chinese embassy a few days ago—which makes us think it's their mole— possible exchange in Mexico—

The final news caught Sweetheart off guard: —might be a criss-cross, Rikishi—

Sweetheart was impressed with the idea that the mole might be out to double-cross his longtime Chinese handlers.

Paul Lang and Dr. Harris Cray had superseded Dr. Christine Palmer as his leading suspects. It fit neatly: Cray as lab contact replacing Grayson and Thomas—and both Cray and Lang connected via Palmer. She was still the best conduit to his prey.

One question remained unchanged: *What was the cost to Sylvia?*

As Sweetheart began to walk toward the silver Mercedes, a dust devil spun out of nowhere. The miniature tornado caught leaves, dirt, trash in its funnel. It picked up speed, heading directly into his path. He closed his eyes and braced for impact. For an instant he felt as though his feet were leaving the ground.

Paul Lang drove the barrio streets slowly. His schedule had been pushed back because the feds were busy looking for him everywhere. They'd just missed him at the motel in Española, and again at the motel on the Santa Fe's south side. He'd had to keep moving every night. There would have been no way to get to Palmer even if he'd wanted—first they'd taken her into custody, then she was staying with friends, and all the time the feds were hanging around.

None of that bothered Lang. His plan was still in place.

He was going to offer them a trade . . .

He turned the corner, following the map in his head. The mud houses made him nervous. He found them ugly, primitive. The arid atmosphere guaranteed an almost constant headache and he kept his sunglasses on until the sun disappeared behind the mountains. He reassured himself that his mission was almost completed.

He counted street numbers, irritated by the lack of ordinal progression. The streets, the houses, the entire town seemed to have been put together without an iota of planning or intelligence. London was bad enough, but this place was hellish.

Finally, after he'd circled blocks again and again, he saw the faded white numbers painted on a mailbox. He kept on driving until he was halfway down the street. He parked, locked his car (aware of three young men loitering by a dilapidated building), and carried his briefcase with him. Normally he would've left the briefcase in the car. But circumstances weren't normal—the young delinquents made him nervous, and the contents of the briefcase were . . . volatile.

As he walked up the driveway of the house, he heard the distant, high-pitched cries of children at play. He looked around, searching for the source of the noise, just as he heard a voice in his ear.

"*Orale, 'mano.* Let's go inside, take a load off."

Paul Lang turned slowly around to find himself staring into a face that was chiseled, weathered, and pockmarked. He said, "I'm looking for—"

But he stopped speaking when he felt the nose of the gun pressed into his belly. The man reached for the briefcase, but Lang jerked it away without considering the possible consequences. "If you don't mind, I'll keep it for now," he finally whispered.

The man stared at him, then nodded. "Whatever, *chinga. Andale.*"

Although Lang spoke little Spanish, he knew he'd been given the order to move. He nodded quickly, signaling that he understood and would comply with orders—at least for now. He began to walk with the man toward the house.

redrider: it's happening / too late to back out

alchemist: do you know what to do?

redrider: yes

alchemist: *no!* new plan / look in the usual drop

Ninety minutes after Sylvia was officially discharged from the Albuquerque hospital, the meeting took place in the safest location she could think of—not the U.S. marshal's office, not in a maximum security cell, not in a bunker. Instead, she chose the middle of Santa Fe's Canyon Road Park, where Frisbee champs, dog lovers, and tai chi practitioners were out in full force.

Christine Palmer was waiting at a small picnic table in the shade of two cottonwoods in the northwest corner of the park. Special Agent Simmons was seated next to Palmer. S.A. Darrel Hoopai stood nearby. Twenty-five feet away, the sluggish and paltry Santa Fe River bordered the grassy turf and Alameda Street.

Sylvia noted these details from the security of the Ford as Matt approached the park's entrance on Alameda. He turned in, slowing, then braking to a stop.

"You don't have to do this," he said quietly.

She reached across the seat to place her hand over his. She felt the reassuring warmth of his skin; her own fingers were unnaturally cold, her hands almost numb. The constant sense of floating, of detachment, made it difficult to stay present. She hadn't told him about the moments of total darkness—waking moments—when the paralysis seemed to return, leaving her body frozen and helpless.

She said nothing now.

They shared the silence of the car's interior for a moment before she opened the door and stepped out into soft, clear air. They'd already agreed he would wait for her, but he said it again, to remind her of his vigilance. Just before she shut the door, he said, "I won't take my eyes off you."

The desert sky was cloud-washed; the sun broke through, disappeared, reappeared. A constant dance of light and shadow.

Sylvia left the parking lot and began to cross the open grass. From this distance, Palmer and the feds were anonymous figures; while they didn't look particularly casual, they weren't definable, not yet. It was possible to imagine they were a group of business associates—acquaintances, not friends—waiting for the food to arrive, the picnic to begin.

A yellow Frisbee spun past her ear; she could hear the wiry buzz of object moving through atmosphere. Someone called out to their child or their dog: "Rudy!"

The fall air was probably scented with the bite of piñon wood smoke—she couldn't tell because she hadn't recovered her senses of taste and smell.

When she was a hundred feet from Palmer and the agents, she stumbled, then caught herself. Continuing on. Narrowing her focus. Too late now—there was no way to pretend these were normal people on a normal Saturday afternoon. Life and death. Biotoxins. Spies. Serial poisoning.

It was all too damn bizarre.

· · ·

Sylvia sat at one end of the table, keeping her distance from everyone, not just Palmer. Special Agent Simmons offered a barrier between the two women. Hoopai stood roughly ten feet from the table, marking a perimeter.

"The body search has been completed," Simmons said.

Sylvia nodded.

"Are you comfortable with this arrangement?"

"No—but it will do."

Palmer looked thinner, edgier than when they'd met at the Tesuque Market. How long ago—not even two weeks? It seemed like a lifetime, almost had been a lifetime. She was thankful to be alive. Which brought her back to the point: the meeting between victim and perpetrator. An exchange of data. Details on what it was like to die—almost fucking die—in trade for information on a spy, a traitor.

Sylvia caught sight of herself in Palmer's round, white-rimmed sunglasses. She saw an angular face, dark hair pulled back into a braid, high cheekbones too defined, the face of a woman who had been recently ill, the face of someone who had not yet recovered.

The image vanished abruptly when Christine Palmer reached up one slender hand, wrist linked with delicate gold filligree, and removed her sunglasses. She set them down on the picnic table. Her eyes glittered. Her gaze was speculative, intensely focused.

"Dr. Strange, thank you for coming," Palmer said. "I hope this meeting isn't too much for you. I know you're just out of the hospital. But there is a temporal issue—for the FBI as well as for you."

A round, dusty leaf fell from its branch, spiraling down to settle on the middle of the table, where it was quickly blown into the air again by a sharp gust of wind.

The dance of the leaf on the air, the minute lesson in physics, gave Sylvia what she needed—a moment to gather herself, to move away from a position that was largely defensive.

She nodded coolly at Palmer. Her hands, which had been tightly clasped together, relaxed. "You're right, there is a *temporal* issue."

"I imagine you feel rather fortunate," Palmer said. "From what I've heard, you suffered through an ordeal."

"An ordeal cau—caused—by the poison you put in my body."

"I'm guessing you were exposed to a neurotoxin." Palmer shrugged, apparently puzzled. "Without more information, I can't—"

"Which neurotoxin?"

"I really can't say."

"You can if we agree that it came from your lab."

"If that were the case, we would still have to narrow it down." Palmer paused. "Off the top of my head, I can think of at least a dozen possible toxins."

"Take a wild guess," Sylvia said. A rigidity of voice, a stiffening of muscle telegraphed a shift in intensity. Both agents changed stance. Special Agent Simmons was prepared to intervene.

"Even for a wild guess, I'll need more information," Palmer said. A faint smile lifted the corners of her lips. "I'm a scientist, not a psychic."

She turned toward the river, and Sylvia followed her lead to see Edmond Sweetheart crossing the sluggish flow, creating a path over the largest stones.

He moved easily, keeping his loafers dry, dressed in dark slacks and a sweater the color of lemons.

Palmer watched his approach, her gaze keen, her attitude expectant.

Sweetheart focused on Sylvia, taking the seat next to her when he reached the table. Without thinking, she took his hand. She was grateful for his presence. The world shifted, righted itself again. She felt his fingers tighten around hers, and then he let go. For the first time since his arrival, he looked directly at Christine Palmer.

Her eyes met his. "Hello, Edmond." She turned her cold gaze on

Sylvia, but she was still addressing Sweetheart. "It's been a long time, my friend."

No one said a word. Sounds echoed across the park—dogs barking, a child calling. The world disappeared in shadow, then slowly returned to light. Sylvia stood and stepped away from the table. She wasn't going anywhere but *away*—from danger, from lies, from betrayal. She moved toward the river. She'd covered fifteen feet when she sensed Sweetheart at her back.

He said her name and she stopped.

"Why?"

"Please understand—"

"I do understand. You can't exist without lies. You're incapable of the truth. Where did you meet her?"

"Japan." Sweetheart shook his head, a gesture meant to dismiss either the encounter or his omission. "Three years ago, the Masuma Hayashi case."

"She must have made quite an impression."

"We were in the same place at the same time for a total of seventy-two hours."

She stared at him, silent, unblinking.

"It was a circus," he said. "Everyone was there, swarming over this little Japanese suburb. End of story."

"End of story? You betrayed me, Sweetheart. You left me out in the cold. You made me vulnerable to her poison."

"You're just in time for the ground rules," Christine Palmer said when they were seated again. "It's very simple. The success of this endeavor depends upon a smooth and mutual flow of information." She slid her gaze from Sweetheart to Sylvia. "Is that understood?"

"Yes."

"Good." Palmer took a breath. "You're missing crucial data from a hard drive, and physical product as well. Then there's the matter of the MI-6 analyst and my colleague Dr. Harris Cray. I believe I can help you recover what you seek."

She slid white-rimmed sunglasses over her blue-smoke eyes. The delicate bracelets glistened on her wrist. "If your intelligence sources tell you the product has not yet changed hands, I believe they're correct."

"How do you know?" Sweetheart asked sharply.

"At the moment I can't give you any more information."

"How can you expect us to take you seriously if you won't volunteer some indication of your sources?" Sweetheart's body contracted slightly when Palmer stood, apparently signaling the end of the meeting. "You talked about the flow of information, Christine."

"The *mutual* flow," Palmer snapped.

"You're not leaving," Sylvia said, rising to her feet just as the federal agents stepped forward. "Tell me why I'm still sick." She followed Palmer, her voice low and harsh. "How was I poisoned?"

Palmer held out both hands, palms raised protectively. For thirty seconds the women stood no more than six feet apart. No one else moved until Christine lowered her hands and said, "It's possible the acute symptoms you experienced were not synchronized with the preliminary dosage."

"What the hell does that mean?"

"The onset of acute symptoms may have been stimulated by the last dose, not the *first* dose." Palmer spoke carefully, as if addressing a difficult child. "There's a very good chance you were exposed to the neurotoxin over a period of time—hours, days—in contrast to one episode of acute exposure."

Sylvia stood mute, trying to understand what Palmer had just told her. She barely heard the woman's next words.

"I'm sorry, Dr. Strange," Palmer said. "I'm sure it can't be easy for you." She began walking backward away from the group, and Special Agent Simmons followed in her wake.

"*Christine.*" Sweetheart called to her, warning. "Give us something to work with."

Palmer slowed. "There's an issue to settle before this meeting can resume. I requested copies of your medical transcripts from the hospital, Dr. Strange. The request was refused. I informed them that you would be calling to have copies delivered to me by five o'clock this afternoon. That gives you roughly forty-five minutes to meet my request."

Sylvia stared at Palmer. This whole thing was a violation.

"I understand your dilemma," Palmer said, turning to walk away. "But I think you'll reconsider when I remind you that time is an issue where your long-term prognosis is concerned. I need to review your records *immediately*, Dr. Strange."

Sylvia took a deep breath. *You are a piece of work.*

But she said, "Yes."

At 4:30 P.M., on a narrow street fronting the river on Santa Fe's west side, a child strayed into the yard of a large ramshackle adobe. It was the child's fifth birthday, and his classmates at the day care center had celebrated with cupcakes and songs and games. One of his presents was the kickball that he now pursued down the slope to the front door of the adobe.

The door stood open, moving slightly in the breeze, and with each back and forth, the faint squeak of hinges sounded like the mewing of kittens or the chirping of birds. The boy picked up his ball, clutching it in both hands, and then he stepped closer to see inside. The man on the floor was sleeping. But when the boy stood on tiptoe, craning his neck, he smelled the stench of sickness and he saw a dark stain on the ground.

The boy backed slowly away. He had been warned to stay away from this house. He might be scolded or even spanked if he confessed his sin. It was best if he kept the secret to himself. The sick man was probably drunk—the boy had seen drunk men in the parks and even on his own street. His mother had told him to leave the drunk men alone, not to talk to them, never to go near them.

The boy made up his mind. As he climbed the embankment to return to the yard of the day care center, he decided would tell no one what he'd found.

At twenty minutes past five, Sylvia and Sweetheart were seated once again at the park table when Christine Palmer returned with Special Agent Simmons.

Impending darkness and rain (a slow, lazy drizzle that spit minimal moisture down to earth) had driven all but the most determined visitors from the park.

Two dogs ran loose. A man sat by himself at the crest of a small rise, lotus position, probably in meditation. A glistening raven danced from the lid of one trash can to the next, obviously enjoying itself.

Sylvia had her backup: Sweetheart and S.A. Hoopai—and Matt, who'd spent the break with her.

Palmer held up a thin file. "Your records arrived by fax twenty minutes ago. You're been having fever spikes, memory lapses, blackouts."

Sylvia said nothing as Palmer produced a small pill bottle from the pocket of her orange sweater. She set the bottle on the table. "These should help—but there's a window of effectiveness."

Sylvia stared at the bottle, at the shadowy pills inside.

"A distillation of herbs," Palmer said. "Not an antidote but a detoxing remedy used by the indigenous people of Indonesia in response to ciguatera poisoning—another neurotoxin. They're potent. I spent two months analyzing the chemical content." She paused. "You can have a lab run an analysis, but I'd suggest you not wait more than twenty-four hours."

Sylvia picked up the bottle before Sweetheart could stop her. She opened it, tipping it so that several pearl-shaped pills spilled onto her palm.

"One pill, three times a day," Palmer said. "The only possible side effect would be slight feelings of anxiety and dry mouth, much like you might expect from a decongestant."

Sylvia selected one pill. She held it up in the rain and said, "Let's get this straight—you poisoned me. I know it, you know it."

Palmer extended one hand, and Sylvia dropped the pill into the woman's palm.

"In the wake of neurotoxic exposure, paranoia is a common symptom," Palmer said calmly, swallowing the pill. "You should be aware of that, but you shouldn't be ashamed if it's difficult to regain your confidence in your own perceptions. Give it time."

Sylvia pushed herself from the table. "No. Leave me alone."

She strode twenty paces, stopped, and took a deep breath. Sky, clouds, rain—all held a hallucinatory edge, as if another, deeper level of the material world had become visible. The sensation was acute, extraordinary, but not frightening. In the past few days she'd had other moments such as this. *A new level of perception.*

Sweetheart was watching her, she could feel his eyes. And Matt—he was sitting a hundred yards away, in his vehicle, and yet his thoughts seemed tangible. She felt his love, knew he was with her. She looked up, saw the raven in flight, heard the sharp cut of wings through air, *heard the message.*

When she took her seat again, she was prepared for whatever came.

Palmer wasted no time. "When did you feel the first acute symptoms?"

"The day of your arrest."

"What happened?"

"I'd had a headache the night before, then all day. Gradually, I became disoriented. I was confused. Sensitive to light."

"Did you feel any change in motor response?"

As Palmer pursued the questions, Sylvia contained her feelings of violation; they were valid, they were real, but they wouldn't serve her in this situation. She needed information. She simply responded yes or no when offered a closed-ended question; but usually Palmer asked open-ended questions that demanded consideration, assessment, evaluation. After about twenty minutes, Palmer changed tack.

"At some point you were physically blind, Dr. Strange."

"Yes."

"You lost your sense of identity, your sense of self."

"Yes."

"You reached a point where the experience was so terrifying, so excruciating—" Palmer stopped.

"So excruciating there was no possible course but surrender," Sylvia finished. "I died. My system shut down. My lungs refused to expand. My heart stopped. The light went out in my mind."

"And?" Palmer's breath had quickened.

This is her orgasm, Sylvia thought, *this is how she gets off.* Even now Palmer exuded a primal energy that was magnetic and horrific at the same time.

"And there was nothing," Sylvia whispered. "I ceased to exist."

Palmer, obviously expecting more, looked disappointed.

"Why did I pose a threat, Dr. Palmer?"

"You're asking me to speculate about something I'm not party to, but I would assume there was an issue of trust." Palmer looked uncomfortable. "Perhaps even a misreading."

"You're saying I was poisoned by *mistake?*"

"I said it was speculation. Perhaps you represented a false threat."

"The poisoner miscalculated?"

"That's not what I said."

"Then I'm confused. What are you saying?"

"I don't make *mistakes.*"

"*You* don't make mistakes."

Palmer sat rigid for several seconds before she said, "This is a waste of time. We're playing speculative games. I can't speak for your attacker."

"I see. I didn't think it was a waste of time. I found it interesting." Sylvia tipped her head, considering her next move. "A minute ago you asked what happened at the point of surrender. I said I ceased to exist—which I did. Except I was completely conscious, hyperaware. I was watching myself. And I experienced a wave of sense memory, a triggering, that can only be described as *phenomenal.*"

"You felt no pain, no neural sensations?" Christine asked, excitement flushing her cheeks. "You were paralyzed—"

"Enough," Sweetheart cut in. "You've had your go, Christine. That's enough. You have information. Use it and help this investigation."

"Edmond." Palmer raised her eyebrows. "You're not in the sumo ring, so stop behaving like a *kohai.*"

When he offered no opposition, *no fight,* she nodded, apparently satisfied. "I'm perfectly willing to change topics and discuss my *innamorato.*"

"Your *what?*" Sylvia asked.

"My *fan.*"

.   .   .

"He sent me the first e-mail after Dr. Thomas died." Palmer dipped her head, smoothing one hand across her slender neck. "Since then he's been remarkably faithful. In all, I'd say there are roughly a dozen communications."

"Certainly you reported the fact that someone was writing to you," Sweetheart pressed.

"No."

"According to policy and procedure at any secure facility—"

"I *ignored* policy and procedure. Spank me, I've been bad." Palmer stared hard at Sweetheart—seconds passed. She took a slow breath and spoke softly: "I've had stalkers, death threats, marriage proposals, other fanatics who wrote to me. It can happen to anyone who publishes, especially when the area of research is controversial."

"Did you try to track him down?" Sweetheart asked.

"I did some probing." Palmer paused. "I've worked before with an agency that specializes in computer security—but he uses Internet cafés, aliases, false log-ons, always covering his trail. The investigator said he was very skilled." She shrugged. "At first I was vaguely intrigued. I wondered if it was someone I knew." Her eyes had been focused on the bracelet she was fingering, but now she gazed up into Sweetheart's face. "I wondered if it was someone who knew me. He said he did. I had the feeling we'd met before. Perhaps we'd even . . ." Her voice faded. She shrugged. "Ultimately, he began to bore me. I am his Alchemist. He believes I can transform his life," she said, smiling maliciously, "and make gold from shit metal."

"What did you say to him when you wrote back?" Sweetheart asked.

"I played him along."

"How?"

"The usual way—I'm sure *you've* had occasion to play someone along, Edmond."

Sweetheart inclined his body toward hers. "What makes you believe it's Paul Lang?"

"Paul Lang, Harris Cray, I don't know who it is," Palmer answered. "That's your job—with your *psycholinguistic talent show,* where you compare signatures, a dotted *i,* a curly *y.*"

"For the moment let's assume it's Lang," Sweetheart snapped. "How do you get from fan letters to a stolen hard drive?"

"He told me he had access to the alkahest—the power of transmutation. When things started to unravel, I took a best guess he was after the manufacturing formula." She raised her eyebrows, aware of the effect she'd caused. "Keep in mind, he's a *cryptic* fellow—not unlike you, Edmond."

"When did you receive the most recent message?"

"The day I was released from custody, a message was waiting." She widened her eyes. "He warned me to be careful. You can see for yourselves—I've kept a file on my computer, at my house."

Sylvia felt the world begin to shimmer, and she spoke from a distance. "He warned you about me, didn't he, Christine? He sicced you on my trail."

Was it possible Christine Palmer hadn't poisoned her? What if Palmer had colluded with this spy, this thief, allowing him to do her dirty work?

She saw them staring at her, saw their confusion. She ignored it, focusing on Palmer. "Did he tell you I was a target? Did *he* poison me?"

She saw Sweetheart try to catch her attention, and she heard Palmer's husky voice: "You're not making sense, Sylvia."

Then the world shifted on its axis.

Palmer spoke calmly, clearly, loud enough for all to hear. "I poisoned you, Dr. Strange. Do you think I'd trust someone else to do my dirty work?"

Sylvia reached out for Sweetheart's arm. "Did you hear her?"

But he kept his back to her, walking ahead—he didn't turn.

. . .

Christine Palmer lived in a two-story white-shingled alpine-style home. It occupied a cul-de-sac, backed by a private forest of forty-foot pines that had been spared by the Cerro Grande fire.

Palmer led the way up five steps to the landing, through a door-way encased by plate glass windows, and into a hallway and living room. Sylvia followed, trailed by Sweetheart.

When Palmer had refused to let anyone else inside her house, Sylvia convinced Matt to wait with S.A. Hoopai in the FBI's van. After an initial stalemate, he'd agreed. Special Agent Simmons had remained behind in Santa Fe to follow up a possible tip on Paul Lang's whereabouts.

It was going to be a very long night.

"Dr. Strange can stretch out on the couch," Palmer said, tossing her jacket over a white leather armchair. She disappeared into the adjoining kitchen. The faint sounds of cupboard doors opening and closing and the chink of glassware were audible.

"I don't need to lie down," Sylvia said just as Palmer reappeared. She waved away the offer of a glass of water and a cool towel. "I don't need anything." She closed her eyes, welcoming the blackness.

Palmer watched her closely, then turned to Sweetheart. "Make yourselves at home. There's a guest bathroom next to my study. I'll take a few minutes to freshen up."

Sylvia opened her eyes to see Palmer disappearing down the hall.

The living room was spacious, low-beamed, shades of eggshell, alabaster, ivory. Both the back and front walls were plate glass, offer-ing respective views of pine trees and street, now shrouded in dark-ness. One interior wall opened into Palmer's study.

"People who live in glass houses," Sylvia said softly. "Imagine the show she put on for the surveillance teams."

Sweetheart was examining shelves of books. "Biographies," he said. "Carl Jung, Marcel Duchamp, Wassily Kandinsky."

Sylvia moved to his side. Glancing over his shoulder, she noticed titles: *The New Mysticism, The Transcendent in Art, Sacred Geometry.*

But Sweetheart was reading a dedication in another book—an elegantly bound collection of medieval poetry: *For Christine, undefinable, unforgettable, untouchable. Always, Fielding.*

"Her father," Sylvia said.

"It's a cruel inscription."

"Sweetheart . . ." She turned away from him to stare out the window at the shadowy world. Her senses felt sharp as glass. "I'm going to fill in the blanks. You met Palmer in Japan, just like you admitted, but it wasn't by chance. The encounter was intentional, it was part of your investigation." She raised her eyes to meet his. "How am I doing?"

Sweetheart's face was impassive. "I looked for the opportunity to spend time with Palmer."

Sylvia let the seconds pass, then spoke in a voice that was too calm, too controlled. "What you couldn't expect was the way she would attract you. You became lovers. How many days did you have together?"

"Three."

"Only three days. But when it ended, when you went your separate ways, you couldn't get her out of your mind."

Sylvia couldn't meet his eyes; anger made her throat ache. "Why the hell did you accept the profiling job?"

"I know her as well as anyone. I have an advantage."

"That's pathetic. You're pathetic." She moved past him, then stopped, whispering the words. "She's a killer. That's all you need to know."

Alchemist

You touched me with your poison—the beginning of transmutation.

You created the monster—the government released it from its cage.

I watched you—invisible—knowing you're so much more than they give you credit for.

You know me through word / thought / action.

I hold the alkahest.

My gift? I'll wait until you are ready.

Sylvia looked up from the printed page. "Who chose your screen name?"

"I did," Palmer said. She'd positioned herself across the room near French doors that opened onto the rear deck. "I've always been interested in the early alchemical texts. I've used that, how do you say, that *handle*. I've used it off and on for years."

"He didn't just write you a fan letter," Sweetheart said. "That's a letter of *commitment*."

Palmer didn't blink. A white paper lamp provided backlight; beyond the wall of windows night had fallen, and the starless sky blanketed the shoulders of slender, shadowed pines. She'd changed clothes and was wearing a pale, soft-woven caftan that fell in folds around her bare feet; her hair was loose around her shoulders; she stood out like gold thread against black velvet. "A dark commitment, then," she said softly.

Sylvia watched them from the couch; a place she'd monopolized off and on for the past hour. Sweetheart—blue-black hair pulled into a braid, exotic eyes now outlined by exhaustion, slash of cheekbones, wrestler's body. He looked like a refugee from another world, another time. Palmer's beauty had a frozen quality that made Sylvia think of the inscription they'd just read.

"A penny for your thoughts, Dr. Strange."

Sylvia blinked up at Palmer. She pictured a golden child raised without a mother, a father's daughter. She could see a basic resemblance to Fielding Palmer, could imagine an almost perfect childhood, a close relationship into adulthood. But the pictures stopped cold when she reached the moment when Christine administered poison into her father's body.

"I was thinking about attachments," Sylvia began. Abruptly she stood, shrugging off the vision, her inertia. "I was thinking about the implications of your fan's reference to the alkahest—the alchemical elixir. Does he mean the missing toxin? Or is he referring to something much more ephemeral?"

"Love?" Palmer said the word quickly, as if it stung.

"Or as close as he can get to love. It's obsessional, possessive—it's also a threat." Sylvia crossed the room to sit in the chair next to Sweetheart. The images on the monitor blurred, only slowly returning to focus. She said, "The threat is implicit throughout the body of the communication."

Sweetheart took over, reciting the text: *"You know me through word / thought / action. I hold the alkahest . . . I'll wait until you are ready."*

For the past hour, he'd dominated Palmer's desk, computer, study; he was driving the keyboard, entering commands. "The fact that Paul Lang was born in the U.S. but educated in England blurs national syntactical and lexiconal distinctions," he said, barely lifting his eyes from the screen. "That makes it more difficult to eliminate or confirm him as the author of the communications."

Sylvia frowned. "How do we know he's not ten thousand miles away, making a deal with Iraq or Libya as we speak?"

"What's your gut instinct tell you?"

"He's still in the area."

Sylvia thought, *If the missing toxin is in Lang's possession, what does he plan to do with it? Would he use it as a bargaining tool? If so, does he want Palmer in return?*

Sweetheart grunted. A mind reader. "Our job is to figure out his agenda before it's too late."

And what about Harris Cray? A man obsessed—but was he infatuated with Christine Palmer or fixated on his own obscurity?

Again Sweetheart effortlessly picked up the unspoken thread. "Harris Cray has spent years living in America, he's worked all around the world."

"And now he's gone missing," Sylvia said.

"Definitely not a point in his favor." Sweetheart flipped screens, cutting between several communications. "The subject's parsimonious loyalty to the alchemy-alkahest theme represents threat . . . analyses concept categories of potency, destruction, order. Under the interpersonal processes we see a system of hostile personal reference." Sweetheart expelled air through tight lips.

"When do we hear back from Luke?" Sylvia asked.

"Not soon enough." Thirty minutes earlier, Sweetheart had arranged live feed to his own office in Los Angeles. MI-6 in London had agreed to transmit samples of Paul Lang's written communications for linguistic comparison, and Luke was working the computers at that end, already running hastily gathered samples of Dr. Harris Cray's papers and memos through MOSAIK.

The problem: MOSAIK had spit out their feed with editorial criticism—*insufficient data for valid content analysis for personality inference.*

But that didn't stop *human* analysis from continuing in the meantime.

Sweetheart glanced at Palmer as she approached. He said, "We *can* run this content through a representative corpus, a threat dictionary, but the gross analyses—"

He broke off when Christine Palmer placed her hand on his arm, their first physical contact all day.

She said, "Let Dr. Strange have a go." She turned and walked away, widening the space between them again.

Sweetheart looked up, caught Sylvia's eye, waiting for her signal.

For a fraction of a second she balked; then she gave her answer. She took Sweetheart's place in front of the monitor. She studied the communications silently, splitting screens to pull up and highlight earlier sections. All the while she was attempting to compose herself. Her hands trembled, so she kept them moving.

"If we review multiple communications, issues come to light." She dove in. "Obsessive personality traits, control-related issues expressed in his use of lexicon, syntax, morphology, manipulated to reduce internal anxiety—his obsession with alchemy and the tie-in with your cyberhandle. His theme is transformation—this is a man who desperately feels the need to evolve, to *escape*." Her voice faded away. She'd been following Sweetheart's analysis, but now she felt herself floundering.

She tried again. "Taken as a whole, the letters communicate the tension between conflicting goals of possession and destruction."

"He loves me, he hates me?" Palmer suggested dryly.

"Something like that." Sylvia swallowed, keeping her eyes on the screen. "He's gotten darker, more fatalistic, with each communication. He has intimate knowledge of you—of your actions."

. . . I understand what you were made of—before heat and light—and I understand what you will become when you are ready to transform.

What a rare thing in this life to meet a kindred spirit. Do you understand what I am offering? Km.t. True partnership until the end.

The letters blurred, the lines merged. Sylvia blinked again. Her eyes lingered on the last line, and she asked, "'Km.t'?"

Palmer ran slender fingers through blond hair. "One theory for the origin of the word 'alchemy' is that it comes from the Egyptian word for Egypt, which is *khemet,* black land or black earth." She stretched her arms overhead, and the sleeves of her robe slid down, revealing toned muscles, golden-brown skin. "The hieroglyphics for *khemet*—"

"Are 'km.t,'" Sweetheart finished. "That simply tells us your pen pal knows how to use an encyclopedia."

"If we bring up the initial communication—" Sylvia typed a command, then stopped. "You said the first e-mail arrived the day after Dr. Thomas's death, correct?" Glancing at Palmer for clarification, she turned back to concentrate on the text that filled the screen:

I can read your mind . . .

There is always the hunger to understand:

—while poison courses through veins, is absorbed into organs, reaches the cells and synapses of the brain.

Where does it hurt the most? Are you shivering from heat, or cold? Is that flickering of your eyelids the first sign of the convulsions to follow? Is your mouth dry? Is your brain exploding with pain? Is your stomach tied into knots? Are your thoughts fractured? Are you going blind and deaf?

Do you know death is with you . . . do you know death is with you . . . do you know death is with you?

Are you afraid?

Sylvia pulled back in the chair, turning away from the words to refocus on Palmer. "Who is he talking about? Samantha Grayson? Doug Thomas? One of the others?"

"Who can keep track?" Palmer's smile was cool.

"You think this is funny?"

"Sarcasm is my way of dealing with an unpleasant topic," Palmer said carefully. "I'm sure, as a psychologist, you can understand that particular defense mechanism."

"I don't give a shit about your defense mechanisms," Sylvia said. She turned back to the screen as Christine Palmer stood and walked from the room.

"What will you win if you alienate her?" Sweetheart asked, studying Sylvia intently.

"It's too late to *win* anything," Sylvia said, angered by his interference. But most of all, silently enraged by his deliberate denial of Palmer's poisonous confession in the park. She'd been holding back her emotions, and now she pulled back internally again. "Don't ask me to stick to morphological structure."

"I'm asking you to maintain communication."

"Something you're so good at."

"Something I'm not good at—which is why I need you."

Abruptly Sylvia felt dizzy, and it took all her energy to stay where she was, to ride out the wave of vertigo. She tipped her head toward her knees, then straightened.

In time to see Palmer, a glass of red wine in each hand, pass by. She set one glass on the desk next to Sweetheart as she sipped from the other and crossed to the loveseat.

"I apologize for my rudeness, Dr. Strange," she said. "You asked a serious question. I didn't give you my full attention. But I will."

Sylvia found herself staring into Palmer's blue-gray eyes. Her mouth had gone dry, but she didn't break off contact as Palmer said, "I believe he was talking about my work on a particular project."

"Which project?"

"You won't find it on my résumé. It was classified. Military."

"What was the nature of the research?"

"We were experimenting on antidotes for biochemical agents that had been used—or might be used—in combat situations."

"Was the research successful?"

"The results were erratic," Palmer said. "The project was terminated."

"Why?"

"We can talk in circles all day, Dr. Strange."

"You said it was an antidote for a biochemical agent. How did you test your antidote?"

Images flashed through Sylvia's mind: the videotape she and Sweetheart had watched in a London hotel; a pathetic laboratory monkey with psychotic eyes; obscure words on a sheet of white paper.

"Project Alkahest." She stood slowly, letting her gaze shift to Sweetheart, then back to Palmer. Confirmation was written in Christine's face—in the eyes, the shape of the mouth, the delicately flared nostrils, the sharp pulse where throat met jaw.

Sylvia's mind made the leap. "My God . . . you experimented on human subjects. Who were they? Military? Were they soldiers? Who were your guinea pigs?"

Palmer opened her mouth, shook her head, then ran her tongue around her lips. "They were British. And they were American. A joint project." She pushed herself out of the love seat, moving restlessly now. "The alkahest was delivered with a dozen other injections. It's done all the time—the Gulf War, UN troops—it's routine. The assumption was made that it worked. Questions arose only later."

"What happened—" Sylvia broke off. Words evaporated and reformed. "I need to know about the *alkahest,*" she whispered.

"It's no doomsday weapon." Palmer began to pace a narrow path in the center of the room. "It's a neurotoxin, a class of biotoxin. Others on the market deliver much higher lethality. What makes it valuable is the manufacturing process. We've enhanced it, made it *desirable* because it's malleable. Dispersible through topical absorption, through ingestion, but at its best when it's aerosolized. In asymmetrical warfare, when biologicals are used, the issue is always dispersement. And destructive potential. Alkahest isn't intended to kill, although it certainly can. In the correct dosage it causes neurological damage, damage to the cortex—the symptoms may mimic those of encephalitis, severe psychosis."

Detached from the reality of suffering and death, Palmer was describing the strengths of a specially gifted offspring. She was delivering an impassioned lecture to the uninitiated. "It's advantageous in biowarfare to *maim*." Her breath quickened. "The resources of an enemy are taxed by caring for victims—the enemy is demoralized. The living are haunted by the deformed and dysfunctional more than by the dead. Insanity, paralysis, acute pain—these are difficult to ignore."

She turned now, retracing her steps. Her voice, her body had taken on new energy. She was almost smiling as she said, "The latest generation of the toxin has a very brief window of contagion. Inhaled, absorbed, it will remain in human cells, but it's unlikely to linger in the air. That's the beauty of this particular biological agent. It is selective, allowing a short window of acute toxicity, harming only the immediately exposed victims. Unless, of course, it is stabilized in some other form—in which case it remains potent until it is ingested." Palmer came to a standstill in front of the windows. She stared past her own reflection into darkness. The only sound was the gusting wind and the click of branches against the house.

Finally she seemed to hear a question and turned abruptly toward the others. "Do you actually believe there's some perfect line that divides the moral from the immoral in my world? Those rules don't apply. My world is *amoral*. This is science, the search for the holy grail, chemical, nuclear, biological in all its forms, ugly and beautiful. My work saves lives."

"Christine," Sweetheart warned. "That's enough."

But Sylvia, intent on Palmer, had already risen from the chair. "You stand here talking about saving lives. You tried to kill me—you even confessed to my face." She turned recklessly toward Sweetheart. "And you heard her. Back there, as we were leaving the park, she said she poisoned me—but you did *nothing*."

"What are you talking about?" Sweetheart was staring at Sylvia, and his eyes held fear. "Christine never confessed to poisoning you— not here, not in the park. What are you saying?"

"I heard her—you must have—you're lying again."

"Listen to me, Dr. Strange," Palmer said softly. "Hallucinations, delusions, are not atypical in this type of case."

"But I heard you."

"You imagined it, Sylvia." Sweetheart was walking toward her.

"Get her away from me," Sylvia whispered. *They were telling her the truth.* She stumbled toward the glass door, stepped out onto the deck, gripped the railing.

Sliding into a world she'd discovered through poison.

She turned her face to the sky.

Rain-slicked bark and needles. The plaintive cry of doves. Brittle wind.

The hiss of the sliding glass door.

She turned to see Palmer's face, cut in half by shadow, a Picasso, an abstract of eye, nose, mouth; lips pulled back to reveal a slick glimmer of teeth.

Saw Sweetheart standing just a few feet away behind glass.

He would do whatever she asked.

But she was ready to deal with Christine Palmer on her own.

"Dr. Strange, you need to go back inside."

"No."

"You're ill." Palmer's voice softened.

Sylvia stepped toward Palmer, studying each detail of the other woman's face, her physical presence, as if she might absorb understanding as easily as light through pupil; as if *insight* could be honed by cornea and lens to form a perfect retinal image; as if the nerve impulses zagging from retina to brain could produce anything more than superficial illusion.

"Alkahest," she whispered. "What you described—it's inside me, isn't it?"

Palmer took one step back, then another, as if she might avoid a precipice.

Sylvia moved with her. "Can I have children?"

Palmer stopped, reaching out with one hand.

Sylvia flinched and Palmer pulled back.

But Sylvia gripped Palmer's wrist. "Is the damage part of my DNA? Will I pass it on?"

Palmer came to life—ice breaking—freeing herself.

Sylvia stood in place. It seemed as if she'd gone numb, but when she examined her emotions, she realized she was *calm*. As if she'd stepped through some portal and was now standing on the other side, looking back at herself. "You made a mistake when you didn't kill me, Christine."

"It doesn't matter if you—"

Sylvia slapped Palmer's cheek. The sound of impact, of skin on skin, was sharp and loud.

For a long moment, Palmer didn't move. Then, slowly and with care, she touched her hand to her reddening jaw. "The answer is yes. Your DNA is damaged. Yes, you will pass it on."

She pushed past Sylvia, gliding down redwood steps to the soft wet mat of pine needles. She kept walking, her bare feet following a familiar path, her caftan billowing as she disappeared between the dark trees.

Sylvia followed. Into the darkness. The mist was beginning to turn to rain again. The wind had a bite, snapping at pine branches until the forest was a dark, undulating sea.

Sylvia made her way along a rough path. She moved quickly, her running shoes sliding over slick ground, then snagging on roots and rocks.

She spun around to see Palmer.

"Walk away, Dr. Strange." Palmer's hair was darkened by rain, the thin fabric of her robe soaked through. "Raw courage isn't enough to get you through this. Look at yourself. You're hearing things, imagining confessions. This was just a warning. It could be much worse."

The rain felt like hot ice on Sylvia's skin. She and Palmer were inches apart. Instead of stepping back, gaining distance, Sylvia moved closer. "Why did you come after me? What threat did I represent?"

"I thought you were the one with the answers." Palmer had raised her voice to be heard above a particularly strong gust of wind. "I thought it was your job to explain this mythical creature, this homicidal Dr. Palmer, to the FBI, to Edmond. Was I mistaken?"

"I have some of the answers," Sylvia said. "You poisoned your father and your lover. Mercy killings, that's what you told yourself, because their cancer was so horrible, their deaths so excruciating. I believe they asked—perhaps *pleaded*—for death. And you granted their wishes." Sylvia wrapped her arms tightly around herself, shivering as the cold cut through her sweater. "But at night, in the dark, you wonder if you killed for mercy or for pleasure."

Palmer had gone still. The world seemed to move around her, as if she exerted her own gravitational force. But Sylvia leaned closer to whisper in her ear: "I don't really give a shit *why* you're a sociopath. Narcissism, attachment disorders, abuse, a chemical imbalance—let's just chalk it up to some cocktail of pathology. But it must have been an incredible moment when you realized you held the power of death over life."

Somewhere close by, a feral cat gave a sharp cry. Sylvia pushed herself, riding a final wave of energy. "So you convinced yourself you were killing *bad* people. Cheats, spies out to steal national secrets. That was a true stroke of genius—you playing the *good* psychopath. Samantha Grayson deserved to die because she was a thief. So was Dr. Thomas."

"They were stealing *my* research," Palmer hissed abruptly. Her eyes gleamed, dark and dangerous. "They were selling *my* toxin for profit, they didn't care—"

"But you did?"

"Yes. *Always.* Even though I've never possessed my father's moral certainty." She shook her head, looking lost, physically smaller.

Sylvia saw it suddenly—Christine was sweating, breath quickening. Fighting fear. But she wasn't afraid of Sweetheart, she wasn't afraid of the FBI investigation; she still seemed untouchable, unreachable.

What would terrify her—

"You don't know how to maintain a simple relationship, and that scares the hell out of you. You don't know how to *connect*—not with friends, not with lovers, not with your own kin—except by killing." As she spoke, Sylvia looked into Palmer's eyes, and she saw nothing, just an emptiness that was breathtaking.

"Japan was different, wasn't it, Christine?" Sylvia asked. "You felt a connection—it actually hurt after he'd gone. And when you found out I knew Sweetheart, you saw me as a threat. But you were mistaken, he and I never—"

"You've got it all wrong, Dr. Strange. I don't love him, and I was never jealous of you. I said before, it was a mistake."

Sylvia's eyes went wide as the belated insight finished crawling down the neural pathways, no minuscule bolt of lightning; a slow dawn.

"You didn't poison me."

Christine Palmer faced her, not moving.

Finally Sylvia whispered, "*Lady Macbeth*. I know what you're afraid of. Yourself. Afraid that in the end, your guilt will drive you mad." She caught her breath. "I can't tell you you're safe."

Sharp sound of branches snapping.

Both women turned to see Sweetheart, his face all but obscured by darkness.

"Somebody tipped the feds," he said. "It looks like Lang found a buyer for the alkahest."

Dead men in a house in a Santa Fe barrio. A suspected biological agent on the premises. A request for help from Los Alamos National Lab.

Instantly Sweetheart, Palmer, and federal agents went into high gear, everyone praying that Paul Lang and the missing computer data were inside that barrio house.

Palmer disappeared for a few minutes to change clothes and collect what equipment she had on the premises. Sweetheart coordinated with the FBI agents to rendezvous in Santa Fe at the emergency site.

Sylvia was out of the picture—after exposure to the neurotoxin, her nervous system was hypersensitized. Even mild reexposure could cause a serious reaction.

Matt was waiting for her. But she had one last thing to do.

She stood by the doorway of Palmer's study, watching Sweetheart as he gathered the contents of his briefcase. He felt her presence and looked up.

She spoke first. "It's not over. Not until he gets what he wants. When you're face-to-face with your spy, be very careful. He's torn between destruction and possession. He needs her, needs to believe he can possess her. Don't stand in his way. If you try to stop him, he'll take you with him. You and a thousand innocent people."

"Why can't he leave her behind?"

"Don't you know?" She watched his face, the faintest contraction of the pupils, the barely perceptible tightening around the eyes, and she felt a stab of fear. For him. For the future. "The alchemist will bring him peace." She saw he didn't quite understand. "The alchemist will release him—she'll bring him death."

She turned, starting toward the door.

"Where are you going?"

"Home."

"Sylvia . . ."

"Don't let her blind you, Sweetheart. Your test has just begun. But you can't do it alone. You've got to trust Christine Palmer. *Trust her.* That's your only choice. That's *our* only way out of this."

She left him standing there, feeling his eyes traveling with her, knowing he was afraid she was hallucinating, delusional, out of her mind.

Was she?

She walked quickly toward Matt's dark blue Ford idling at the curb.

The anonymous call had come through emergency dispatch at 5:10 A.M.; it was routed to the Santa Fe Police Department: *Possible 10-53—man down.*

The responding police officers had recognized the address: a two-story adobe next to the Santa Fe River, the family residence of a known drug offender, a small-time meth dealer, currently doing jail time. One of the officers also remembered that the repeat felon had a grandmother, a mother, and three brothers all living at the residence. Another officer knew there was a cousin who'd done a stretch for pushing heroin and cooking meth.

After an initial assessment, they'd updated the call to a 10-54, a possible dead body, this one in a clandestine meth lab. Using extreme caution, they'd braved the rain and entered the scene at 6:07 A.M.

What they'd found: suspicious equipment, bottles (some empty, some filled with liquids), burners, rubber tubing, canning tubs; multiple dead bodies, male and female—victims' faces contorted, tongues blackened, foam and vomit caked at the corners of mouths.

It had been warm inside the building. Muggy and stifling with heaters at full blast. And quiet except for the buzz of flies. Crazed flies. Vibrating, circling, gorging on the end product of death.

First count, seven dead.

They didn't wait around to do a second count.

Outside the building in the drizzling rain, at 6:26 A.M., they radioed a request for the Santa Fe Fire Department's HazMat team to deal with possible hazardous materials—hazardous death.

The director of SFFD's HazMat team had twenty years of experience in the field; as soon as he heard the descriptions of the bodies, he knew this wasn't the usual gang-related deaths or a meth manufacturing accident. They were dealing with what the orange bible of Haz-Mat, the Department of Transportation's emergency response guide, classified as a highly toxic *unknown*—the stuff a lot of the guys simply dubbed "ethelbutylbadstuff."

For the next half-dozen hours, the team's mission would be summed up with the ancronym SIN: *S* for "scene safety"; *I* for "isolate and deny" (access and egress); *N* for "notify" (residents and—when appropriate—media).

HazMat officers were divided into two teams. The first would deal with the crime scene, the second with the kids from the day care center as well as the first police officers on the scene.

By 7:13 A.M. the order was issued to evacuate the neighborhood within a three-hundred-yard perimeter. Officers would evacuate downwind; the command center was located upwind. The hot zone (demanding maximum-level protective gear) included everything within 150 yards of the building; the warm zone (medium-level protective gear and precautions) included anything within 150 to three hundred yards of the building; beyond three hundred, street clothes were considered safe.

Meanwhile, the HazMat team was using chem-bio books from the U.S. Army's college in Georgia to make a judgment call on vector. From the obvious crime scene information, it looked like a fast-acting inhaled or ingested chemical or biological agent. From the symptoms, the first guess was an inhaled neurotoxin. *Acute exposure.*

By 7:19 A.M., the Los Alamos Fire Department received a call requesting aid. Another call was made to LANL—the lab had its own HazMat team.

Thirty minutes later a leading expert in neurotoxins, Dr. Christine Palmer, arrived on the scene to offer support. The toxicologist was accompanied by Edmond Sweetheart.

They were part of the third wave of personnel to enter the premises.

Christine Palmer was used to the full-body protective suit, Sweetheart less so; he was sweating beneath the weight of the heavy material. The hiss of the breathing apparatus sounded loud to his ears. The mask was fogging, the heat almost unbearable. Two members of LANL's HazMat team entered the building with them. Although fire departments and HazMat teams could be as touchy about turf as the next guys, in this case they welcomed assistance.

HazMat went first, Palmer and Sweetheart followed, moving slowly, with care.

The adobe was old, ramshackle, a debris-filled maze of dark rooms. It was obvious from the scene that the small-time meth cookers had had no clue what they were dealing with when they unleased the alkahest.

The bodies were still in place. Palmer was busy assessing the damage and the symptoms of the dead. Sweetheart was searching for anything connected with the theft of the biotoxin and the missing formula.

What he found was Paul Lang.

Or at least he found what he *believed* were the remains of Paul Lang. This corpse had been pushed into a closet in the last room. Unlike the other victims, this man had been shot. At least two bullets had entered through the front of his skull, leaving the victim's face so damaged that a positive ID would be accomplished only through forensics.

It wasn't difficult to piece together a probable scenario. Lang had delivered the toxin to the house at some point within the previous thirty-six hours. (A child had confessed to his parents and teacher that he'd seen "sleeping" men in the house just the day before.) Judging from the gunshot wounds, the deal hadn't gone down the way Lang expected. Perhaps he'd been told he could use the address as a safe house. Sweetheart had to guess about Lang's ultimate agenda: trade the toxin for Palmer; use it to create enough publicity so that this time she wouldn't get away with murder.

But things hadn't gone according to plan.

Somewhere along the way there'd been a double cross.

Sweetheart leaned over the dead body; the weight of the suit threw him off balance, and he was forced to use the corpse for support. He looked down, his gaze settling on the dead man's hand. There was a ring, a family crest.

Hadn't he seen Paul Lang wearing that ring in London?

Sweetheart mouthed a quick prayer.

Outside, where it was still raining, he fought claustrophobia as he waited for release from the suit. He was used to death, but from a distance.

When he was finally free, he watched—grateful for the cold gray drops pelting his skin—while Christine Palmer briefed the HazMat teams on contamination probabilities. He heard her telling them there was a very good chance the site was safe, or soon would be. The window of exposure might be very small depending upon the type of biotoxin. The actual cleanup would be left to the HazMat teams under the watchful eye of LANL.

In the midst of the emergency, the conflicts flared over turf. The local HazMat people accused LANL of neglecting to inform local authorities that a toxin was missing. The FBI—S.A.C. Hess, S.A. Hoopai, and others—were desperately trying to gain control of the crime scene. Local police were caught between their duty to protect and inadequate training for the current situation.

Sweetheart stood alone, watching—thinking that they were still missing what might be a disk containing a highly classified manufacturing formula for the alkahest; thinking that no one really knew how much deadly toxin had been stolen from the lab—when the call came in on his cell phone.

They were also missing Dr. Harris Cray.

A male voice whispered: "Bring Palmer, leave the feds behind, take I-25 south. Do what I say, I'll let you know what's next."

Sweetheart's cell rang again as the silver Mercedes was passing the rain-slicked bypass exit on I-25.

"Your plane's taking off from the City Different in fifteen minutes. Before you call for backup, think about Fiesta Street, what happened to those people, what can happen again."

Sweetheart barked out, "We need twenty minutes," but the transmission was dead.

He accelerated across the interstate divider, tires tearing out mud, chamiso, and scrub juniper, oncoming traffic scattering, drivers cursing the man behind the wheel.

In the passenger seat Christine Palmer braced herself, sucking in air as a twenty-foot-long U-haul slammed on the brakes, only to skid toward them along wet highway. Sweetheart and the Mercedes cut into the next lane to run a slalom between a pickup truck, a shuttle, a limping Gremlin.

Palmer released her breath with a curse. Sweetheart took one hand off the wheel and reached for the leather seat.

"We'll lose him if you call in the feds," she said.

"No feds, no calls." His fingers gripped seat belts—his, then hers—testing strength before he accelerated. "Hold on tight."

A small cloud of sparrows dove past the windshield, wings barely escaping wet glass. Water and wind friction created a muffled hiss outside the Mercedes. Ahead, the interstate was clear for a quarter mile, and Sweetheart rode the pedal, speedometer hovering just beyond a hundred miles per hour.

They'd used up eight minutes by the time they were on the bypass.

Seven minutes to go.

Four minutes on the bypass, another twelve seconds idled away before Sweetheart carefully ran a *slow* red light. (It wasn't the time to pick up a cop escort.)

A sharp left—only to skid onto the oily airport road—and ninety seconds before they could see a small jet bursting into flight.

The sky above the Santa Fe airport was a sheet of smoky glass, a reflection of the rain-slicked asphalt below. True nightfall was hours away, but the sun, trapped behind clouds since dawn, had conceded defeat, and the small Spanish Deco terminal glowed against the horizon like an artificial sun highlighting contrived darkness.

Beyond the terminal a flock of molded steel birds had gathered on the tarmac—private jets and commercial commuters, wings spread, in pecking order, bound for Denver, Albuquerque, Dallas, and other, not so exotic destinations—on schedule or making up time.

Sweetheart slowed the Mercedes in response to the sudden red glow of taillights twenty feet in front of them on the airport road. He was thinking of Sylvia as he glanced over at Christine Palmer. Her manicured hands rested on the thighs of her black leather pants. (The only sign of nerves—faint streaks in the leather where her tapered nails had clamped down.) A single strand of diamond chips shimmered around her left wrist. It occurred to Sweetheart that diamonds, cold as ice and razor sharp, were exactly right for Christine.

Neither of them spoke, and he welcomed the silence—he had nothing to say, but he kept needing to touch her visually.

Christine refused to meet his eyes. Her back was straight, her chin slightly raised, attention focused impatiently on the scene ahead. Her profile was a study in classic composition, a just right balance of shadow and light and line, but her beauty was cold, just like the diamond bracelet. He thought of Sylvia, of her description of Riker as a man *who made me touch a place within myself that knows no compassion, no mercy, no humanity.*

A cold, dark place where nothing lives, he thought.

He tried to summon a comparison to his own relationship with Christine. But it was different—the places he'd touched with her had been dark and hot and very, very dangerous. In spite of Sylvia's plea, he could never trust Palmer, never turn his back on her. Too much was at stake. He was closing in on the man he'd been pursuing for years. He was closing in on a spy, a traitor.

"Christine." He didn't know he'd actually spoken her name aloud until she shook her head, a gesture so small he almost didn't catch it.

When he gave the Mercedes gas—heard the low throb, felt the engine responding, and cut into the left lane to pass a line of traffic—he had an odd sense of going nowhere.

Minutes earlier, when the second call had come through, he'd worked the calculation in his head: it would take at least twenty minutes before the feds could get here—and when they did, they'd bring disaster.

Sweetheart didn't intend to play it that way.

A horn, blaring and indignant, brought him back into his body. He slammed on the brakes to avoid hitting a battered Toyota hatchback.

In his peripheral vision he saw Christine brace herself against the seat as the Mercedes jolted to a stop. He took a breath as the Toyota completed a turn; behind the rain-marred window, the driver was invisible.

He thought he heard a whisper, and he glanced over to see if Christine had spoken. This time she met his eyes. He wasn't prepared for what he saw: some private blend of hurt and contempt.

He accelerated, speeding the last quarter mile to the terminal.

The rain had begun to fall in heavy threads, drumming against the roof of the Mercedes. Even before he'd cut the engine, Christine thrust the door open, stepping out into the deluge. She jogged across the parking lot and was soaked through by the time she reached the terminal doors. Sweetheart was only a few feet behind her, moving quickly.

The interior of the terminal, brightly lit and smelling of damp clothes and bodies, was a throwback, something out of the 1940s. Clusters of people loitered on benches and around a small snack bar. A line had formed in front of plate glass; passengers boarding an Eagle Express flight stepped reluctantly from the shelter of the terminal into cold gray rain.

Sweetheart watched as Christine scanned the small crowd. She moved quickly past families and solitary travelers. He followed.

There was no place to hide. He walked through the small terminal, winding his way through the crowd, catching a glimpse of a face, a gesture, a smile, hearing a word or a phrase—in English, Spanish, even German.

He stayed ten feet behind Christine, trailing her toward the glass doors that opened onto the tarmac. And then he saw her freeze.

Dr. Harris Cray was crossing the terminal, briefcase in hand. Sweetheart caught it the instant it happened—Cray realized he had company. Haggard, haunted, the scientist stared back at Sweetheart, who was ready to launch an assault, whatever it took to close in on his quarry.

To his shock, Cray began striding, half running, directly his way. Sweetheart glanced over, but Christine had disappeared. He'd lost her.

Why isn't Cray running away?

Instead, Harris Cray stumbled past pedestrians, finally lunging desperately for Sweetheart, clutching his sleeve. "I got the message—that you'd be here. She told me you could get me to a safe house—where no one could find me—until this was straightened out." Cray sounded hysterical. "I never stole anything—they can't arrest me, can they?"

"Who told you?" Sweetheart growled, shaking the man roughly. But he already knew the answer.

"I thought—wasn't it—" Cray's eyes were wide, his face puzzled. "Dr. Palmer."

Crisscross—that's what flashed through Sweetheart's mind.

Special Agent Darrel Hoopai swerved into the parking lot of the Santa Fe Municipal Airport, braking next to Sweetheart's silver Mercedes. He shot from his sedan, not even slowing to slam the door shut. As he raced across the slick asphalt, he told himself his instincts had been right when he made the decision to follow the profiler and Dr. Palmer. He only hoped he wasn't too late.

Passing pedestrians, Hoopai raced through the terminal doors into bright lights and more people.

Sweetheart pushed Dr. Cray out of the way. He took a dozen steps, turning instinctively toward the glass and the tarmac.

Only to catch sight of a ghost seen through rain and glass.

Shock waves traveled through his body.

He didn't stop. He kept on moving, and the doors parted, allowing him to pass into darkness and a world of rain.

He'd been wrong—blinded by assumption, missing the obvious.

Drew Dexter—LANL's deputy director of security—with his Louisiana drawl and his sharp eyes turned now on Sweetheart. Watery red neon light spilled across Dexter's close-cropped hair—the red light seemed to splash onto wet asphalt.

Christine had played them all perfectly—Cray, Sylvia, himself—as fools.

Now she walked straight out the double doors and right up to Dexter.

It took Sweetheart another two seconds to react, even then in slow motion.

Dexter sidestepped Christine. He stood calmly, almost casually. By the looks of it, he had no obvious physical weapon on his person.

Sweetheart wasn't surprised. A primitive weapon like a gun wouldn't effect his plan. But Christine Palmer would. A stolen supply of biotoxin would.

Watch your back, Rikishi—a double cross.

He'd had the chance to play it another way: close down the airport at the command of the feds and the FAA, risk a hot-shot cop setting Dexter off, risk a hostage situation or worse.

Dexter's voice echoed again in his head: *Before you call for backup, think about Fiesta Street, what happened to those people, what could happen again.*

He saw that Christine had accepted a briefcase from Dexter. She clutched it by her side, watching both men. As three points of a triangle, they were equilateral; a dozen feet separated each from another. A stranger watching from the terminal would never guess anything out of the ordinary was about to happen . . .

Sweetheart took a step toward Dexter. The rain had let up slightly, and now the drops felt like faint pinpricks. He blinked, clearing his vision.

"That's as far as you go," Dexter called to him. "We can do this without trouble."

Palmer managed to gain a few paces in the direction of a small plane, a two-seater, a red-and-white Citabria, parked at the edge of the tarmac.

Dexter followed; so did Sweetheart.

One step at a time.

"You don't want to push me," Dexter warned. "There was more than enough toxin left for another round of Fiesta Street. Only this time, a whole lot more people could die."

"Just do as he says and it will work out," Christine said. She was still backing toward the airplane.

Sweetheart shook his head. "I can't let you go."

She shrugged. "You don't have a choice."

"She goes with me." Dexter's voice had turned hard. "Once we're out of here, I'll send you a message on where to find the alkahest."

Christine took a step in Sweetheart's direction. She stopped and smiled that icy smile at him. "I thought you'd recognize when you're *yorikiri.*"

"What?" Dexter asked, his voice sharp with suspicion.

"Sumo. He's been forced out of the ring." She turned quickly, carrying the briefcase to the Citabria's mounted step.

Dexter backed away from Sweetheart, following in Palmer's wake.

Again Sweetheart moved with him. It felt like a weird dance, an outdoor performance, rain or shine. At the corner of his consciousness, he realized the rain had stopped and, a jagged sliver of blue sky had appeared high in the distant sky.

He called out to Dexter, "We know about the years, your dealings with the Chinese."

Dexter shrugged. "My life as a spy. That's all in the past. It's harder for you to let go than it is for me, Sweetheart." A slight smile crossed Dexter's lips. "You've been after me too long. As for my extracurricular activities, that's easy—my government *owes* me." He gestured toward Palmer, standing on the step of the airplane, still holding the briefcase. "The disks are my privately negotiated pension. It's that simple. I make sure there are no secrets because the *bad guys* get the same recipe as the *good guys*. I'm so fucking sick of government sanctity."

"What about your family?" Sweetheart called. "Your wife and children?"

"What about them? They'll be taken care of—I made sure of that. But they've never understood me."

While Dexter talked, Sweetheart had been gauging the distance. He'd gained some ground—he was barely eight feet from Dexter now. In turn, Dexter was another eight feet from the plane and Christine.

Sweetheart kept himself talking. "And you think Christine understands you?"

"Yes."

"Don't be a fool."

Dexter laughed. "Speak for yourself."

Sweetheart knew the most vulnerable moment would be when they climbed into the cockpit—that was when he'd have a chance.

Dexter read his mind. "Try to stop us and you'll never find out where I left the second load of toxin. You'll have to live with the nightmares."

Sweetheart stopped. Poised between the moment of action and nonaction. He could stop Dexter and Palmer, he could bar their escape, but Dexter still held the winning hand. Sweetheart couldn't risk more innocent deaths.

Sylvia had warned him not to get in between Dexter and his ultimate goal. And she'd warned him about Christine.

Don't let her blind you, Sweetheart. Your test has just begun. But you can't do it alone. You've got to trust Christine Palmer. Trust her. That's your only choice. That's our only way out of this.

But he couldn't play it Sylvia's way. He knew Palmer too well, knew he could never trust her.

"Just tell me where you left the alkahest," Sweetheart called. "Let me make sure no one is hurt—I won't interfere."

Dexter had reached the steps, and he smiled. "Of course you won't."

Christine called to Sweetheart, "You lost. I won. I'm out. It's time to end my career, and this is the graceful way. I simply disappear. Things always turn out in the end, haven't you learned that by now? Ask your friend Dr. Strange. I know what she asked you to do—and she was right. Trust is always a dangerous game." She climbed into the plane.

"Ah, yes, Strange," Dexter said. "I don't know why she survived." He reached up to balance himself on the Citabria's wing. "That was never my intention."

Sweetheart heard those words, the arrogant edge in Dexter's voice, and he started to move, ready to kill the bastard with his bare hands.

He never got the chance.

He heard the sound of running feet, saw the gun in Special Agent Darrel Hoopai's hand—and he threw all his weight at the federal agent. Both men went down, the gun slid onto slick asphalt.

As the Citabria's idling engine roared to life, Sweetheart growled at Hoopai, "Let them go, damn it."

Both men followed the plane's progress to the end of the runway. As Sweetheart watched the red-and-white Citabria cresting sky like the winged creature she was, floating, reaching altitude, touching the clouds—free as a bird—he knew there was nothing left inside him, no air in his lungs, no thought in his mind.

It was Darrel Hoopai who said, "My God, what have you done?"

It arrived in a thick cardboard mailer. No return address.

Two CDs slid out.

Followed by an envelope.

When Sweetheart slit the onionskin—when he gingerly spread both edges—a single news clipping floated to the floor.

A one-column item clipped from the *International Herald Tribune.*

It was worn, slightly yellowed, dry.

It was dated three weeks earlier.

CARACAS, Venezuela—The death of an American retiree, David Atlas, 46, who was found dead in his hotel room, has been ruled an accidental death at inquest. Atlas, who has no known relatives in Venezuela or America, apparently died from ciguatera toxin ingested from contaminated shellfish. He had been ill for several days before his death. Witnesses from the hotel said his only visitor since his arrival had been a woman who was described as an attractive, middle-aged American. Since her departure a week before the body was found, David Atlas had no more visitors. The case will remain open. Officials from the American embassy were notified. Authorities request anyone with information to come forward.

Printed by hand in the margin:

It's over. No more surprises waiting for you. Yours, C

Sweetheart slipped the newspaper cutting back into the envelope.

For a moment, he closed his eyes. When he opened them again, he found himself staring out at the Los Angeles landscape, but his mind was traveling across oceans.

He thought of Sylvia—remembered the promised he'd made to her.

The job was done.

EPILOGUE

Weddings are best when the bride and groom both show up, when the ceremony is brief and to the point, when there's plenty of food (including three kinds of cake) and drink and great music.

It was a beautiful late-fall afternoon in La Cieneguilla. Unseasonably warm.

Los Vaqueros warmed up with a Cuban rancheros tune, they served up salsa and two-step for a main course, folk blues for dessert, and finally, for an apertif, they played tango.

Rosie Sanchez—in stocking feet, the ruffles on her tight hot-pink suit sticking out like fresh hibiscus—made the first toast. Her husband, Ray, held ruler-straight by his tuxedo, made the second. Sylvia's mother made the third. Serena made the fourth.

As tradition dictates, Sylvia danced the first dance with Matt. He guided her firmly across the floor, his hand hot against the small of her back. He kept it there—as if now that he'd finally succeeded in coaxing her to the altar, he was afraid to let go.

Sylvia didn't mind. She was in the mood to be held. Warm and mellow from too much wine, punchy from wedding cake, and barefoot like her matron of honor—the future looked good.

She danced with Serena next—Rosie joined in, tugging Sylvia's mother to the dance floor—while Matt, Ray, and a group of men gathered by the edge of the tent to talk about the things men tend to talk about at weddings: sports, women, and sports.

When Sylvia was searching for Serena's tiny beaded handbag somewhere among the presents on the vast, linen-covered table, she noticed a small silver-wrapped package. She knew, even before she read the card, who it would be from.

There are many dangers in this world, Dr. Strange, but as far as you're concerned, I am not one of them. Congratulations, CP

Sylvia opened the package slowly, with great care, and inside she found a tiny pink plastic case.

Familiar. The size of a very small compact.

Like a million similar cases, it contained birth control pills. Like the brand Sylvia had discontinued two months earlier.

She'd never be certain when Drew Dexter had managed to contaminate her own packet—the motel in Los Alamos? But it was also possible he'd done it that first night when they toured the lab.

She shook off the sudden chill of memories, and then she opened the case.

All the pills were in their tiny plastic cases—except for the first three, which were missing.

A perfect place to hide a little bit of poison . . .

ABOUT THE AUTHOR

Sarah Lovett worked as a researcher at the New Mexico state penitentiary. Her previous novels are *Dantes' Inferno, Acquired Motives, Dangerous Attachments,* and *A Desperate Silence.* Raised in California, she now makes her home in Santa Fe.